THE
OUTSIDE

THE
OUTSIDE

LAURA BICKLE

Houghton Mifflin Harcourt
Boston   New York

To Jason.
"All my love, for all my life."

www.hmhbooks.com

Text set in Bembo.

Library of Congress Cataloging-in-Publication Data
Bickle, Laura.
The outside / Laura Bickle.
p. cm.
Sequel to: The hallowed ones.
Summary: Kicked out of the safety of her Amish community, teenaged Katie must face the dangerous vampire-infested outside world.
ISBN 978-0-544-00013-1
1. Amish—Juvenile fiction. [1. Amish—Fiction. 2. Christian life—Fiction. 3. Coming of age—Fiction. 4. Vampires—Fiction. 5. Horror stories.] I. Title.
PZ7.B4727Ou 2013
[Fic]—dc23
2012040065
Manufactured in the United States of America
DOC 10 9 8 7 6 5 4 3 2 1
4500427453

Acknowledgments

Much gratitude to my editor, Julie Tibbott, and agent, Becca Stumpf, for creating such a wonderful space for this story to grow. There would be no book without you.

Special thanks to the other wonderful folks at HMH who supported this story throughout the process: Karen Walsh, Joan Lee, Alison Kerr Miller, Roshan Nozari, and the fabulous team in marketing and publicity who've been so good to me. Thank you for the beautiful cover image created by Shane Rebenschied with the model Alena Follestad-Jutilla, and for the cover design by Carol Chu.

Thanks to my crit partners, Jeffe Kennedy and Marcella Burnard, for all your help and good humor. Writing is a lonely business, and I've been very blessed to have you two to call writing sisters.

Chapter One

The hard part about the end of the world is surviving it, surviving when no angels scoop you up to fly you away to heaven.
God doesn't speak. But I kept asking.

"Unser Vadder im Himmel . . ."

My breath was ragged in my throat, my voice blistering
around the words of the Lord's Prayer. I spoke in Deitsch, the
way my people always did when we prayed. It didn't matter if
evil understood me, only God.

". . . Dei Naame loss heilich sei . . ."

I opened my arms, my coat and dark skirts flapping around
my legs and wrists. I stared out at a field, holding a sharpened
pole in each fist. One had been a garden hoe in a previous
life and the other a shovel. The metal had been stripped from
them, but they were still tools. Weapons. A crumpled piece of
paper was fastened to my chest with straight pins, the writing
growing faint and illegible in the gathering darkness.

Darkness with eyes.

"Dei Reich loss komme . . ."

I strained to see into the night. Shapes seethed. I knew that
something terrible was out there. The bullfrogs had stopped

chanting and the late-season crickets had gone silent. I heard crunching in leaves, saw something shining red.

"Dei Wille loss gedu sei."

My knuckles whitened on the wood in my hands.

"Bonnet, c'mon!"

My head snapped around, my bonnet string slapping my chin. I could see two familiar figures retreating behind me. A short, round woman scurried through the field. Her platinum hair was bright against the night, almost appearing as a moon bobbing along churning water. She reached a nervous white horse who was pawing at the earth, clambered clumsily onto its back. Between her and me, a lanky shadow in a dark jacket gestured at me with white hands. Alex.

Bonnet. That was Alex's nickname for me. My real name is Katie.

Alex said that God did not rule the end of the world. Alex said the end of the world was ruled by sun and Darkness. By time. And time was one thing we had very little of. The light had drained out of the day, and we were vulnerable.

I saw Alex taking off his jacket, wading through the grass toward me. I swallowed. That meant that he sensed the same thing I did, that the hair also stood up on the back of his neck, that he was ready to fight.

He stripped off his shirt. My heart flip-flopped for a moment and my grip on the stakes slackened for a fraction of a second. His pale skin was covered by black sigils that seemed to blur in the twilight. It was cold, but for them to work well, the creatures pursuing us needed to see them—the same reason I'd pinned the petition to God to my chest.

I worked the prayer through my teeth, one eye on the horizon, at the roiling shadows in the east.

"... *Uff die Erd wie im Himmel.*"

"Damn it, Bonnet." He grabbed my elbow. He tore the white bonnet off my head, stuffed it into his pocket.

I snatched at the strings. "Don't ..."

"This thing makes you a target. I could see you from all the way back there." He stabbed a thumb at Ginger's retreating figure on horseback, melting into the grass. "It shines like a beacon."

I lifted my chin. "*Ja.* Maybe it should."

This was an argument we repeated often. Though the end of the world had come, I adhered to the old ways. I was born Amish, and I would die Amish.

But hopefully not tonight.

Alex's eyes narrowed and he looked over my head. I could feel his hand grow cold through the sleeve of my dress.

"They're here," I breathed.

He swore.

Alex pulled me back, back into the tall grass disturbed by a breeze.

My breath hissed behind my teeth:

> "*Unser deeglich Brot gebb uns heit,*
> *Un vergebb unser Schulde,*
> *Wie mir die vergewwe wu uns schuldich sinn.*"

I ran. I felt the grass slashing around my skirts as I plunged into the gathering night. The landscape slipped past, and I had the feeling of flying for a moment, of hurtling through that striped shadow in which no crickets sang.

But I knew that a more solid Darkness gathered behind me. I could feel it against my back, the way the air grew thick and cold, the way it felt above the earth right before first frost.

The last lines of the Lord's Prayer slipped from my lips:

> *"Un fiehr uns net in die Versuchung,*
> *Auwer hald uns vum ewile.*
> *Fer dei is es Reich, die Graft,*
> *Un die Hallichkeit in Ewichkeit . . ."*

Evil hissed behind me, crackling like ice popping over a fire. I felt the thread of a spider web slip through the grass, breaking on my hands.

"Amen."

I turned, swinging the hoe in an arc around me. It whipped through the grass with the sound of a card trapped in bicycle spokes. A pair of glowing eyes leapt back, but claws scrabbled around the makeshift stake. I lunged with the second weapon in my left hand. The point struck home into something solid, and that something shrieked. I fought back the urge to shudder.

Nothing human made a sound like that. It was a sound like a bobcat wailing at sunset, mourning the loss of the day. Only this shadow mourned the loss of flesh.

Alex, ever the anthropologist, had a theory about that sound. In the calmer daylight hours, he speculated that this shriek had been at the root of the banshee myth, in an earlier, more orderly age. Once upon a time, when there had been civilization. I'd never heard the myth before, but I knew that inhuman sound all too well now.

The stake broke off in my hand, and I stumbled back with only splinters in my fist. Something swept up from the grass and ripped at my sleeve with claws.

I howled, smelling my own blood. The scent would bring more of them.

I twisted in its grip. The letter pinned to the front of my dress rustled and the creature with the glowing eyes hissed. It loosened its hold, enough for me to jam the ruined stake into its face.

I was no longer a pacifist. I meant to kill.

I was no stranger to death. We Amish lived close to the earth, under the watchful eye of God and all of his kingdom. I had helped with the butchering of pigs, mourned the loss of dogs at my kennel in whelping. I had stood at the bedsides of my grandparents when they died. I'd held my mother's last child, a stillborn, and witnessed a neighbor die during childbirth. Those things had happened in normal life.

But when life stopped and God's kingdom fell into shadow, I saw death in an entirely different fashion. I had dressed the bodies of women in my community for burial, only to be forced to cut their heads off before daylight's fingers of sunshine had left them. I had seen children torn asunder, reduced to unrecognizable smears on a ceiling. I had slain men who were once like brothers to me, impaled them, and burned them.

I had seen too much.

I had seen true Darkness.

My heart thudded against the fabric of my dress and the holy letter pinned there—small defense against the undead, but still a defense. I thrust down with all my might to jam the stick into the face of the creature twisting beneath me in the grass.

This was not murder, I had decided. This was doing the Lord's dirty work. Putting the dead back in the earth.

"*Bonnet!*"

I glanced up to see a pale face with a gaping maw hurtling toward me. I saw fangs, red eyes, little else. I flung my right hand with my remaining stake up before me, but the creature slammed against it, buffeting me back to the sea of grass. I landed on my backside, my feet tangled in my skirt. Its cold shadow passed over me, blocking out the pinpricks of starlight in violet sky. It smelled like blood.

"*Food,*" it rasped. "*Lovely food . . .*" It reached toward my face, gently, reverently, almost as an intimate might. It was a very human gesture, rendered savage by the greed in the red eyes. By hunger for the blood that slipped down my arm and pooled in my palm.

"*Get away from her!*"

A black and white blur passed between me and death. Alex. From behind, I could see the familiar tattoos stretching across his skin: a Djed pillar, sacred to Osiris. And on his chest, an ankh made of scars, which he told me was the symbol of eternal life.

It was nothing like the carefully scripted letter pinned to my dress. It was called a *Himmelsbrief,* and had been made for me by my community's Hexenmeister, a petition to God on my behalf. But any symbol of divine power behaved in the same way, the way that crucifixes and holy water did. God, in whatever guise he chose, did have some power over these creatures.

The vampire reached for Alex with an expression of longing.

"Food," it whispered, with a nearly palpable sorrow.

But its hands were stilled just above the ankh burned on Alex's chest. It was as if this was an invisible barrier it could not cross. The vampire froze in puzzlement, and I could almost imagine that some thoughts still rattled around its head as it had learned what was safe to eat and what was poisonous.

"Not food," Alex responded. There was a subtle jerk at his elbow, and the flash of a silver knife plunged between the vampire's ribs. The creature clawed, scratching at the edge of the ankh. I could hear the sizzle of his flesh, a sound like bacon frying. Black blood flowed over Alex's wrist. He shoved the vampire down to the grass, and I could see his knife slashing, the black droplets of vampire blood clinging to the tips of the grass stalks like dew. I was still mystified by it, by its lack of redness, by its soft, inklike consistency. It smelled like iron, though, which was enough to tell what they had once been. Alex speculated that iron oxidized in their blood, darkening it.

That black blood was on my wrist. I smeared it against my skirt as Alex's fingers wound around my hand. "We've got to go. There will be more."

I nodded. This was no time to contemplate biology or humanity. This was time to act, to move. To survive.

We ran, hand in sticky hand, sliding through the grass like ghosts.

I could see the bright helmet of Ginger's hair and the stark white figure of the horse far before us. We'd given them a head start, which was good—Alex and I had the only really effective weapons against the vampires. Alex had his tattoos and I had the *Himmelsbrief.* They were more of a deterrent, Alex said, like spraying mace at a perpetrator. The startlement they created sometimes gave us enough opening to run away. Or kill.

"Where are we going?" I asked, casting my gaze about the dark landscape. It was suicide to be out in the open like this. "We can't fight until daylight."

He shook his head, mouth pressed in a flat line. "I don't know. The sign said that there was a church back there, but all we saw was burned timbers. Useless as shelter, if it was desecrated by the vamps."

"We'll have to find someplace else," I decided, nodding sharply to myself.

"How do you feel about sleeping in trees?" His face split open in a lopsided grin, his teeth white in the darkness. There were some at the horizon we could possibly reach, but none in the field.

"I'm quite sure the vampires can climb trees."

"Maybe not if we set fire at the roots . . . they don't like fire."

I made a face. "I don't much fancy the idea of being roasted alive in a tree."

"Reminds me of a movie, *The Wicker Man* . . ." he began.

I glanced at him blankly. I had never seen a movie.

"Never mind, then. I'll tell you later."

Ginger's horse was climbing a slope ahead of us. This part of the meadow wasn't cultivated, and the grass and weeds swelled over this rill in the earth, perhaps five feet tall, stretching east to west.

My skin prickled. In the far distance, I could see more glowing eyes gathering. They had heard us. They smelled blood. I pulled at Alex's sleeve and pointed.

Ginger had reached the top of the hillock. She was panting, and her glasses slid down over her nose. She was dressed as an Amish woman, but she was not one of my people. She was an Englisher, like Alex. She was an old friend of my family who had lost everything: her husband, her children. And she was the only part of my old life I had left. I clung to her.

The horse stared to the south. His ears flattened, and his eyes dilated black as obsidian. His nostrils flared, and his tail swished back and forth. He pawed the earth, pacing nervously. I had found him back on Amish land with an empty saddle, smeared in blood and with his former rider's boot still in the stirrup. We had discovered that the horse had a sixth sense about the vampires. Perhaps he could sense them the way dogs could sense earthquakes. Or perhaps he was merely a nervous horse and vampires were everywhere.

Alex had named him Horus, after an Egyptian god of the sky who defeated evil. Ginger and I just called him Horace.

"They're out there," Ginger said, staring out at the dark and patting Horace's sides soothingly.

"*Ja*. They're coming." I climbed up the hill, gazing at the flattened trail of grasses we'd left.

Alex scrambled to the top of the hill. Ginger and I made to rush down the slope on the other side, but he said: "Wait."

I looked up at him, my brows drawing together. "What do you mean?"

Alex shook his head. He squatted, and squinted to the beginning and the end of the strangely squiggling formation of land.

"Alex. We've got to go." Now it was me urging him on.

He slipped on his jacket. "We wait here."

Ginger's head popped up above the grass line like a platinum gopher. "What are you talking about? We've gotta get moving." She tugged at Horace's reins, but he would not budge. He stood on the pinnacle of the hill as if he were a statue.

Alex shook his head, and he pressed his hands to the ground. He was smiling. "No. We wait here. On the hill."

I bit my lip. Perhaps the stress of running from vampires for the last several weeks had caused Alex to finally lose touch with reality. Perhaps he had some desire to make a last stand. I confessed to myself that I felt like that often. I hadn't been baptized, so I wouldn't get to heaven, but it was sometimes peaceful to imagine not existing in this chaotic world any longer. I didn't *think* I'd be sent to hell, but I just wasn't sure.

In any event, I wasn't quite ready to test theology.

"Alex," I said. "We need to go if we're to have any chance of—"

"Do you trust me?"

He crouched on the top of the hill, looking at me with

an infuriatingly jovial smile. I felt myself frown, but I reached down for his hand. Behind me, Ginger sighed and scrambled up the grass bank.

We sat on the crest of the little hill, looking down, as dozens of glowing eyes converged upon us.

"We're screwed," Ginger said.

I didn't disagree with the sentiment.

Those luminous eyes drew near. I counted more than two dozen pairs. My heart hammered, and my mouth felt sticky and dry. I fingered the rough edge of my makeshift weapon. I might be able to kill one vampire with it. Not dozens.

Jagged silhouettes of people pulled themselves from the grass, like spiders extricating from webs. I braced myself, clutching my puny staff. Their eyes swept up the hill. I expected them to rush to us like water in a trench after a rainstorm.

They reached up with pale fingers that smelled like metal. Their lips drew back, hissing, and I could see the thirst in their eyes. But they made no move to climb the hill.

I sidled closer to Alex. "What's stopping them?"

"Holy ground," he said, grinning.

My brows drew together. I didn't understand. I saw no sign of any human habitation here. No church. No graveyard. Just this oddly shaped hill that rose up out of the field.

"How?"

Ginger started laughing behind me. She turned on her heel and surveyed the sad little hillock. "I see it now," she said. She huddled in closer with us when a vampire snarled at her.

"See what?"

"We're on an Indian mound," Alex said. "A holy site built by any one of a number of tribes in this area. They were used as burial mounds, ceremonial sites, astronomical measurements . . . some, we have no idea what for."

"How did you know?" It looked like just a rill in the land to me. A bump.

"See how it's sorta shaped like a snake?" He gestured to the west. "It's hard to see underneath the tall grass, but notice how it undulates in the ground?" He swished his hand back and forth like a snake swimming, and I could see some of the suggestion of a reptile in it.

"I saw a mound one time that was shaped like a big serpent eating the moon." He cocked his head and started to walk off down the snake's back. "I wonder if this one is like that . . ."

Ginger snagged the back collar of his jacket. "No exploring in the dark with the monsters down below."

"What do we do now?" I leaned on my staff. The hissing and bright eyes below were unnerving. Pale fingers combed through the grass.

Alex sat down. "We wait for morning."

I sighed and knelt down to pray. I could feel the chill of the earth beneath my knees, dew gathering. My skin crawled at the thought of the creatures, only feet away. I shut my eyes, trying to prove that I trusted God. He had kept us safe so far. He would keep us safe as long as it suited his purposes.

That was part of what I believed—what the Amish believed. We believed in *Gelassenheit*—surrendering ourselves to God's will. It was difficult, at times like this. I struggled to keep my eyes closed, seeing crescents of light beneath my lashes; I could not quite make myself trust the darkness.

"Unser Vadder im Himmel . . .

. . . dei Naame loss heilich sei . . ."

"Damn. I wish I had a harmonica," Alex grumbled.

CHAPTER TWO

One does not sleep in the presence of evil. Not when you can see it and it can see you.

We sat on the top of the hill and watched the stars spin overhead. It's funny the way that they shone as they always did. I took some comfort in that, that heaven was still the same as it always was. Watching, but remote.

The all-purpose prayer of the Amish was the Lord's Prayer, recited in Deitsch. It was vanity and belligerence to ask God for anything. But I couldn't help it. I had too many questions:

Is this the end of the world, as you meant it to be?

Where is the Rapture, this thing that was spoken of so often by the Englishers?

Did you forget us, or did you deem us unworthy?

I knew that God was still here, that his power was felt on the evil in the world. Holy symbols and places kept us safe from the plague of vampires that had been released weeks ago. We didn't know how or why. I had heard snippets from Ginger's cell phone and radio. We had been safe in my little Amish settlement. We had believed ourselves to be protected from evil. That we were favored among God's people.

We had committed the sin of pride.

The evil infected our community. Ginger, Alex, and I had fought it, in our own ways. We had the help of the village Hexenmeister, the man that Alex called our "wizard," the man who painted our hex signs and who had the authority to write *Himmelsbriefen*.

And it wasn't just the evil of the vampires. It was the evil of man. The Amish Elders, in attempting to quash panic, kept a stranglehold on the community and denied the truth. Ginger, Alex, and I had been shunned, thrown out of Amish land and into the world to certain death.

I missed home. I missed my mother, my father, my sister. I wondered if they would survive. If the Hexenmeister, who had stayed behind, would be able to protect them. My vision blurred when I thought of them, and I wiped away tears with my knuckles. I was not the only one who had lost.

Alex knelt at the edge of the hill, sharpening his knife with a rock. The flash of the silver illuminated a hardness in his jaw that I had come to recognize when he was thinking of those he'd loved who had been killed. I didn't ask about his old girl-friend, Cassia. We were both, in many ways, forced to move past that.

Instead, I placed my hands in his blond hair and kissed the top of his head. His jaw softened. He reached up for my hand with the one that wasn't holding the knife.

Ginger was huddled with her arms around her knees, hands tucked into her sleeves. Unblinking, she stared through her glasses at the creatures clamoring below. Most of it was inar-ticulate hissing and howling, but phrases could still be heard:

"Come here. Let me release you."

"Pretty thing. You can't run forever."

"Nothing can protect you. We are legions of legions, and you are so very few."

"Aren't you tired of fighting? I promise that it won't hurt."

I sat beside her, put my arm around her shoulders. I didn't want her staring at them for long. They had the power to reason, and also a kind of glamour. Though we were theoretically shielded from them on this hill, I didn't want her to be tempted. And I didn't want her to begin to view them as people.

She reached up to rub her eyes beneath her glasses. "I keep thinking," she said. "About Dan and the kids, that . . ." She gestured to the twisted faces below.

I squeezed her shoulders. "That hasn't happened to them. Dan's safe with the other soldiers. And your daughter is at the kibbutz in California with her friends."

"But my son . . ." She shook her head. "The college surely doesn't know how to deal with this. Didn't," she amended.

"He's smart. And Dan is looking for them." That was the last we had heard. Before the Elders had destroyed Ginger's cell phone as a symbol of the contagion from Outside. Before the end of the world, Ginger had been visiting, and she was accidentally trapped in our settlement when the end had come.

"I hope . . ." She fell silent. Articulating hopes in this world seemed futile.

Hands in the darkness crooked toward her, beckoning.

"God is watching," I said firmly.

The eastern horizon grew pink and the stars began to fade. As gold began to lighten the undersides of clouds, the vampires started to slip away, like pale eels. They growled and snarled as they receded, sliding into the protective shade of the tall grass. Horace blew and snorted at them.

I tipped my face to the sun, feeling its light upon my skin. I scrubbed my fingers through my hair, wanting it to soak into my pores. The sun felt like love. I unpinned the *Himmelsbrief* from my breast and folded it carefully away in my pocket for safekeeping.

I prayed again, as I always did: at dawn and sunset. At sunset, I prayed for protection. At dawn, I prayed in thanksgiving that we had lived to see it once again.

"We should get moving," Alex said. He stood and shifted his weight from foot to foot. "Get as far from them as we can before nightfall, lose the scent."

I wearily climbed to my feet.

"How far today?" I asked. We had decided to go north, to Canada. Alex had family there. Perhaps vainly, we hoped that the contamination hadn't spread as quickly in sparsely populated areas.

He squinted north. "As far as we can get before the sun goes down."

———

"Do you think that it will always be this way?"

I heard hopelessness creep into Ginger's voice. We'd convinced her to climb up into Horace's saddle to save time while Alex and I walked. Her fingers were tangled in the horse's white mane and the reins, and her gaze between its ears was unfocused.

"No," I said. "The Rapture is brief. Then there are the Tribulations before the Second Coming of Christ."

"I must have missed the Rapture part," Ginger said, bitterly.

"We don't know that," I insisted. "Some people could have been taken away to heaven." But I didn't really believe it. Though the world seemed empty, it seemed its inhabitants had been taken by darker forces.

"I wonder how many people were seriously expecting to be taken away from this," Alex said. He walked through the sunlit grass with his hands jammed in his pockets. "Did they just sit down and pray, waiting? Why?"

It was in his nature to question. He had been an anthropology graduate student before the end of the world came. He knew almost as much about the Bible as I did, but viewed it through the lens of a curious detachment, as an artifact and not the word of God.

I frowned. "I don't know how many righteous children of God there are. I thought . . . I thought that we were faithful." I squinted up at the sun. "I thought that my community was good. That we were doing as God commanded us. We followed the *Ordnung,* the rules."

"I thought so too, Katie," Ginger said. "We were all safe there . . . well, in our way," she amended, glancing at Alex. Ginger had been safe until the Elders had caught her contacting the Outside world with a cell phone, had been accused of going mad. A bit of that had been true. She'd been safe as long as she was quiet and said nothing.

"They just locked you in a room," he said. "Me, they threw out, once they found me."

"That was my fault," I said. I violated the Elders' rules. They ordered that no one was to come into or leave the settlement. Alex was hurt when I found him. I brought him inside, and pulled the wrath of the Elders down on all our heads. And I had done more than that. I had lain with him, and they had discovered us. I had used up my virtue on an English man outside the bonds of marriage.

He kicked a stone. "I feel bad for that. You'd still be safe there if it wasn't for me."

I shook my head. "No. The vampires had come in anyway." That was the fault of a boy I'd been intending on marrying. A boy who saw the brothers he thought were dead resurrected as vampires beyond the fence, and foolishly let them in. Elijah had betrayed me, turned away from me and toward something I didn't understand. I was pretty sure it wasn't God.

"The ground is no longer holy," I lamented.

But I still ached for home. Before the end of the world, I could not wait for my *Rumspringa,* the testing of the Outside world. I was looking forward to being able to experience a different kind of life. Sit in a movie theater. Wear jeans. Perhaps learn to drive a car. And now . . . now that I was in the Outside world, it was more fearsome and terrible than I ever could have imagined.

I remembered when we'd been exiled, when we had been cast beyond the gate of my community. My family and the Elders had watched. I felt their sorrow pressing against my back as we walked down that dirt road with the horse, feeling the horizon too large before us and my familiar life shrinking behind.

I shook my head. "Something happened. I don't understand. It wasn't just that the vampires glamoured their way in. Something changed in our land."

"Evil," Alex said. "Not just the contagion. When people are forced into a crucible like that, they start biting each other like rats. Power becomes an end unto itself. Evil is an inevitable sociological fact."

I frowned. I could not dispute that idea with logic. "I don't believe that everyone is corruptible."

"Everyone is corruptible. We all just have different limits."

We walked in silence for some time before Ginger said: "How many do you think have survived? If this is a biblical thing?"

I knew that she wanted comfort. She wanted to believe that her husband and children were alive. Just as Alex wanted to believe that his parents were. As I wanted to believe that my parents and sister would live.

"Revelations says that a third of mankind will be killed." I couldn't lie to her. That was what the book said, but doubts crept in on me. "The rest will flee to the mountains. There will be the End Times of Tribulation, and then Jesus will cast Satan out for a thousand years."

"The idea of End Times isn't specific to Christianity," Alex said. "Islam, for instance, believes in a Judgment Day. At that time, terrible creatures called the Gog and Magog will slaughter everything they can get their hands on."

"Sounds familiar," Ginger said.

"There's also the idea that a mystical smoke will descend on the earth. Nonbelievers are stricken with grave illness, and believers only get a case of the sniffles. Allah then sweeps a wind over the earth, which steals away the lives of the believers, leaving the nonbelievers behind until judgment.

"Mormonism has the idea that darkness will cover the earth, and that the evil will burn in fire."

"If we were only that lucky," Ginger muttered.

"Hinduism believes that there's a cyclic life and death in the world, moving from purity to impurity. It's not really an End Times in the Western Protestant sense, but there's also the idea in Buddhism that the teachings of Buddha will be forgotten and that people will degenerate into a destructive cycle until the appearance of the next Buddha," Alex said. "So there may be some grain of truth in many traditions about what's happening here."

"I struggle with this," I said frankly. "I know that this keeps me safe." I patted the pocket containing the *Himmelsbrief.* "But your tattoos also keep you safe."

"And before communications were cut off to the rest of the world, we knew that people were safe at the mosques, Shinto shrines, synagogues, temples," Ginger said. I'd fallen back to walk beside her heel, and she leaned over to pick bits of grass from my hair. Motherly fussing. It felt normal, and I relished it.

"I'm struggling with it too," Alex said, scratching self-consciously at his chest. "I never thought I really believed in God, deep, down deep, like you do." He gazed at me with eyes the color of winter skies. "I've got a healthy respect for the religion of ancient Egypt, you know. But nobody really practices it anymore. It is, for me . . . an intellectual curiosity, I guess. The idea that Osiris rose from the dead, that there is some concept of eternal life . . ."

"But you believe, in some fashion," I said. "Or else it wouldn't work." I touched the back of his hand. "I guess I don't understand how we can come from such different perspectives and have the same result."

I was accustomed to thinking that there was one right way to live, one way to achieve favor. "Evil" for me had been a broad category once upon a time. Evil had included transgressions great and small, from murder to failure to submit to God's will with grace to immodest dress. Now . . . now I found that my definition of evil was shrinking. I feared that rather than rising to the challenge of the Tribulations and becoming strong in my faith, I was growing weaker. Decaying, like the rest of the world. And that frightened me.

His fingers closed around mine. "I don't know," he said helplessly. "But it works."

In some ways, I think that I loved him.

And I shouldn't have.

He was an Englisher. Wholly inappropriate, based on just that fact. He wasn't even Christian. He was older than I was, by a handful of years. Worldlier. He had seen and experienced things I couldn't even imagine: the ocean, airplanes, computers. His world had been much bigger than mine, glamorous and exciting.

But now our world was the same: bleak and frightening.

Alex shook his head. "In the Gnostics' Gospel of Thomas, Jesus said: 'If you bring forth what is within you, what you bring forth will save you. If you do not bring forth what is within you, what you do not bring forth will destroy you.' What's in me is not gonna save anyone."

I gazed at him. "I believe that what you have within you is good and beautiful."

"I wish I could believe that," he said. I heard the doubt and fear in his voice.

"I believe for you," I said.

The sun always seemed to move too fast.

Growing up Plain, I had always been conscious of the sun. We rose with it, conducted all our business under its light. The cows were milked, fields plowed and harvested, and animals fed with its warmth on our faces. We went to bed when it set, when the crickets and spring peeper frogs emerged in the warmer seasons. During the short days of winter, we would sometimes play checkers by lamplight for an hour before submitting to the moonlit darkness muffled by snow.

This was the same, but different. Then, it had been an easy connection to nature. We told time in the fields by squinting at the sun. I still did, in fields not so different from those, but for much different reasons. I could feel Darkness bearing down on us, behind every shadow and patch of shade.

We were running. There was no objective other than simple survival now. No livestock that needed us to care for them, no fruit that would rot on the vine without our intervention. We just needed to find enough to eat and keep from being eaten.

We waded through the fields until the sun pushed our

shadows long to the right of us. I shivered, with the knowledge not only that night would come soon, but that frost was coming. Frost would kill the last of the blackberries and gooseberries that I'd found for us to subsist on. The acorns were long gone. I'd been lucky to find a crab apple tree three days ago, but I didn't think that we'd be that fortunate again. The animals, like birds and squirrels, who had been accustomed to scavenging the leftovers of humans, were now stripping trees and bushes bare.

The animals had known that Darkness was coming. I remembered when I had been back home, before any hint of evil. The ravens had known, taking wing in huge flocks that blotted out the sun. I saw no sign of any of them as we traveled.

I squinted, spying something white in the distance: a structure, with a gravel road leading up to it.

Alex and Ginger and I traded glances.

"What is it?" I asked, narrowing my eyes. I had never seen a house washed that white.

"It's a church," Alex said.

"If it hasn't been defiled, this could be good." Ginger sighed happily.

I regarded it closely as we approached. Plain folk didn't have churches. Our worship services took place at our homes, on a rotating basis. We'd listen to sermons in backyards and on front lawns. In that way, our whole space had been sanctified. We lived and worked with God.

I had never been in a church before. The white structure was small, perhaps a story and a half, with wooden siding covered by paint that was beginning to peel. The windows were peaked, but closed with shutters. A large cross was nailed to the peak of the roof, and the gravel drive led up to the front door. A small stream meandered behind it. I doubted that it could contain half as many people as were held on my backyard on Sundays.

A hand-lettered sign on the front lawn read CALVARY PEN-TECOSTAL APOSTOLIC CHURCH. ALL ARE WELCOME.

I shuddered. I hope that wasn't enough invitation for the vampires.

I ran my fingers over the black painted letters of the sign. I knew that the Pentecost was when the Holy Spirit descended upon the disciples of Jesus, after his resurrection. "A Christian church, then," I said, comforted a bit by the idea of a traditional God that I could recognize.

Alex stared at the sign. "Yes," he said. "Pentecostals have an experiential belief in God. They believe that the Holy Spirit can move within them, work miracles, make them speak in tongues, grant special rapport with animals . . ."

I pressed my lips together and thought about what that might mean. "Interesting." Plain folk believed that God and man were separate. My body seemed confused and crowded enough with just my spirit inside. How strange it would feel to have God inside me as well . . .

Ginger climbed the steps. "Let's see if anyone's home."

She rapped on the whitewashed front door. It was tall with black hinges. We waited, hearing the sound echo in the structure. A mourning dove was disturbed from one of the gutters and flew away in a flurry of cooing.

She knocked again.

I heard thumping inside, creaking, like something come to life. I held my breath as the door opened.

Ginger gasped and backed away.

An old man stood in the doorway, covered in snakes. The reptiles wreathed his head and shoulders and outstretched arms: blacksnakes, garter snakes, copperheads. He said something unintelligible, his rheumy eyes taking us in.

"Oh, yeah," Alex said. "I forgot to mention the snake handling."

CHAPTER THREE

The old man's eyes fixed on us. The garbled words from his mouth untangled, and he clearly said:

"Welcome, friends."

His voice boomed like a drum, and he smiled beatifically. His beard and mustache were white. A tiny garter snake peeped out and disappeared in the knotted mass, possibly down the collar of his flannel shirt. His eyes were so brown that they were nearly black.

I stood, rooted in place. I was afraid—I could feel the hair standing up on my arms—but also fascinated. The snakes seethed over his shoulders, wrapping around his arms. I was reminded of an old tree I knew as a child that had been struck by lightning. Half of it had turned black and rotted. The other half sprouted green leaves in winter. In the rotted half, snakes had moved in: large blacksnakes that wound around the wood, making it churn and still seem alive. Our Hexenmeister said that it had been touched in a bad way by lightning, by God's wrath.

We all avoided that tree.

"Hello," I squeaked.

Alex held up his open hands. He wasn't holding his knife. That was probably a good sign. I took his lead. "We don't mean you any harm."

"We're not vampires," Ginger said, unnecessarily.

The old man laughed. "Darkness hates sunshine. You aren't Darkness."

I shuddered. He reminded me a bit of my old Hexenmeister. Though this man seemed hale and barrel-chested, there was something about his laugh and the way that he looked past us, through us. Something . . . that made me think he saw things that I couldn't.

"And what have we here?" The old man walked down the wooden steps, regarded each of us in turn.

He paused before Ginger. He took in her borrowed Plain clothes, glasses, and her short haircut. "A mother without her children."

"I'm Ginger," she said softly. "Ginger Parsall." She laced her hands behind her back. I was pretty sure that she didn't want to shake hands.

He looked Alex up and down. "A lost scholar."

Alex nodded. "Fair enough. I'm Alex Greene."

He approached the horse. "This is your prophet."

Horace didn't react to the snakes. Most horses I knew were terrified of them. This one simply looked at the man through his pale lashes.

And then he turned to me. "And a Plain girl who is not yet filled with God."

I swallowed, lifted my chin. "*Ja.* I am Katie."

The old man mumbled to himself, again in the unintelligible

language. He squinted at the sun lowering on the horizon. "I'm Pastor Gene. You'd best be getting inside before the sun sets."

My hands wound in Horace's reins.

"And the horse, too. The Darkness will come and tear him apart if you leave him."

He turned and disappeared inside the church.

Alex, Ginger, and I stood rooted in place. None of us wanted to go first.

"Snakes or vampires?" Alex asked.

"The snakes . . . I don't understand." I shook my head.

"That's part of the Pentecostal belief system. He believes that the Holy Spirit keeps him safe from venom," Alex explained.

"I hate snakes," Ginger said. I could see the pulse thudding along her collarbone and sweat prickling her brow. "But I hate vampires more."

"*Ja,*" I said. "The least of the things to fear."

"'And the serpent said to the woman, 'You will not surely die.'" Alex's mouth turned down. "That's what they said in Genesis, anyway."

"*Ja,*" I sighed.

Alex climbed the stairs first, and we followed him into the shadow of the doorway.

It took some time for my eyes to adjust from the gold gloaming of the sunset to the shade of the church. I smelled dust and roses. For a moment, I was blinded in red sun shadow, and all I could hear was my breathing in my ears and a low sibilance.

My vision cleared to show a boxlike room with benches on the right and left of a center aisle. The floor was scarred pine, and light poured through the windows in broad orange shafts. In the ponds of sun on the floor, I saw a rat snake sunning itself. An altar at the front was decorated with brittle white roses, dried up and crumbling. A wooden cross adorned with a dove looked over the shattered flowers, a copperhead curled around it. Bits of the ruined flowers were strung in garlands on the pews, dropping petals on the floor. A blacksnake slipped beneath the altar.

Pastor Gene was walking up the aisle, heedless of the snakes. "Don't mind the reptiles. Or the décor."

Ginger was frozen in the doorway. I took her hand and tugged her inside. Horace's hooves clomped on the old boards. Alex closed the doors behind us.

"How did . . . how did they get here?" I asked.

Pastor Gene reached out and grasped a white rose at the end of a pew, pinched it. The petals dissolved. "We were going to have a wedding here when the End Times came."

"I meant the snakes." My voice was timid, echoing up to the dark ceiling.

The snakes had begun to drop off of the pastor, the heavy weight of them striking the floor, slapping the boards with echoing thumps. They slithered off beneath the pews. Behind me, Ginger whimpered.

"They began to show up shortly after the Darkness fell. When the news anchors were reporting that an infectious agent had been released on the East Coast, were telling everyone to stay indoors, I came here to pray, and noticed all the snakes on the bank of the creek." He pointed through a window. "This is the creek where we do baptisms. Sunday Creek."

Minding where I stepped, I peered through the thick glass. The creek shimmered in the sunset. I saw ribbons of snakes in blacks, browns, and greens knotted in a mass on the bank. The sight transfixed me—it was like watching living water.

"I knew it was a sign," he said.

I swallowed. "Back in my community, the ravens all left."

He nodded. "God speaks to the animals."

I glanced at the garter snake staring at me, unblinking, beneath his beard. "Do you . . . talk to them?"

He chuckled. "No. I don't. But I have no reason to fear them. The Holy Spirit moves in me. It's one of God's gifts. The Bible tells us:

> And these signs shall follow them that believe: In my name shall they cast out devils; they shall speak with new tongues. They shall take up serpents; and if they drink any deadly thing, it shall not hurt them; they shall lay hands on the sick, and they shall recover."

"From the Book of Mark," I said.

He smiled. "You're a good student of the Bible. And: 'Behold, I give unto you power to tread on serpents and scorpions, and over all the power of the enemy: and nothing shall by any means hurt you.'"

"Luke," I said.

His eyes shone, and I wanted to believe him. The garter snake flicked its tongue out at me.

I flinched in the face of that evidence.

"Do you feel the Spirit dwelling in you?" he asked.

I stared out the window, at the last bit of sun reflected on the baptismal water of Pastor Gene's creek. "I . . . I have not been baptized." My cheeks flamed. "Amish are not baptized until they are old enough to choose the church of their free will."

"And you didn't choose to?" His dark eyes searched me. "Or didn't have time?"

"My parents wanted me to be. But . . ." I struggled for words. "Before the end of Outside, I had intended on going on *Rumspringa*. With some of my friends, and a boy."

Pastor Gene glanced at Alex. "That boy?"

I shook my head, and my blush deepened. "No. An Amish boy. Elijah. We were to be married." I could hear the words coming out of me in a flood, like the stream below, didn't try to stop them. "He was baptized in a hurry after we learned of the end of Outside, before the Darkness. I wasn't ready. I was too . . . rebellious."

The corner of Pastor Gene's mouth quirked up. "That boy, Alex—was he part of your rebellion?"

"*Ja*. In a way. I found him injured beyond the fence of our property. The Elders told me to leave him there. They knew that the Darkness had come, but I couldn't leave him to die." I folded my hands at my waist. "I could not accept the *Ordnung*, the rules, and be baptized while harboring a fugitive."

"And the woman, Ginger? Was she also a fugitive?"

"No. She just happened to be on our land when the order to close the gate came. I breed—used to breed—dogs, and she sells them for me in the English community."

"I see. And your community?"

I shook my head. "The vampires were let in. Not by me, but they are inside. The Elders put us under the *Bann* . . . turned Alex, Ginger, and me out. So I don't know what happened after I left. I hope that our Hexenmeister can help them."

"What's a Hexenmeister?" His brow wrinkled and he lingered a bit on the first syllable.

"He does the Lord's work," I explained. "But not in the way that clergy does. He paints hex signs and writes letters to God—*Himmelsbriefen*. He knew about the vampires, tried to keep us safe."

"I've known some Plain folks in my time, and I've never heard of that." His words were slow, a bit suspicious.

"Our community is a bit different from other Plain communities, in that way," I said. "The Hexenmeister came over with the Pennsylvania Dutch. We have always kept a remnant of those old ways." I stared at my reflection in the glass. "It may be a good thing. If they listen to him."

It was a while before Pastor Gene spoke. "My parishioners are baptized at a young age," he said, without judgment. "Usually in summer, when the water's warm."

"You walk in the creek?"

He shook his head and lowered his hands. "All in. The Spirit dwells within all of us. Baptism fills us up with God. The Lord washes us clean of our sins. And then there's a picnic."

I could picture it: a sunny day, by that cheerful creek, people playing in the grass rather than snakes, the smell of good food.

"Where are your parishioners?" I asked. "And your family?"

His gaze was far away. "I tried to tell them. They were afraid. A lot of them thought I was crazy—that I was one of those doomsday prophets talking about the end of the world. I think that much of it was that we've been moving too far into the future. In the modern world, God exists as an abstract. Everyone wanted to believe in sunshine. But not the Darkness. Not in evil."

"They all . . . they all left?"

"Most of them went southwest, to the nearest military base. Some wouldn't let their children be this close to the snakes." He smiled sadly. "They didn't believe."

I swallowed. I understood. In a strange way, it was hard to believe in an absolute good when I knew there was absolute evil in the world.

"When the evil came close . . . when people were being slaughtered in their sleep, they came here to the church. But they heard their friends and families calling to them from outside." Tears filled his eyes.

"The glamour," I said. "They came to us. They called to their families too. Convinced them to let them in . . ."

Pastor Gene shook his head. "I kept them from letting the evil in, but I couldn't keep them here. One by one, the Darkness called them. They called my wife, my sons."

"And they answered."

"They did. They slipped outside and became part of the Darkness. Became vampires. Those they don't devour completely become part of it."

"But not you."

"No . . . I heard only the hissing. Just the snakes."

I screwed up my courage, reached out and touched his sleeve. The garter snake slipped down over his elbow and flicked its tongue at my fingers. "I am sorry for your losses, Pastor Gene."

He shook his head. "I thought I was the last one on earth. Meant to suffer, like Job."

"No. There have to be more," I insisted.

His fingers closed over mine, and the striped green snake fell into my palm. I reflexively caught it. It was no larger than a pencil, warm and dry in my hand. I could feel the articulation of its spine as it moved.

It reminded me of when I was a child. Elijah had found a little garter snake in the barn. I'd taken it from him and set it free in a field. It had given me some satisfaction to see it vanish into the green grass, melting into the world.

"We shall have to take that as an article of faith."

Pastor Gene brought us a loaf of sandwich bread and canned meat from the church cellar. We fell upon it, ravenous. We sat in the first pew of the church, our feet tucked beneath us, one eye on the snakes and the other on the setting sun. Clouds were gathering in the west, blotting out the gold.

When the last of the light drained from the windows, Pastor Gene lit an oil lamp and set it on the altar.

"I sleep in the dark," he said. "But I thought that you might not be so used to the snakes."

"Thank you," I said. I had my feet on the pew before me, my arms wrapped around my knees. I could see the reptiles moving, hear them. It was more awful in the dark, not knowing where they were. I was not as afraid as I had been when I'd entered the church. But I was always unsure about the strength of my faith.

Ginger rubbed her arms. She kept turning her head right and left—I knew that she couldn't see well through her glasses in the dark, and the faint light sparked off the lenses.

I reached for her sleeve. "We should pray," I suggested.

"Yes. We should," Pastor Gene said. "The vampires are coming soon."

I bowed my head beside Ginger. I could see Alex silhouetted beyond us. He bowed his head respectfully, but his voice did not join the Lord's Prayer. Ginger and Pastor Gene spoke in English, and I spoke in Deitsch. I heard a tapping on the rafters above us, the beginnings of rain.

"Our Father, who art in Heaven . . ."

The pastor's voice was lovely, a large baritone. I thought to ask him if his church sang. Ours did, in our curiously chant-like way.

Rain pattered on the thick glass. Somewhere inside the church, I heard a trickle of drizzle from the roof. A copperhead slithered from the altar to a puddle forming on the floor.

I heard a huff in the back of the church: Horace fidgeting. His white shadow turned toward the window, and he tossed his head. The snakes began to hiss.

A soft scraping began at the window. I tried not to look, but I couldn't help it.

The glass was black and wet, and a white hand was pressed against it.

CHAPTER FOUR

"Don't look," Pastor Gene ordered.

I was certain he'd said that many times before. More white fingers made trails in the runnels of water on the glass. I caught a glimpse of a wristwatch, of a wedding ring, a ponytail. It reminded me that they had once been people. Maybe people that Pastor Gene knew.

The pastor wobbled to the altar. His gait was unsteady. A copperhead snake was wrapped around one wrist.

"Gene?" Alex asked. He leaped to his feet to follow.

The pastor turned. His eyes were vacant and garbled speech poured from his mouth. It sounded like gibberish, but his voice was loud and insistent, as if he was issuing a sermon in another language. He didn't seem to be speaking to us, didn't even seem aware of us at all. It was as if he'd dropped deep within himself, had closed himself off to the world and the terrible tapping on the windowpanes.

"I don't understand," I whispered.

"No one does," Alex said. "He may not even understand himself. He's speaking in tongues. The Spirit speaking through him. A gift."

I cocked my head. Why would God speak in a way that no one could understand?

"He's crazy," Ginger whispered. I took her hands in mine, squeezed.

"Quite possibly," Alex agreed. "But I'm not sure that matters at the end of the world."

I shuddered at the sound of the squeak of fingertips on the window, the scrape of a fingernail. I heard high-pitched pleas outside. I wondered if Pastor Gene's wife and children were there, if he'd flung himself into this ecstatic state to keep from looking at the chalky woman with the fathomless eyes behind the glass.

"They can't get in. They can't call us. They don't know us, have no tie to summon us. We're safe here," Alex said.

A fat copperhead slid along the back of the pew, and Ginger's nails dug into my palm.

Her gaze was wide behind her glasses. "I'm not convinced."

"As long as God is convinced." I screwed my eyes shut as a snake tongue flickered on the back of my sleeve.

Thunder rolled in from the west. I tried to sleep but fell into a rigid doze, punctuated by Pastor Gene's mumblings and pacing, the slither of snakes, the hiss of rain, and the wails of the vampires. I was afraid to let my feet touch the floor, but exhaustion dragged me under. I would nod off and start awake, hearing the roar of thunder and feeling each rustle of my dress and twitch of Ginger's hand as the movement of a poisonous snake. At some point during the night, I felt Alex come sit beside us, the reassuring warmth of his side against mine.

And the oil in the lamp burned out.

This must be hell, I remembered thinking. I sat on the pew between Ginger and Alex, my fingers intertwined in theirs. Pastor Gene's speaking in tongues had grown louder, almost furious. I heard the hissing of the snakes but couldn't tell where they were. I saw vampires slipping against the wet windows. They reminded me of the fish one of my friends won at a carnival on *Rumspringa,* swimming against the plastic bag and brushing against the glass bowl.

I prayed under my breath, prayed for morning to come.

I prayed for the snakes to leave us all alone.

I prayed for sleep.

I prayed for the vampires to go away.

I knew that it was wrong to ask for specific things from God. But I think that God heard me.

The dim light outside the church began to lighten almost imperceptibly. I recognized that light, despite the rain. It was a fine change in the graininess of the dark, but it signaled that morning was coming.

I blew out my breath, thanked God.

Thunder crashed overhead, deep enough to rattle the pews and the timbers of the church. Pastor Gene paused in his hoarse litany. The hair on the back of my neck and arms rose. My body tingled. I smelled something metallic in the air.

My heart leaped. I felt surreal. Light. Almost floating. As if God was close. I looked skyward, hopeful that perhaps this terrible Darkness was at an end.

A blinding flash of lightning seared through the windows, and a deafening crash struck the roof.

I jumped to my feet, jerking free of Alex and Ginger, and nearly stepped on a snake. I stumbled back and slapped my hand on the back of the pew. I felt something small and sharp sinking into my hand. I cried out, tripped. Alex caught me, and I could hear him swearing under his breath. I smelled something burning.

I glanced upward. A dull orange glow was emanating from the roof. A spark drifted down, and a snake slithered away from it.

"Lightning!" Alex shouted. "We have to get out of here."

"But the vampires," Ginger said. "We can't."

"It's almost dawn," I said.

I turned to look for Pastor Gene. He was facing the altar, reduced to a black shadow in the lurid light. I smelled smoke, and it moved between us. "Pastor Gene!"

His silhouette half turned toward us. I could feel snakes seething along the floor, like water flowing downstream. Orange light glistened along their scales. They sensed that fire was coming. Surely Pastor Gene could be shaken from his trance. The snakes were dropping from him as the smoke filled the tiny church. In the flickering light, he blinked at us, dazed.

Alex lunged up to the altar, grabbed his arm. "You have to come. Now."

Ginger and I made our way to the back door. My vision was filled with yellow flames shining on black smoke. My eyes teared up, and I couldn't breathe. I reached for the pawing white shape by the door, for Horace, and Ginger shoved the door open. Cool dark air sucked into the structure, shoving my skirts and the smoke behind me.

I turned, and saw fire racing all along the roof of the church. Alex and Pastor Gene were stumbling toward the door. My hands were wound in Horace's reins, and he dragged me out. My feet barely touched the steps as he lunged down, down into the dark.

I gasped for air, wavering on my feet, coughing. Rain spat on my face. I heard Ginger coughing beside me. I braced myself to feel the bright pain of vampires tearing into my flesh, but no pain came. Through slitted eyes, I saw a bright ribbon of gold under gray clouds at the horizon.

Dawn.

A terrifying crash sounded from the church as the roof collapsed in on itself. The roof was too wet to burn, but the old timber beneath it went up like dry pine. This was like a fire that I'd seen as a child. A neighbor's barn had burned to the ground in the winter, devoured by a conflagration that killed three men. The men in our community had rebuilt that barn, but I knew that wouldn't happen with this church. Fear lanced through me when I realized that Alex wasn't behind me.

"Alex!" I screamed. I took two steps toward the door of the church, but Ginger grabbed me around the waist.

"No!" she shouted. I struggled against her, screaming.

Two dark shapes appeared in the ruined door frame, and I gasped in relief. Alex was supporting Pastor Gene, and they clambered down the burning steps to the cool of the grass. The last of the rain spangled the gloom and fire.

I moved to embrace Alex, but my legs felt rubbery and didn't obey. My hand burned. My heart pounded like the thunder and my breath came quickly.

I stumbled. I fell to the ground and tugged up the edge of my sleeve to stare at my hand, dimly remembering the sting in the church. It had blossomed into a terrible pain, and blood trickled down my wrist into my elbow.

My fingers spasmed, and I turned over and vomited into the wet dirt.

I felt a shadow over me and cool hands on my wrist. Ginger ripped open my sleeve above the ripe, swollen flesh. Alex cradled my head in his lap. I could see Parson Gene above me.

"She's been snakebit," Ginger said. "Did you see what kind of snake got you, sweetie?"

I shook my head. That gesture caused my head to swim.

"How bad is it?" Alex demanded.

"Bad." Pastor Gene's face was white, white as a vampire's. "It's poisonous. Runners of poison are moving up her arm. I saw this once before . . . my uncle got bit by a copperhead when I was a boy."

"How did you stop the venom?"

"We didn't."

I blinked up into the drizzling dawn. I had not imagined that I would die this way. It was laughable, really. I expected to be chewed to pieces by vampires. Not poisoned by the bite of a snake.

But a part of me had hoped that I'd survive this, that my faith would be strong enough to see myself and my friends through the Darkness. I wanted to believe that I was indeed favored by God and that I would eventually be united with my family in heaven. I wanted to believe that I was special. Loved.

But that was impossible. Tears blurred my vision, and I

hiccupped back a sob. What I had told Pastor Gene was true: I had not been baptized. But I had not told him what that meant. I was caught out. My baptized friends and family back home would go to heaven. Since I had not accepted God, I would be separated from them forever. In Darkness, alone.

"We have to help her!" Alex gathered me in his arms and rushed toward the horse. The movement made me nauseated.

"No." I heard Pastor Gene's voice. "There's no one within riding distance who can help her. You'll be carrying a corpse."

"We have to do something," Alex said. I could feel him trembling, hear his heart roaring in his chest. "We can't just let her die."

"Bring her here." Ginger's voice. I was tangled in arms and felt the ground beneath me. I heard a tearing sound, saw her tie white fabric from her apron around my shoulder.

"She'll lose her arm if you put a tourniquet on . . ." Alex began.

"Better she lose her arm than die. Unless . . . that stuff that they show on television about sucking out poison works." Ginger turned on Pastor Gene. "Does it?"

"No. It's a myth. The only thing that can save her from poison is to be full of the Holy Spirit. We have to pray."

"You . . . you shut up." I could hear the fury in Alex's voice. "This is your fault. You and your damn snakes."

"The Spirit hadn't filled her up yet, so the snake—"

I heard the thud of flesh on flesh. A blow. Alex had struck the pastor. I winced, tried to speak, but my lips felt swollen and rubbery.

From some distance away Alex shouted, "This isn't her fault! She's the most pious person I've ever met."

I struggled to turn my head, to mouth the word "Stop."

Pastor Gene picked himself off the grass. He rolled up his sleeves. I saw the puckering of scars up and down his forearms. "I've been bit before. She can survive it. The Spirit is in her, just not filled her."

"How?" Alex demanded. "And don't tell me to pray."

"I'll pray, damn it. If that's what it takes." Ginger hovered over me, scraping wet hair from my forehead. "I'm not going to lose another child."

Sorrow and pride stung me. Ginger considered me to be one of her children. And was sad that I would be taken from her. Just like the others.

"Bring her to the creek," Pastor Gene said. "The water can cure her."

Alex lifted me, and I felt the bumping cadence of his walk over the uneven ground. His arms trembled, and I wondered if it was from the strain of carrying me or from fear. I felt grief to know that I would not learn to understand him better. To love him more deeply than I already did, to see where that spark of affection would have led us. With him, I might have had a life beyond the farm and marriage and children that was expected of me. And now I would never know.

I began to pray in my head. I didn't pray for salvation, or mercy—I just wanted to feel the comfort of the familiar words. I could feel my heart hammering so hard that I thought it would break.

"Bring her into the water."

I heard the slosh and splash of Alex wading into the creek. I dimly wondered if the snakes were still there. Cold water dampened my skirts, and I felt the shock of the chill against my back.

My right arm twitched, the muscles cramping up tight. My fingers curled into painful claws, and the hot sting of the venom coursed through my blood. I could feel it reaching, reaching toward my lungs and my heart. Water splashed around me, droplets rattling around. I could feel my jaw clench and hear my own breathing, very close.

"She's having a seizure," I heard Alex say.

Hands brushed my forehead. They were rough and callused. Pastor Gene's hands. Alex's and Ginger's palms pressed my back, supporting me in the water. I swallowed a bit of the creek. It tasted like iron, cold and pure.

"Heavenly Father, please grant us the gift of healing for Katie, your daughter in Christ. Fill her with the Holy Spirit and drive out the venom. In Jesus' name, we pray . . ."

His words grew unintelligible. Maybe he was speaking in tongues again. But it seemed that I couldn't hear what Alex and Ginger said either. Ringing filled my ears. My muscles slackened as I felt the heat of the venom reach my heart. I stared up. I was suspended, weightless, between the prayer and white sky.

I was nothing. I was less than a feather, dark and vanishing in that vast expanse.

CHAPTER FIVE

I don't know that I ever had any particular thoughts or expectations about what heaven would be like. To be honest, I'd always been too caught up in the day-to-day details of life to really ponder it in more than a vague "someday" sort of way. Deep down, I wanted it to be a certainty. I expected it. I believed that I was good. And I believed that I'd have time to make up for all my sins.

But the end of the world had undone all of that.

And now I was going to be undone. Caught out. And lost from those I loved forever.

I wondered if it would always be like this: the searing heat of the venom, the cold of the water, the pearly gray-white of the sky surrounding me. Gradually, it all faded, even the ringing and the sensation of water in my ears, leaving behind that sense of sky.

I closed my eyes, savoring that feeling of the in-between.

And sucked in my breath.

It hurt to do so. It hurt more than anything I'd ever done.

The air in my lungs seemed to sear their interior, but I made myself breathe.

I was not yet done with life. I had too much left undone. I would fight for it.

I stared, blinking. I saw three faces above me: Ginger, Pastor Gene, and Alex. There was such an awful expression of fear on Alex's face that I wanted to reach up and wipe away.

But I started to shiver.

Alex broke into a smile, and his ice-blue eyes glistened. "You with us?"

"Ja," I said, through chattering teeth. "I am."

"She's freezing," Ginger said. "Bring her to the fire."

It took the three of them to haul my sodden body from the creek, up the bank. I was in Alex's arms, and I pressed my ear to his chest as he carried me toward the burning church. I could feel the heat on my back, but I shivered violently. Alex sat behind me, wrapping his arms around me, and rested his chin on my hair.

I stared down at my hand. It was swollen to three times its normal size, gone black and red as a rotten apple. It didn't look like my own body—it looked like something that belonged on a corpse. Pink water drained from the wound. It throbbed, but not with the sharp viciousness as before. Ginger huddled over it and began wrapping it up in fabric from her apron.

"It's a miracle," Pastor Gene said, crouching beside us.

"Ja," I said, too exhausted to argue.

And the four of us watched the church burn down, blackening and curling in on itself in silence.

────────

I fell asleep and dreamed of a snake.

It wasn't just any snake.

In the dream, I was back at home in my village. Night shrouded me in a soft blanket of darkness, and I was walking through the field toward my house. I'd recognize that sharp roofline against a starry sky anywhere. A light burned brightly inside. I ran toward the house, but it seemed that the light kept moving farther away.

Ravens cawed in the sky, darker specks of black against the purple night. They moved as one, south, away from the land I knew and loved. I knew that something terrible must have disturbed them.

But I was determined to make it to the house. At last, I reached the back step. I tugged open the screen door.

In the light of a lantern, I saw a familiar silhouette.

"Elijah," I breathed.

He turned toward me. He was taller than I was, with dark hair and hazel eyes. But his gaze was hooded. I'm not sure of the exact point at which I began to think of him as my enemy. Maybe it was when he had gotten baptized before I did, crossed that invisible divide from ordinary to blessed. Maybe when he had insisted that I do it, as well, and that we should be married without tasting the Outside world. But it was certainly when he found Alex and me together and brought the Elders to my doorstep.

I flinched away from him. "What are you doing here?"

He looked at me from under the brim of his hat. "What are *you* doing here? You don't belong here anymore."

A lump rose in my throat. I had no answer. I wanted to say:

"This is my home. Of course I belong here." But the words would not come.

I heard something beyond him, in the living room. I knew that sound, from the church.

I pushed past Elijah to see what it was. I stopped cold in my tracks.

Something lay in the shadows, bloated and dark. It curled around the room, thick and black as a rotting tree trunk. It was a massive snake, at least thirty feet long. It scraped around the bottom of table legs, behind the couch and wooden chairs and treadle sewing machine, its scales moving against the hardwood floors.

Impossible.

I knew it for what it was. It was no snake. It was pure evil. It was in my house.

I wheeled to Elijah. "You let it in."

He stared past me. The snake's head, as large as a pumpkin, came into view. Its eyes reflected the lantern light like those of the vampires. I could tell that Elijah was hypnotized by it. Glamoured.

I grasped his arm and shook it. "Where are my parents? Where is Sarah?"

Dazed, he pointed to the snake. It gathered its coils to itself, and then I noticed that it had a lumpy, engorged shape.

I stopped breathing. As it slid past me, I counted one lump . . . two lumps . . . three lumps.

The snake turned its head toward me and opened its mouth.

Its fangs were as white as a vampire's, and its hiss was the one I heard from the undead creatures in the night.

The sound of a predator.

———

I woke with a start, against Alex's shoulder.

"Shhh." He stroked my hair. "It's all right."

I felt warmth on my face. But it wasn't the heat of the fire. The church had burned down to black timbers and red embers. What I felt was the warmth of the late morning sun, melting through the last of the gray clouds.

I pulled my bandaged arm into my lap, wincing. It was sore, but the swelling seemed to have gone down. I saw Ginger and Pastor Gene sitting a few yards away, talking in low tones. Horace grazed in the grass beyond.

Beside me, I saw my *Himmelsbrief,* weighted down with a small stone. Alex must have taken it out of my pocket and carefully plucked open the folds to dry it. The ink looked a bit blurry, but it was still legible. I hoped that would be enough.

"I'm going to be all right," I said. I couldn't stand the worried look on his face. I reached up with my uninjured hand and pressed my palm to his cheek.

"I was worried." He turned his head and kissed my fingertips.

I cast my eyes down and blushed. I felt the hand of God in this, but I didn't know how to say this to Alex. I didn't think that he would really believe it, not the way that I did. There was a vast chasm of something between us. Faith. He was still a good man, upright and much kinder than many people of my own sect. But I didn't understand how he could do the right thing without thinking that God was watching. I knew that he had his own moral compass that led him, and sometimes it seemed stronger than my own.

Pastor Gene had stood up and was approaching us.

"How are you feeling, Katie?"

"Weak," I said, honestly. "But much better than before."

He crouched beside me. "It'll take some time before you're feeling normal again. Bites can take a long while to heal entirely. But I think you had some help." He winked.

I felt Alex glowering above me, but I smiled back at the pastor. "Thank you, Pastor Gene."

My smile faded as my gaze tracked back to the burned-out husk of his church. Two walls were standing, with the wet roof caved in over it. The structure was no longer habitable, and the vampires could reach in and pluck us out like sweetbreads if we tried to stay.

His eyes followed mine. "It's just a building," he said. "All the people who were in it are gone."

"Come with us," I said. "We are going north. To Canada."

He shook his head. "It's time for me to come out of hiding, to see what remains of my family and the rest of the world."

My brow knit. "Where will you go?"

His gaze drifted off to the horizon. "I have nieces and nephews out west. And following the sun doesn't seem to be bad advice these days."

He patted my cheek, pressed his hand to Alex's shoulder. I saw the green tail of a garter snake in his beard. He rose up,

took one last look at the church, and walked across the field
with his hands in his pockets.

I gripped Alex's sleeve. "Will he be all right . . . alone?"

"Yeah. I think so. And I don't think he'll be alone."

In his wake, the grass rippled, and I saw the shadows of
snakes following him.

———————

We turned away from the smoldering fire. I carefully climbed
up on Horace's back. I cradled my wounded arm in my lap,
but the jostle of the horse's stride made it ache enough to set
my teeth on edge. But walking was just as bad, and Ginger had
ordered me to conserve my strength.

We headed north, as we always did. I did not turn back
to the burned church. I saw Ginger looking at it sadly as we
moved across the meadow. I imagine that Lot's wife had much
the same expression on her face.

"Don't look back," I said. "It's *Gelassenheit*. God's will."

She shook her head. "It would have been good to stay
someplace for a few days. To rest. But not with the snakes."

I lifted my chin. "And not with the fire. Fire is something
that all Plain people fear."

"Because of no fire department?"

"*Ja*. By the time that someone can run to find a phone, it's
usually too late. And it is a particular fear in the winter."

"Why winter?"

"Because our chores stretch beyond the daylight hours.
And we carry lanterns around many flammable things in the
barn. One overturned lantern can engulf a barn in minutes. It
can kill animals, people . . ."

"I guess I never feared fire much before," Ginger said. "But now that those modern conveniences are gone . . . perhaps I will again."

"It feels strange to be afraid of something so essential to survival," Alex said. "I wonder if Prometheus knew how much we would fear it."

"Who is Prometheus?" I asked.

"In Greek mythology, he was a Titan, one of the old gods that were a generation before Zeus and the rest of the Olympians. Zeus asked Prometheus to create man, but in doing so, Prometheus felt some sympathy for his creation. Prometheus watched man struggle to find enough to eat, to build places to live, and felt pretty darn sorry for our incompetence.

"So he brought us a gift. He stole one of Zeus's lightning bolts and gave it to man. It was the gift of fire. It kept man from freezing to death, helped him cook food. It saved man from a short life of cold savagery."

I shook my head. Alex's stories were exactly that—good stories. But I did not believe in the underlying morality of those old, cruel gods.

Ginger kept walking backwards, looking for the fire. And I resolutely looked forward, remembering how Lot's wife looked backwards, full of salt and tears. No good could come of that.

Within hours, my fear proved to be a prediction.

We smelled the fire before we saw it.

It wasn't the benign, warm smell of wood smoke. This was acrid, chemical. It was the stench of man-made things burning: plastic, gasoline, rubber.

We'd walked through the morning, having found a two-lane road. Horace trotted along the soft shoulder to save the wear and tear of pavement on his hooves. The clop of his hooves on the earth created a mechanical marching rhythm and an ache in my bones. We didn't speak, shuffling along at Ginger's pace. She struggled and wheezed a bit, but we went steadily. There was no traffic. No cars. Just buzzards circling in the distance. And a dark haze on the horizon.

The road fell away at a crossroads, and we plodded over a hill that seemed to go on forever. When we reached the crest, we stopped.

A city lay below us in the valley, burning.

I sucked in my breath. I had never seen a city before. I had imagined that it would be as I had seen in books and newspapers: skyscrapers laced with gray ribbons of road and overhung with the glitter of electric light shining against mirrored glass. It would be towering and vast and glamorous, full of life and movement. This was where I had intended to go on *Rumspringa,* a lifetime ago.

I was here, but this was not what I had pictured. There were tall buildings surrounded by a black cloak of smoke. Orange flames reflected on broken glass. Stilled cars blocked congested streets.

I stared ahead. "Should we go down there?"

Ginger's fingers knit in her coat sleeves. "There might be people down there. Radios. Survivors."

My stomach growled.

"And food," she added. "Supplies."

Alex frowned. "It could be infested. Probably is. Dangerous."

"It's daylight," Ginger said. I could hear the yearning in her voice for news. For hope.

"They can be awake during the daytime," I reminded her. "All they need is shadow, indoors, away from the sun." I had encountered a nest of them before in daylight hours, on an excursion from my old home to the nearby town. They had nearly killed me.

"It's too dangerous," Alex said.

"What if . . . what if we stayed in the open? Stayed on the street . . . found something to eat, and left right away?"

"There aren't only vamps to worry about. Survivors could be just as violent," Alex pointed out. "Especially if they're hungry or desperate. Violence is the first rule after any disaster. We're better off on the road."

I pressed my fingertips to my lips. I didn't want to believe that humans could be terrible to each other. But I'd seen what a disaster could do to even a small community, like mine. We had turned on ourselves, begun threatening each other with expulsion and dogma.

"We have to try," I said. "There's not going to be much more forage. Frost's coming."

Alex sighed and kicked at a rock. "Maybe we can find a car or something that runs."

I leaned protectively against the horse's neck. "We can't leave Horace behind. All of us or none of us."

He reached out and tenderly touched my cheek. "Horace will be fine. We can't—"

He saw the ferociousness in my face. My grip tightened on the reins. "All of us or none of us," I repeated.

His hand dropped and he stuffed it in his pocket. "It'll . . . it'll work out."

We descended the hill and walked down a highway off ramp together. Horace's hooves rang loudly against the pavement, piercing the silence. My heart clunked unevenly in my chest as we approached a truck stop that spread out by this, the first exit to the city. The blacktop lot was mostly empty, but my spirits lifted when I saw a few tractor trailers parked there and imagined that Horace could fit in the back of one of them. A convenience store, gas station, and deli were housed in the same building. A sign listing prices for diesel and unleaded fuel stood above advertisements for sodas, cigarettes, and sandwiches.

I could tell that the place had been abandoned. My heart sank. A chain was run through the handles of the front door and fixed with a padlock. Ginger grabbed the pay phone receiver and shook her head. "No dial tone."

The locks on the building had done little good. The glass in the window was shattered, and I could see a toppled display of fruit pies inside. I slid down from the horse and found my stake in his gear. I tucked the weapon into the crook of my right elbow, pressing myself forward against the dizziness creeping into my skull. I reached with my left hand through the ruined window, conscious of the hollowness in my belly.

I snatched a lemon fruit pie from the display, clutched it to my apron. I peered into the half shadow inside.

Sunlight streamed inside the store about four feet. The only things that moved were the dust motes. I could make out toppled racks of candy and bottles of car fluids. I smelled stale beer spilled on the floor and wrinkled my nose.

"I think we can get in there," I said, gesturing to the broad safety of the stripe of sunshine.

Alex looked inside. "I'll go first, see if it's clear. If it is, you can come in after."

I opened my mouth, closed it. For all of Alex's foreign manner, he did try to be chivalrous, to protect me.

I nodded, gripping my stake with my good hand.

Chapter Six

Alex stepped through the shattered window frame. I held my breath, watching as the sunlight washed through his blond hair and poured over his shoulders. I glimpsed the reflection of sun on his knife. As he moved away from me, into the darkness, the daylight drained away. I could hear his footsteps crunching in the glass, but soon even that soft pulverizing sound fell silent.

I balanced my wounded palm carefully on a shard of glass in the window frame and strained to see beyond the silhouettes of ruined displays. I smelled curdled milk, tobacco, and sour coffee. Lottery tickets had been dragged from behind the checkout counter like streamers. The cash register was broken open on the floor, surrounded by glistening change.

"Alex?" My hand tightened on the shard, summoning a trickle of blood. I snatched my hand away, pressed the heel of my palm to my mouth to stanch the flow. I tasted blood—warm and coppery. It turned my stomach. How the vampires found sustenance in such thin liquid baffled me.

I heard steps crunching back in the glass and candy. Alex's lanky silhouette came into view.

"It's clear," he said, and I could hear the relief in his voice. "And there's food."

Ginger and I clambered though the window. I felt a tiny pang of guilt as I scavenged down the aisles, filling my apron pockets with packages of food. I tore open a candy bar, stuffed it into my mouth without really tasting it to quell the rumbling in my belly.

Alex had ripped open a door in the refrigerated section and was pawing through the sticky cans.

"No beer," he mumbled. "I would really like a beer."

Ginger gave him a dark look. "You'd have to fight me for it." She lifted a bottle of clear liquid. "The vodka's all mine."

Alex swore. "Damn it. Looks like looters already got the rest of the good stuff."

Funny how we didn't consider ourselves to be looters. Just survivors.

I paused before a glass door. Behind it was a display of red and white Coca-Cola bottles. I had developed a sweet tooth for Coca-Cola on my excursions to the local English-run general store back at home. I reached in and grabbed a bottle. It was warm. I twisted off the cap and took a slug. It tasted hot and unsatisfying.

I turned toward the counter, stepping through ribbons of lottery tickets. I spied the aspirin, Band-Aids, and medicines behind the counter and figured we would need those.

And as I came around the edge of the counter, it was clear that the occupants of the store no longer needed them.

A rust-colored stain covered the gray speckled tile. It was

large, as if someone had bled a great deal, but faint, as if it had happened a long time ago.

I crouched down. There were small swipes and rills in the stain. Sweat prickled the back of my neck. I had seen that pattern before, when I'd spilled milk on the floor and the dogs had licked it up.

"They've been here," I said.

"There are more in the city than in the countryside. Simple math. Which is why we shouldn't linger," Alex said, reaching past me for a bottle of aspirin.

I nodded and retreated. I left my Coke on the counter, having lost my appetite. I stared at a stack of very thin newspapers. They were from six weeks ago, and the headline was "SUS-PECTED VIRUS INFECTS EASTERN US — RESIDENTS URGED TO STAY INDOORS." Only one page was printed. I scanned the article:

(AP) In a press conference from a bunker in Greenbriar, West Virginia, the president urged residents to remain calm. A highly contagious blood-borne pathogen with symptoms similar to rabies has infected major metropolitan areas in the eastern U.S., while similar reports of outbreaks are developing worldwide.

"We are working on a way to control the epidemic," the president said. "But it is critically important to stay calm. The world's top researchers at the Centers for Disease Control are working on a way to identify and isolate the pathogen. In the meantime, stay indoors and do not open your doors for anyone after dark."

When asked if there was any truth to the rumor that the pathogen arose from germ warfare, specifically Tuesday morning's detonation of a dirty bomb in Washington, D.C., the president said that he could "neither confirm nor deny" such reports. He issued a similar response to rumors that the pathogen developed in Chernobyl, Fukushima, or nuclear testing sites in the Middle East.

The National Guard will be enforcing quarantine orders in the following affected areas: New York, Baltimore, Washington, D.C. . . .

I tucked away the paper to read later. It was old news, but perhaps we could glean something useful from it. I had been calling the creatures we were fighting vampires. The Hexenmeister had simply called them Darkness. It was useful shorthand for what we saw. But there was still doubt among Alex and Ginger about what they really were, of what fusion of myth and technology blighted our world.

Alex reached under the counter, began fiddling with a black machine with knobs, a radio the size of a large breadbox.

Ginger was beside him instantly. "Is the radio working?"

"I think the battery's about gone."

The two of them began poking and prodding the machine. I heard a low hiss, varying in volume as they changed the numbers on the dial.

Ginger grabbed a handheld device wired to the radio box and spoke into it: "Mayday, is there anybody out there? Over."

Alex continued to fiddle with the dials. Perhaps they could summon a voice out of it, some hope that we were not alone.

"Mayday, mayday, is anyone out there? Over."

I heard only the dull, rushing hiss. They continued to try to work the machine. Once, it seemed like there was a garbled human voice at the other end.

I held my breath.

"Repeat that? What's your twenty?" Ginger's fingers tightened on the microphone.

The voice sharpened and then faded.

"There are people out there," she said, her knuckles white on the black plastic. "Probably in the city."

"That's a great way to get killed. We can't fight a city of vampires, even in the daylight," Alex said.

"But we have to find out what happened," she protested.

"We may never know what happened," Alex charged. "The only thing we can do is survive."

Ginger threw the corded plastic microphone down on the countertop so hard that it bounced and struck a reel of lottery tickets. She stormed away to the back of the store.

Alex moved to follow her, but I caught his sleeve. "Give her some time," I said, as soothingly as I could.

He grunted and went back to rummaging through the medicines.

I gravitated toward a strange contraption in the corner. It stood on four legs, and had a glass tabletop with colored bits of enamel and springs inside.

"It's a pinball machine," Alex said.

I blinked. "It makes . . . pinballs?"

"No. It's a game. You put in a quarter." He pointed to the slot. "A ball gets loaded here." He gestured to a rod with a spring wrapped around it and pulled. It made a startlingly loud noise in the silence.

I jumped back, and he chuckled. "It's a lot more fun when the power's on. The ball hits the bells, and it lights up. You score points based on how long the ball's in play."

I leaned curiously over the glass. "Interesting." I met his eyes. "You actually pay money for this?"

"Remind me to show you Pac-Man sometime."

I frowned. "We play checkers or chess back home . . ." My voice trailed off. "Or, we did."

Alex squeezed my shoulder. "Maybe we can find a chess set somewhere along the way."

"There's water!" Ginger exclaimed.

I turned, clutching my apron full of goodies. Ginger had emerged from a hallway marked SHOWERS. Her hair was wet, and she held a bottle of shampoo. She looked overjoyed.

"It's working?" Alex's face split into a grin. He let out a spontaneous whoop and tore off his jacket.

"Yes! I don't know if it's still what's left in the pipes, but there's water. And it's even kind of warm."

I scurried down the tiled hallway. Ginger had started a fire in a wastebasket, and the flames illuminated a bathroom. Lockers stood on the left side, sinks on the right. And beyond them, shower stalls. I wrapped my apron up, kicked off my shoes. I peeled off my dress, mindful to keep track of the pins that fastened it together, threw my bonnet and the rest of my clothes in a pile, and skidded into the nearest stall.

I turned the handle and held my breath.

A blessed stream of lukewarm water flowed out and over my head. I scrubbed it through my hair and over my face. I felt filthy. Not just from the grime of the journey. From the evil and destruction. From hopelessness. It clung to me like a corrosive film. I could feel evil creeping into my pores, feel my morality slipping down the drain. Each day, I was slipping further and further away from my faith. I had begun to demand things of God. I had surrendered to fear and doubt.

I choked back a sob. I felt that I was falling. Failing. I squeezed my eyes shut. I couldn't tell if there were tears on my face or just the warm water.

The sweet smell of violets assaulted my nose. I took a deep breath, savoring that innocent scent.

I felt hands in my hair, the soft lather of shampoo. Startled, I twisted back to find that Alex was massaging my scalp

Naked.

I felt a flush crawling over my cheeks. "I . . ."

It wasn't as if I hadn't seen him in the nude before. I'd given myself to him back home. I knew that it had been wrong, violated every rule I'd been taught. But I cared for him. Not in a romantic, head-over-heels kind of passionate longing I'd seen glorified in the English magazines. Instead, I felt a deep steadiness when we were together, a quiet reservoir of strength. It made me wonder whether there were different kinds of love, for different kinds of people.

But it was still new, and I was still shy. My hands curled over my chest to cover myself, but my eyes roved over the water sluicing down his shoulders. The scarred ankh on his heart contrasted sharply with his fair skin, and I could see the black Djed pillar creeping up his neck in ink.

I don't know that I could say that we were "in love" the way that they talk about in books. But it was the end of the world. "I thought you'd like this." He held up a bottle of scented shampoo. Water dripped down his chiseled chin and he grinned sheepishly. "It says it's 'violet wisteria water blossom, with ylang ylang.' I don't know what that is, but it sounded girly, eh?"

"Where's Ginger?" I managed to croak.

He jabbed a thumb behind him. "She's out there, playing with a musical toothbrush."

I could hear tinny jingling and happy chortling behind the trickle of water.

He tenderly wiped a glob of soap from my eye. "I . . ."

The water suddenly dropped in temperature, and I squealed. I thrust my soapy head under the cold water to finish rinsing off, then stepped back for Alex to do the same.

I beat a hasty retreat to the room with the wall-mounted hair dryers. Ginger was wrapped in a towel, bobbing her head along in time to her musical toothbrush.

I snatched up a towel from a pile in the corner and began to dry myself off. I'd gotten myself pinned back in my dress by the time Ginger had made herself decent. I looked down at my apron full of food and set about tying the corners together. Ginger didn't mention the flush that still clung to my face, but I could feel the heat.

And that couldn't be good. Not for me, and certainly not for the fragile state of my faith.

We'd scavenged through the convenience store in less than an hour, stuffing everything we could carry into plastic grocery bags and some mildewy-smelling laundry bags that we'd found in the shower area. We'd come away with some good first-aid supplies, some food, fresh water, and some lighters. Those would be helpful—though I could start a fire without one, it was time-consuming and very dependent upon the weather. I'd also found a small collection of brooms and mops that would make good stakes. And we'd found maps. Those were the most valuable things.

My heart soared a bit at our good fortune, and I set about tying the bags to Horace's tack. He pressed his head into my chest and I rubbed his forelock.

"I promise not to leave you behind," I murmured.

He seemed nervous, pawing and fussing at the packs I'd tied to him. I took this to mean that he wasn't used to being used as a pack mule. But I was still eager to move on.

I glanced at the city skyline on the horizon, and longing welled up within me. I had always wanted to see the city someday, but it seemed that "someday" would never come. Not that my faith needed any more tempting.

Alex had hopped up into the cab of the nearest truck. It had a big, boxy trailer. I stared at the one with a cylindrical trailer parked next to it. I had seen trucks like this one at one of the bigger commercial dairy farms near my old home. But

I didn't think this one had milk in it. It bore a placard with an orange flame on it marked FLAMMABLE.

"No keys," Alex announced, jumping down to the pavement.

I frowned. I wasn't sure he could even manage to drive such a huge vehicle. Though I supposed that there were few penalties now if we hit anything.

"But I found something useful." He threw a piece of black plastic at me.

I caught it, turned it over in my hand. It had jagged edges, as if he'd pried it out of the dashboard with a knife. It was a compass.

"How about this one?" I pointed to the flammable truck's cab. I didn't know if there was a way that we could switch out the trailers to accommodate Horace.

"There were keys in the tanker truck, but gas got siphoned from it. I already checked."

I glanced at the puddle below it, wondering if it was gasoline. Squinting closer, I could see dripping from the metal seams.

Alex crossed to the back of the truck trailer. "Maybe there are some things we can use in here. If we're lucky, it's hauling a fully gassed-up Maserati."

I didn't know what a Maserati was, but it sounded like a good thing.

"Don't hold your breath," Ginger said. "I think we used up our luck on the candy bars."

Alex reached up for the handle of the trailer door and pulled it down. "Probably not. If gas was scavenged, then there's probably nothing else left for us to use."

The door swung open, and Horace whinnied. The hair rose up on the back of my neck.

"Alex, don't!" I screamed.

Pale hands reached out of the darkness of the trailer and dragged him inside.

CHAPTER SEVEN

I snatched up a broom and dug a lighter out of a bag with shaking and swollen fingers. I ran to the door of the truck. Chalky hands were already trying to pull it shut, but I saw that they smoked in the sunlight. I smelled burning meat.

I lit the bristles of the broom with the lighter and thrust it into the darkness before me. The vampires shrieked and hissed, recoiling from the fire. I swept the broom right and left.

I scrambled up on the edge of the truck trailer and plunged inside.

My vision took a moment to adjust to the darkness, and I was blind in the glare of the makeshift torch. I felt a spider web stretch across my face and break, the very sensation of evil, and I couldn't stifle a shudder.

This was a vampire nest. Thin filaments of something like spider silk streamed from the top of the cavernous trailer. Shadows moved in the guttering torchlight, skittering across the floor and crawling up on the ceiling. I was reminded of a nest of daddy longlegs that my sister and I had disturbed while cleaning out a barn. The vampires gathered on the ceiling, hissing, bobbing, the fire reflected in their cold red eyes.

"Give him back." I heard my voice issuing the command, and it sounded so much more assured than I felt. I reached into my pocket for the *Himmelsbrief.*

Something snickered above me.

I stared up into the reflective eyes of a vampire. He wore a flannel shirt and a hat with an advertising logo on it. I wondered if he might have been the trucker who owned the vehicle. "Your fire will burn out, girlie. Then you're ours."

My eyes slid to the guttering flame at the top of the broom. It was burning fast, the bristles blackening and curling.

I thrust the flaming bristles into his face. The vampire howled at the sparks and batted it away. The broom spiraled away in the darkness, and I lunged for it. I singed my fingers trying to pick it up.

An aggrieved yowl emanated from the far darkness at the front of the trailer.

"Alex!" I shouted.

I grabbed the last of my makeshift torch and advanced toward the writhing shadows, my heart in my mouth.

A pale figure flopped and writhed toward me. I moved to jam my torch in its face, but I saw familiar markings on the flesh. Alex's tattoos. His jacket and shirt had been torn from his shoulders and he was crawling toward the door, slashing with his knife.

I swept the broom right and left over his head as we backed to the opening, toward daylight.

"It's not going to be that easy, girlie. We're too hungry."

The trucker vampire slammed the door shut behind us, blotting out the sunshine. My heart stopped—I could hear it stop over the clang of the door.

"Get behind me," Alex muttered.

The light from my broom faded to sparks, and I heard the *thunk-thunk-thunk* of vampires dropping from the ceiling like too-ripe apples on the ground. I could feel the weight of the creatures' eyes upon us. They seemed almost human, palpable in their need, except for the red glow of the sparks in their eyes. But I knew that they were not like us, that they had left humanity behind a long time ago. I felt the strand of a spider web brush across my face, and I shivered violently enough to shake the last of the sparks from the broom.

"Come here, girlie." I smelled fetid breath. I knew that this was a vampire's attempt at glamour, at seducing a victim with its voice. I'd seen it before. Men and women could be lulled into a lassitude, follow the vampires and bare their flesh to them. But the holy letter I held insulated me from it, just as Alex's tattoos made him resistant to that siren call.

Before, I'd been grateful to God for such a boon. Now, that might serve only to make us painfully aware of a slow, agonizing death. We'd be lucid rather than walking blindly into death in a soft dream state.

I began to pray beneath my breath.

And my prayer was answered in a blinding flash of light.

White-hot brightness flooded the compartment. The door was torn open, and a short silhouette stood in the open void. And that figure held fire in her fist.

"Leave those kids alone," Ginger's voice bellowed.

The vampires turned toward her, snarling. She held a bottle in her hand with a flaming rag trickling from the top. I dimly registered it as her prize — the bottle of vodka she'd scavenged from the convenience store cooler.

She hurled the bottle into the trailer. It sailed over our heads and struck the far wall with a sound like a gunshot. It exploded into glass and flame.

I ducked, trying to shield my eyes. Fire blistered from the makeshift bomb, and raced over the wall in a liquid rush of blue and orange flame. I heard howling, smelled burning meat . . .

. . . and there were hands tangled in my apron straps. Alex hauled me through the door of the trailer, into the daylight. I landed on my shoulder on the blacktop, gasping as the wind was knocked out of me.

I felt Alex land on top of me. I rolled back, under his arm, seeing shadows seething at the mouth of the trailer through blurred vision. I clutched his arm, struggling to breathe.

Ginger stood before the opening of the trailer. In each hand, she held a bottle of lighter fluid. She twisted open the cap of one bottle and hurled it into the conflagration.

Squeals and screams echoed from inside. I wanted to clap my hands over my ears. It sounded like the screaming of pigs. The neighbors' barn that had burned when I was a child held two dozen pigs inside. It was not a sound I'd ever forgotten.

"Burn!"

Ginger's glasses reflected the fire inside the truck. Her face was twisted into something I didn't recognize. I had always known her to be motherly, passive. She'd faced the end of the world with a soft shock, hesitating and confused.

But now . . . now, she was wrathful.

She hurled the second bottle into the truck. The open neck of it arced into the air. Flame licked from the interior of the trailer, igniting those clear drops. They splashed on the pavement, burning in a puddle.

Ginger turned her back on the truck, her gait stiff as she approached us. She seemed a different woman now, full of the power of anger that sang through her.

"Ginger," I wheezed. I could barely squeak, so I pointed behind her.

Something was crawling out of the trailer.

She turned, her skirt swirling in the backdraft. A flaming creature clawed beyond the lip of the truck, slipped to the blacktop like a bat startled during daytime. It scuttled right and left, flopping, as fire crackled along its spine.

But it was daylight. And daylight was just as deadly to these creatures as fire.

Ginger stared at it as its blackened jaws opened and closed, as its fingers spasmed and curled in on themselves like burning paper.

"Burn!"

I saw then that her eyes were damp beneath her glasses. Of all of us, Ginger may have lost the most. And I could see that she wanted these creatures of night to suffer.

My eyes fell to the trickle of lighter fluid on the pavement. The burning creature scuttled to the nearest shadow — the underbelly of the next truck.

The one with fire on the placard.

I drew half a breath to scream at her. Alex pulled me to my feet. I saw understanding cross Ginger's face, and she began to run.

We ran to Horace. The horse had begun to retreat, cantering along the shoulder of the road, away from us. Away from the evil. And away from what he could smell coming.

Thunder roared behind us. I skidded to my knees and covered my head. Gravel rattled along the side of the road. Behind the ringing in my ears, I could hear bits of metal striking the blacktop parking lot.

I turned, gripping my bonnet strings.

The tanker truck was an open shell, burning. The fire soared beyond the roof of the truck stop. I heard a thin, high whistling in the wreckage. I didn't know if that was the sound of something flammable under pressure or the keening of something dying. For good this time, hopefully.

And more black smoke poured up into the sky, darkening heaven.

———

"I'm all right."

I reached for Alex, placing my hand on his cheek. I felt stubble growing there and a worrisome smudge of blood on his lip. A bruise was darkening over his right eye, and I could see a piece of metal jutting out from the top of his thigh.

"I'm all right," he repeated.

We were relatively unscathed. Ginger had cracked her glasses, but no one had been bitten, and there were no broken bones. Ginger plucked the piece of metal out of Alex's leg without warning him, and he swore at her.

Nonetheless, we truly had God's favor.

Except the horse was gone, with all our gear. Horace was understandably spooked, and had run off with all our scavenged supplies. I was the fastest runner and took off after him. Alex and Ginger followed, but fell behind. Alex limped along, pressing his hand to his leg.

I chased Horace, a receding white speck in the distance. He raced away from the city, away from the fire and the smoke. I chased him past the road we'd come in on, through a field pocked with drainage ditches, across an empty freeway. My snakebitten hand still throbbed with every step. I whistled and called for him, but he galloped as if the Devil himself was after him. I lost sight of him once or twice, beyond the edge of the horizon that kept falling farther and farther away.

Outside was much larger than I'd ever dreamed. Endless.

I knew that Horace's panic would drain away, that he would stop at some point. He had to. It happened to all of us. The poor horse was without any logical explanation for what was happening to him, to us. He knew only fear.

But even fear gave way to exhaustion.

I found him, at last, in a soybean field. The yellow leaves curled against each other like closed fists. I could see his white figure standing beneath a hickory tree at the edge of the field. His pack was askew, and there were leaves tangled in his mane and tail.

I approached him slowly, well within his sight. He was breathing hard, his nostrils flaring as he watched me.

I sat down on a grassy spot beneath the hickory tree, opposite the horse. I pressed my back against the trunk. Shade made me nervous, but the early November wind had stripped almost all the orange leaves from the tree.

I picked up a hickory nut and thumbed the ridges of its shell, found the sweet spot that would release the meat when struck. I took off my shoe and crushed the nut against a root.

Horace flinched, but his ears pressed forward.

I tossed him a piece of the nut meat. He lipped it up from the ground, blew out his breath. I threw another piece, closer this time.

I continued to crack the nuts, feeding him the pieces. I took a few too. When a raven fluttered down from the naked tree, I tossed it a piece as well.

I regarded the raven as it grasped the piece of nut and wolfed it down. The ravens had been the first to sense something was wrong, to flee the apocalypse. They had left in great masses, blotting out the light in the sky one morning. My father had told me that the correct term for a group of ravens was *an unkindness*. It sounded strange to me, imputing an impure motive to an animal.

But this one seemed all alone. A straggler. When I looked closer, I saw why he had not fled — the feathers of his left wing were bent back. He was injured and could not fly far.

I tossed him more food. He was one of God's creatures, after all. And I knew that for all his intelligence, he was unable to crack hickory nuts. I had seen some very clever ones back home who would drop nuts on the stone lid of our well at great heights to break them open. But I saw no such stones here.

Dragging his reins on the ground, Horace approached me. He stood over me for a moment, looking down his long nose with his sad brown eyes.

With a sigh, he came to his knees. When a horse does so, it's a sign of exhaustion and surrender. I had rarely seen one do so outside of foaling or illness.

Horace laid his nose on my knee. I stroked his broad forehead, watched the raven bob and weave among the spiky grass to find the last bits of hickory nut.

The sun was warm on my face. I closed my eyes, relishing this small moment of solitude and peace.

I just listened to the thin breeze in the branches. I wondered how God's creatures interpreted all that had happened —was happening—to them. I thought of all the cats and dogs in houses in the city. And I began to miss my dogs. Back home, I bred golden retrievers. Sunny had just given birth to puppies. I hoped that my little sister was caring for them as I'd showed her.

I missed my family. I missed my mother, with her gentle work-callused hands, and my father, with his calmness and equanimity. I missed Sarah. I missed sleeping in my own bed, and eating hot mashed potatoes. I missed clean clothes and fresh water and the sense of ordinariness that my old routine brought. I didn't appreciate it enough then.

But now, now that I had been shunned and cast out into the Outside world . . . now I knew an inkling of the value of such things. Even though they had been spoiled when I left by the incursion of the vampires and the stranglehold of denial the Elders were beginning to exert on the community, I missed what had once been.

And I wondered if it would survive, ever to be again.

When I dreamed, I knew that I was dreaming.

I dreamed of blue sky with the tatters of white clouds, of sun on my face. I dreamed that I was in my backyard, doing laundry with my mother and sister. I was scrubbing clothes in a basin with a washboard and lye soap. I handed a dress to Sarah, who rinsed the garment and handed it off to my mother. It was my favorite dress—a dark blue the color of gathering night. My mother wrung the dress dry and fastened it to the clothesline with wooden pins. She was a future version of myself, with the same straight, light brown hair, gray eyes clear and smiling. The apples of her cheeks glowed with contentment. She and Sarah were singing as we worked.

My mother commented, "*Ja,* we should make you a new dress before winter."

Sarah clapped her hands. She was just learning to sew. "Can I help?"

"Of course you can!" I told her. I was perfectly capable of making my own dresses, but it went so much faster with my mother's help. And Sarah took the cutting so very seriously that her eyes crossed.

I glanced around the familiar yard. My dogs, Copper and Sunny, were stretched out in the grass. Sunny was nursing her greedy little puppies. Copper was halfheartedly chasing a chicken. He'd chase but never kill.

I could smell supper cooking through the back screen door, and my mouth watered. There would be savory ham and sweet potatoes and my mother's delicious pumpkin pie with fresh butter and cider.

After supper, we'd read from the *Ausbund,* the Amish prayer book. We might play checkers in the light of the oil lamps until it was time to go to bed. We'd sleep under quilts my mother and I had made, warm and secure in the knowledge that to-morrow would be the same as today, which was the same as yesterday.

My father was walking down the dirt road. I could see his smile above his beard, and I waved. He smiled and waved back. He was carrying a bushel basket of squash. Beside him walked Elijah, who grinned at me over the heavy basket of vegetables he carried. He waved at me and said something I couldn't hear.

Then, I heard a raven's hoarse caw.

I peered through the swirling laundry: the dresses and aprons, the bonnets, my father's britches and shirts. The sheets flapped in the breeze, and it made my skin crawl. It reminded me of something . . . something ghostly . . .

A raven landed on the clothesline. It cocked its head to stare at me, unblinking.

I looked up at it. It opened its beak as if to speak, but no sound came out. A dark figure advanced through the field, one I didn't recognize. It was a blond English man, wearing a black jacket. The laundry snapped in the rising wind and I reached up to hold it, to keep it from being torn from the lines.

I snatched up pillowcases and shirts before they were lost in the yard. I spun on my heel to look for a basket . . .

. . . and my family was gone.

The silent man stood at a distance. Darkness was gathering behind him, and the raven screamed hoarsely in my ear.

Chapter Eight

Sensing a cold shadow over me, I jerked awake.

My hands balled automatically into fists, and I flinched.

"Katie. It's just me."

Alex crouched over me, tenderly pushing a strand of hair behind my ear. I sucked in a breath, then forced myself to exhale and unwind my fists. I blinked up at him, up at the sky. The sun had lowered a bit.

I looked right and left. Ginger was standing next to Horace, patting him and adjusting his gear, her broken glasses perched on top of her head. The raven fussed with a nut in his talons, cawing softly to himself.

"Good nap, eh?" Alex asked.

I rubbed my eyes. "I can't believe I fell asleep."

"Any time you can catch a wink is a good time." He offered me a hand and pulled me to my feet. "I'm just glad that we found you."

I grinned. "How did you do that?"

"We just headed where there was the most grass until we saw a speck of white." His eyes darkened, and he wrapped an arm around me. "But seriously . . . don't run off like that again."

"*Ja,* I promise," I said. I squinted up at the sun, feeling a pang of anxiety. "We have only a few more hours of daylight left."

"I hope we can find someplace safe to sleep," Ginger said.

The travel was wearing on all of us. We had slept in bits and snatches when we could, but the exhaustion was making us reckless and sloppy. I could feel it in the way my feet slapped listlessly on the ground, in the ache of my muscles.

Alex spread out one of his maps and fussed with his new compass. I tried not to stare at the bloodstain on his jeans.

"Maybe we could find someplace we could stay for a day or two. Someplace quiet." I closed my eyes and imagined home, just for a moment. It ached to do so, but I needed to feel the pain. Because I didn't want to forget. If I forgot, I was pretty sure that I was going to lose all sense of myself, the touchstone to who I was.

And then I'd be little more than one of the hungry shells of the living roaming the world.

We pushed on until the sun moved into the western sky. I felt the warmth shifting from the top of my head to my left cheek, and I knew that we'd need to seek shelter soon. Or hope that we were far enough in the hinterlands that the vampires wouldn't find us.

"Maybe we can find a barn," Ginger said.

"A hayloft," I agreed. "Somewhere up high. And a place where we can hide Horace."

"This looks like farm country to me," Alex said.

We followed a dirt road tracking along the edge of a fence.

At first, the fence seemed to be like ordinary barbed wire. But then it grew to more than eight feet in height, chainlink with razorwire coiled like ribbons at the top.

Alex squinted at it. "I sure hope we're not in a prison area."

The barbed wire. It was angled inwardly, as if it was intended to keep something inside. I had never seen a prison. I had occasionally seen pictures of criminals in the police blotter section of the local newspaper when I got ahold of one, but I didn't understand most of the crimes. I was twelve before I knew what burglary was, and fourteen before I understood the word *rape*. I had never understood the point of robbery, since Plain people would give anything they had to a needy person. I shuddered. "Let's hope not."

"There are no paved roads here," Ginger said. "A prison would have paved roads. All paid for with taxpayer money."

"Good point," Alex said. "And that doesn't look like a prison."

He pointed ahead of us to a ramshackle collection of buildings. I saw what looked like a barn made out of corrugated metal, a few outbuildings, a house, and what appeared to be cages. It smelled like an outhouse.

My heart thudded in my chest when I saw a black shadow moving behind the chainlink fence.

"What is that?" I whispered.

"Oh, damn," Ginger said.

I walked up close to the fence, peered in. A languid form slipped between trees, pacing, sinuous. I couldn't get a complete look at the creature, so I moved closer.

It paused, stared back at me with golden eyes.

It was a cat.

A really, really large cat. It was larger than my golden retrievers, with a head the size of a melon. It was covered in black fur, and it was skinny. So thin that its ribs rippled when it walked and its shoulder bones jutted out of its back. I smelled feces in its pen, and the flies were thick in the air.

"What is it?" I asked.

"It's a jaguar," Ginger said.

"It's starving," I said, staring at its empty food trough, overturned, on the ground. I realized that the razorwire fence didn't go entirely around the property. It was in squares and runs—makeshift cages.

"And he's not the only one." I heard Alex's grim tone behind me. He pointed to other enclosures. Tin roofs had been partially torn away by the wind. I saw two bears in one cage. One was clearly dead, covered in flies. The other sat with its back turned to us, its snout on the ground. A pair of wasted striped cats, orange and black, paced agitatedly within another cage. They were as bony as the jaguar.

"Those are tigers?" I asked.

"Yes. But they're not supposed to look like that."

I had only seen tigers in books, on my covert trips to the library back home. Those tigers had been plump and well fed, not these skeletons with stripes. Skin hung from their bones, like some kind of gaudy material in a fabric store. Their bellies and legs were covered in mud, and their eyes were hollow.

I approached gingerly.

I heard a deep growling, so deep that it was almost impossible to hear.

And the tiger lunged for me. Its paws slammed up against the chain link fence with an incredible amount of force, bowing it outward with a crash.

I jumped backwards. Claws larger than my fingers hooked in the fence, and the tiger growled again.

My heart hammered, but the fence held.

Alex grabbed my arm. "Don't tempt them. They're hungry. And we're just meat."

My eyes filled with tears. I knew we were just meat to the vampires. But I saw something different in the eyes of the starving animals. In vampire eyes, I only saw evil. In these, I saw pain.

I heard a thin howling behind me. I wheeled, spied a pack of a half-dozen wolves in a dog run the size of some I'd seen for small dogs. They trotted along their side of the fence, calling, yipping at us. They were dirty, terribly thin, with sores on their paws and tufts of fur missing. Their golden eyes watched me with something like hope.

"Is this a zoo?" I wrinkled my forehead. I had never been to one, but I had heard of them, seen pictures in books. Those facilities had elaborately built habitats, with healthy-looking animals and zookeepers in uniform. This was not what I'd imagined.

"No. This is . . ." I could hear the anger in Alex's voice. "These are some jerks with a private collection. Who aren't taking care of their animals. Or can't." I could tell by the set of Alex's jaw that this infuriated him.

With trepidation, we walked the short distance to the house. It was two stories, covered in vinyl siding with plastic shutters. The front door was painted red. Alex pounded on it.

We waited. No one answered.

He pounded again, tried the knob. "It's locked."

"I don't see any cars or trucks around," Ginger observed. "They must have left." Her hand was pressed to her mouth, and not just to block out the smell of the animals.

Now fury rose in me, too. I had assumed that something had happened to the people. I couldn't conceive of anyone voluntarily leaving their animals in this condition. I had occasionally heard of stories about Amish puppy mills and animal mistreatment in the Plain community, but I had not witnessed that in my own little village. I didn't see how that could be tolerated. My parents had always taught me that animals were also God's creatures and deserved to be cared for with the best of our ability.

"Hopefully the vamps haven't been here," Alex said. "If the people left, the vamps wouldn't tackle a tiger to eat. That's not as easy a snack as a domestic animal."

"There's no sign of a break-in," Ginger said, peering through a ground-level window. She jiggled the front doorknob. "Locked."

I stared at it. "Could it be a trap?" We knew the vampires were smart enough for that.

Alex frowned. "Not likely. If this was a trap, they would leave the door open and let the food come to them."

Alex pulled his jacket down over his knuckles and picked

up a brick from the carefully landscaped border. He hurled it at the window and the glass caved in. He cleared the glass from the lower sash with the sleeve of his jacket and climbed through.

I held my breath, waiting, listening to his steps inside. I heard scraping at the front door before it opened.

"C'mon in, ladies," he said.

I crossed the threshold into the house, sucked in my breath. I didn't see any signs of violence, but the people who lived here had sure left in a hurry.

To my left, the dining room table was covered in empty plastic bags. To my right, the living area held an overstuffed couch and chairs, but a set of shelves was empty below a giant black television.

I walked over plush carpeting to the kitchen. Cabinets and cupboards had been emptied, doors and drawers standing open. A puddle stood at the bottom of the refrigerator, forming a lake on the tile.

I searched for food for the animals. The garage contained a lawnmower, tool chests, and bags of birdseed occupied only by mice. Cardboard boxes marked CHRISTMAS were perched up in the rafters. A chest freezer sat against a wall.

I stared at it, wary. There might be food in there. Or maybe something terrible.

I pressed my ear against the top of the freezer. I heard nothing moving within.

I grabbed a rake. Holding the staff above my head, I opened the lid.

And I immediately turned away in disgust.

There was meat inside, wrapped in white paper turning black as it rotted and liquefied. I slammed the lid quickly and returned to the kitchen.

I heard Alex clomping around upstairs. He returned with a hard expression on his face. "Upstairs has been tossed. Nobody home. Empty gun cabinet, though."

"They left," I affirmed. "They left, locked the door behind them, and left those animals to die. And they didn't even have the decency . . ." I was going to say "to put them out of their misery," but I couldn't speak it out loud. The Elders had wanted to do that to Alex when we found him injured just outside our land.

Ginger reached out to hold my hand. "It's horrible. But at least we have someplace to stay for the night."

I swallowed, stared out the kitchen window at the scrawny animals in their enclosures. "We can't leave them out there."

"They'll eat us alive if we let them go now," Ginger said.

I shook my head. "No," I said. "We can't. I can't, and I won't."

I turned and walked out the front door, my heart hammering in my chest. Righteous anger glowed within me.

I walked to the first cage. The cage with the wolves. I think that they scared me the least. I circled it, searching for a latch to open it.

"Bonnet, wait." Alex rushed after me and caught my arm. "They'll tear you apart."

I wheeled around. "I will not leave them like this!" There

was iron in my voice. It surprised me, and it surprised him. His grip on my arm slackened.

"It's not right," I said.

"I know. But they don't belong here. They'll hurt people if you let them go."

I lifted my chin. I could hear my voice rising, yelling. I felt heat rising in my cheeks. Rage. And not at Alex, but at the circumstances we found ourselves in. "There are no people left *to* hurt. And I'm not going to let this . . ." My hand sketched the broken world around us. "I'm not going to let this change or break me. It can kill me, but I won't let it change me or what I think is right."

He stood opposite me, staring at me. I was certain that he could physically stop me. He could impose his will on me the way the Elders tried, with the threat of violence or restraint.

But he didn't. I knew that he respected me.

"I get it," he sighed. "I don't want to see you mauled by wild animals. But . . ." He spread his hands, and I could see the helplessness he felt in that gesture. "I can't protect you. Maybe being food for an animal is better than dying of snake venom or vampires or starvation."

I stepped up to him and kissed him.

"Bonnet, you are the most frustrating woman on earth."

I lifted my eyebrows. "I know."

He shook his head. "You ever seen *Star Wars,* Bonnet?"

"No."

"Never mind, then."

Ginger knew what I meant to do. From the corner of my

eye, I saw her lead Horace to the house, let him inside as if he were a giant house pet.

I found the latch to the wolf pen. Alex watched warily. The wolves hung back, watching me with their luminous eyes. I flipped up the latch and swung the door open. I stepped back, waited with my heart in my mouth.

One by one, they bolted out of the pen. They glanced at me in passing, and my heart soared to see them go. They trotted down the road, making guttural growls and yips.

One remained in the cage. He was a thin gray wolf with sad eyes. He was smaller than the others, a bit more golden, as if he had some domestic dog in him.

"Go on," I said. I felt a lump in my throat. "I don't have any food for you. Go with the others and hunt."

Alex struck the side of the fence with his boot, making a rattling noise.

The wolf whimpered softly and skulked out of the cage.

"Go on," I told him.

He lifted his nose to sniff the air. For a moment, I was afraid that he would attack me or Alex. And then he took off at a loping pace after his skeleton pack.

I gave them some time to recede beyond sight before turning to the next enclosure. The tigers.

They paced with open mouths, watching me. They'd seen what I'd done for the wolves. They knew.

And they were hungry.

The cage was held shut with two simple push latches. I flipped the bottom one up, then the one at the top. I didn't intend to open the cage. I intended to let the tigers open it for themselves.

And they came lunging toward the door, at me, in a flurry of stripes.

I heard myself scream.

CHAPTER NINE

The weight of the tiger crashed the door of the cage against me, pinning me to the exterior cage wall. It drove the wind out of me, and I was face-to-face with the giant cat. It stood on its back feet, with its paws pressing against my shoulders through the wire. I could feel the heaviness of its body and its claws prickling against the shoulders of my coat. It lowered its head to the level of mine, drawing back its lips to reveal its teeth. Its hot breath smelled like death. Golden eyes burned at me. This wildness was something far beyond my stilted ideas of good and evil. In this beast's world, there was only kindness and cruelty.

Dimly, I was aware of Alex shouting. But that was a background sound, tertiary to my breathing and the tiger's breathing, both short and shallow.

Without warning, it pushed off from the door and released me. It dropped back to all four feet, beside its mate, tail lashing.

It gave Alex a deadly glare, growled. He was holding his knife and standing his ground.

"Don't hurt him," I said. I didn't know if I was speaking to the tiger or to Alex.

One before the other, the tigers turned and walked away. Their massive paws disturbed the dust of the road and their painfully thin shoulders worked beneath their dirty hides.

I released a breath, didn't move until they'd receded beyond sight at the edge of the field, becoming lost in that line of sunset.

"That was stupid, Bonnet," Alex said. "Real stupid."

"Just the bear and the jaguar are left," I said. My voice sounded much more level than I felt.

The bear didn't react initially to the open door. I stood far away, watched as it shambled through the opening. It seemed reluctant to leave its mate, shoved at the carcass with a paw. The display of affection caused me to wipe a tear from my eye.

But it too lumbered away, down the path that the wolves and the tigers had taken.

And then there was only the jaguar. It sat beside the door, its luminous eyes burning into me.

"I hope that you will be better behaved than the tiger," I said.

I opened the rusty door. I saw the jaguar crouching down, coiling like a snake, readying for the chance to flee. When I'd gotten the door half open, the jaguar lurched out. Unlike the others, it ran. It ran as fast as it could, ears flattened, toward the horizon.

I stood, shaking. I knew that I would never see anything that magnificent in my life again.

"I hope we don't meet them on the road," Alex said.

I said nothing. I hoped they would live. All of them.

We had prepared for night the best we could. We'd hauled a cabinet up against the broken window and locked the door. Horace seemed content to occupy the living room, with the couch pushed up against the wall. He chewed idly at the carpet, though I knew that he was full on grass. There was a little water left in the pipes of the house, and I gave him a dishpan full to slurp at.

Ginger, Alex, and I headed upstairs. We did so in the dark: there was no electricity, and we wanted to create no light by which vampires could spot us across the open countryside.

The house held three bedrooms that appeared to belong to adults, a boy, and a teen girl. As if by prior assent, we each took a room. Ginger took the adults' room. Alex took the boy's room, and I took the girl's.

I paused in the twilight, my eyes slowly adjusting to the new surroundings. I could make out a quilt on the bed, smoothed it with my fingers. Unlike all the quilts at home, this one was manufactured—I could tell by the artificially even stitching. The walls were covered with posters of young men and women holding guitars and microphones.

I paused by a short dresser with a mirror. Plain people didn't keep mirrors for any purpose but for shaving. We were told that it encouraged vanity. And it seemed that it did—my eye roved over neatly stacked cosmetics on the surface of the dresser.

In the dimness, I looked at myself. I wanted to know if there was any visible proof that the journey had changed me. I wondered if I carried any outward sign of failing faith, some taint or mark.

I removed my bonnet. I looked pale. Gaunt. I could see shadows around me, under my eyes, around my mouth. But I didn't know how much of that was the venom and the journey and how much was just the dark.

I walked over to the girl's wardrobe and opened the closet doors. My clothes felt stiff and dirty, and I craved something clean to sleep in. I found a soft gray sweatshirt, sweatpants, and socks. The *Ordnung* forbade women to wear pants, but I was cold and tired and needed something warm. There were no metal fasteners on these clothes—no buttons or zippers that I was not allowed to use. They were the simplest garments I could find, and I didn't think that God would mind. I changed clothes, tucking the *Himmelsbrief* into the sleeve of my sweatshirt, next to my wrist.

It had been weeks since I'd slept in a bed. I climbed under the covers. This girl's bedclothes smelled like perfume, unlike the clean scent of lye soap that I was used to. But it was better than hard ground, or a snake-covered church pew.

I expected to fall asleep immediately.

But I couldn't.

My thoughts circled around the idea of the girl who had occupied this room. Was she a victim of the vampires? Or was she still alive? Was she alone, trying to make her way in this world with no help?

I tossed and turned. My hand throbbed, and I was too accustomed to being alert at night to fall asleep easily, even in these soft surroundings.

I slipped out of bed and crossed the hall to the boy's room.

I noticed that the door was ajar. I knocked lightly before entering.

Stenciled dinosaurs decorated the walls, and there were glow-in-the-dark stars shining softly on the ceiling. Plastic toys covered a shelf and were strewn on the floor. I wondered if the boy had had time to choose a favorite to take with him.

"Hey," Alex said. He was sitting up in bed. He was dressed as I was, in sweat clothes. They were too large for him. I assumed that he'd found them in the parents' laundry. "Couldn't sleep?"

I shook my head. "No."

"C'mon." He lifted the edge of the blanket and scooted over to the edge of the bed.

I padded across the floor, avoiding the toy dinosaurs, and slipped into bed beside him. His arm cradled my head, and I already felt better. I had never had my own room. I had shared with my sister. Even out here, Outside, I hadn't slept alone.

A low growl-snort emanated from across the hall. Ginger snoring.

"Not everyone is having trouble sleeping," I said.

"She will bring the undead to our doorstep one of these days." Alex said it lightly, as if he was joking. But there was some truth to that. And nothing to be done for it.

"She won't hear them coming." I laughed softly.

We lay in silence for some time. I felt safe with my head next to Alex's chest, even though I rationally knew that he had no better chance of keeping me safe than Ginger did. I shyly rested the flat of my hand over his heart, where I knew the scarred ankh lay under the sweatshirt fleece.

He broke the silence. "You did a good thing today, Bonnet. A brave thing."

I squirmed under praise. "It was the right thing to do."

"That jaguar," he said. "It reminded me of something. An old myth."

"Oh?" I snuggled in closer. I liked it when he told stories. It reminded me of what he would have been in an intact world —a teacher. And it gave me something to think about other than food and Darkness.

"The Jaguar is sacred to the Mayans. He's associated with a sort of dark star myth. On one hand, his coat is supposed to contain all the stars in the heavens."

I looked up at the plastic stars on the ceiling, faintly glowing, and smiled.

"Jaguar Sun rises each day and paces across the heavens. He starts out as a young jaguar, a cub. He paces from east to west, chasing prey. He ages as he goes, and by the time he reaches the western horizon, he's an old cat with gray in his muzzle."

"He dies?" I asked.

"No. Jaguar Sun doesn't have it that easy. He falls into the darkness of the underworld and fights the lords of the underworld all night long. He emerges victorious in the east each morning, a young cub, ready to begin the fight again."

My eyes felt heavy. "He's strong."

He kissed my forehead. "Indeed. And he hunts and fights day and night, keeping us safe from the spirits of the underworld."

In the distance, I could hear a thin, eerie howling.

I smiled. I imagined that it was the wolves, chasing deer. And that Jaguar Sun was fighting the Darkness while we slept.

"We can't stay."

Alex was right. We all knew it.

For three nights, we had been at the Animal Farm. I called it that first, and Alex and Ginger began to laugh.

"'Four legs bad, two legs good,'" Alex said.

"Or is it the other way around?" Ginger mused.

"I don't get it."

"*Animal Farm*. It's a book by George Orwell. If we find a copy of it, I'll be interested to see what you think of it."

I wasn't sure that there would be much time for reading in the future, but it was a pleasant thought.

We brought Horace outside for supervised grazing during the day, but never once saw any of the wild animals. We knew that they had been there—I'd found the remains of a deer in the middle of the field. The tuft of gray fur stuck to a rib bone seemed to indicate that it was not the work of the vampires. After dark, we heard the howling of the wolves. Each successive night, it seemed that they moved farther away.

The pain and swelling in my hand began to subside. I think that the sleep and aspirin from the convenience store had done it some good, as well as our relatively clean surroundings. I felt guilty about letting Horace poop in the living-room-turned-stable, but I was sure that no was one coming back. Ever.

We had fallen into a routine that felt relatively normal. We slept for more than twelve hours a night and ate the supplies from the convenience store. We found a few canned goods and cereal in the cupboards. I'd gathered rainwater in a bucket and had used it to wash our clothes. I learned to play Monopoly at the kitchen table with Alex and Ginger. Ginger always won.

Ginger had located a photo album of the family in the bottom of the china cabinet. I looked through it with interest. I saw wedding pictures of a man and a woman and pictures of many holidays and vacations with the two children. The girl looked a lot like Sarah when she was younger. There were also some pictures of the animals. I saw the jaguar as a cub and the wolves looking much smaller.

"Why did they keep those animals?" I asked.

"I don't know," Ginger said. "Maybe they thought they were helping, if the animals were abandoned by other owners and they took them in. Like a rescue. Maybe they had a thing for exotic animals." She sighed. "It's hard to get into other people's heads."

I stroked the edge of a picture of the girl who looked like Sarah holding a wolf pup. The photographs made me even more conscious that we were occupying someone else's home. And they made me miss my parents and my sister and my dogs.

So when Alex said it was time to leave, I was ready. We gathered up anything that would be of use to us. I realized, as I was packing kitchen knives into a backpack, that I had become inured to the idea of stealing. And that made me sad, that I had dropped that part of my moral compass in order to survive.

I found pencils and paper and wrote the family a note, just in case they ever returned. It was hard to find the words, but I felt that I needed to do it:

> I hope that all your family is well. I am sorry to have used your house and your possessions in this way. I hope that you return and are able to put things back in order. I hope that we all can return home and put things back to rights.
> We let the animals go.
> —Katie

I came to regret leaving later. We all did.

But that morning seemed cool and crisp and full of hope. My belly was full, my clothes were clean. I tugged the backpack high up on my shoulder and followed Alex out into the clear morning.

As always, we moved north. Inexorably north.

I was certain that the sun had colored the left side of my face more than the right. But not enough to burn. It was growing too cold for that. Our feet made tracks in the grass where they wiped away the frost.

I knew that we wanted to get to Canada before snow. We needed to find Alex's family before hard winter came. We had a long way to go; if we continued to go north and avoid densely populated areas to cross the border, we might have to go as far as Sault Ste. Marie, Alex said. I didn't know how we were going to survive that without reliable shelter. Nor did I have any idea how the rest of humanity would.

I suspected my community had a good chance of surviving the hardships of winter. We Plain people were reasonably self-sufficient, growing our own food and raising our own cattle. One challenge would be getting enough heat; kerosene stores would be bound to dwindle. But they'd figure something out, cut firewood, tolerate the elements as our forefathers had.

But the vampires . . . I didn't know how they would survive them. The Darkness had been let in, and the Elders were in denial. The Hexenmeister had the power to protect them, if only they would listen.

But, always, my horizon was today—the next sunrise or sunset. And then . . . I couldn't see beyond *and then*. I hoped that somehow a cure to the contagion would be found, that we could return to our homes and that life would return to some semblance of normal—if we still remembered what that felt like.

I wrapped my coat tightly around my neck. I could feel the cold air creeping in. I had kept my Plain clothes, but Ginger and Alex had taken clothing from the Animal Farm, changed into jeans and heavy sweaters. Alex had found a replacement for his old jacket among the father's clothes, a jacket made of green oilskin. Ginger was wearing the mother's navy blue sweatshirt embroidered with kittens. I felt even more out of step with them than when we had started.

But I was determined to keep up as we walked along a two-lane road. I saw farmland right and left studded with a few farmhouses with metal roofs to withstand the wind that scoured over the northern part of the state. Trees around the houses nodded east, as if the west wind had pushed them for many years.

Off to the west, I could see a forest on the flat land, with the sunlight slanting through it. I squinted at it as Alex spread open a map. It flapped against his jacket, tearing at the corners as he swore at it.

"There." He pointed to the woods. "That's where we're going."

I lifted my eyebrows and shuddered instinctively. "It's dark there."

"It'll be safe," he promised.

I wrapped my arms around my elbows and followed him.

We turned west and walked down a broad paved lane bounded with chains painted white between concrete stanchions. It was surrounded on both sides by what had once been a manicured lawn. At the end of the lane, a white figure stood.

It was a statue of a woman in a veil with her arms outstretched. It took me a moment to realize who she was. Plain people didn't believe in graven images, but I knew her instinctively to be Mary, mother of Jesus. At the base of the statue was a sign that read WELCOME TO THE SHRINE OF OUR LADY OF PEACE. Frostbitten zinnias wilted in a flower bed at her feet.

"What is this place?" I asked.

"It's a Marian shrine," Alex said. "It's a Roman Catholic pilgrimage destination. If any place is still holy, this is it."

"I was here as a little girl," Ginger said. "I remember. My

grandmother took me. There are all these little grottoes in the woods and a church."

"If it's sacred," I said, blowing out my breath and staring up into Mary's unseeing eyes, "we should be safe."

"C'mon," Alex said. "We're burning daylight."

We made our way down leaf-strewn bricked paths that meandered around bare trees. Tied to the trees were brightly painted sculptures.

"Who are these?" I asked.

"Saints," Ginger said. "This one is Saint Francis, patron saint of animals." She pointed to a figure holding a lamb, then another figure of a robed man holding a baby. "And Saint Joseph."

"We didn't have saints in the Amish religion." I stared up at the robed man holding the baby. He was bearded, like an Amish man, and with the expression of tenderness on his face he reminded me of my father. I had heard of saints before, but wasn't sure I fully grasped the concept. "I know that they're holy people."

"Right. They're special people who lived fully 'in Christ,'" Ginger said.

"How is that different from being full *of* Christ, like Pastor Gene said?"

"Saints usually lived a long time before. And accomplished huge miracles. Like this one, Saint Joan." She pointed to a figure of a young woman in armor. Paint had flaked away from her face, and squirrels had stored nuts in the bottom ledge of her shrine.

"What did she do?"

"God spoke to her. He told her to lead an army to victory in the Hundred Years' War. And she did."

I looked at the figure. She didn't seem very big, or very powerful. Plain people didn't believe in military service—we were pacifists. I couldn't imagine leading an army. And I couldn't imagine God speaking to me.

"Remember that she was also burned at the stake for heresy," Alex chimed in.

"She was a pawn for people in power," Ginger said. "A young girl trying to do as she thought best, as she believed God told her. And she was canonized for it, made a saint. She's one of the patron saints of France. Also of women and captives."

"I don't understand . . ." I struggled to articulate what I felt. "I don't understand putting a mortal person on such a pedestal. Literally."

"Saints are thought to be intercessionaries with God. Roman Catholics pray to them, as well as to God and Jesus. It's just another way of connecting to the divine."

I frowned. I wasn't sure how I felt about praying to ordinary men and women, even if Christ moved through them and performed miracles with their mortal hands. But the Holy Spirit seemed to move in mysterious ways.

We walked down the path, farther into the woods draining of light. I saw a fountain, overhung with ivy and backed by a rock wall. The water in it was still and green. A figure of a woman—another iteration of the Virgin Mary, I assumed—was kneeling before it with her hands clasped in prayer. Behind the wall I could see a rack of burned-out candles in glass containers. Leaves had blown into the doorway.

"What's this?"

"Our Lady of Lourdes. A grotto," Ginger explained. "Saint Bernadette of Lourdes saw an apparition of Mary. Mary told her to dig, and a spring with healing powers was revealed. Some believed in its powers. Some didn't. That's the thing about miracles. They're open to interpretation."

I thought I'd experienced healing water at Pastor Gene's creek, but I wasn't sure. As more time passed, I wasn't sure if that was the Lord or if it was just luck. Time was seeming to cloud the miracle I'd felt. I stared into the green water. "This is the spring?"

"No. The real one's in Lourdes, a town in France. This is a replica."

"It's pretty," I said. But also somehow forlorn in its abandonment.

We continued walking along the bricked paths. Moss had begun to grow over the bricks, obliterating names of people who'd apparently made donations of money to the shrine.

"Why does the path circle this way? Aren't we going back where we came from?" I asked. I was unused to the idea of Ginger being a spiritual guide. But this seemed to be an area of thought that she knew from her childhood. She occasionally stopped to look at sculptures, her hand pressed to her lips, lost in reverie. It was beautiful to see her in this way, touched by memory and faith.

"A lot of religions believe in the idea of labyrinths for

meditation. While the feet are kept busy, the presence of God is felt."

I smiled. That I could understand. Plain people believed that God emerged through hard work and performance of our daily duties.

The sun dipped below the horizon. I could see, sharp against the violet sky, an evening star burning. And before it, the cross atop a church spire at the end of the brick path, a quarter-mile distant.

"That's the chapel," Ginger said. It was good to see her smile again.

The moonlight illuminated a stone mound to my right—it reminded me of the Indian mound we'd stayed at days before. A placard identified it as the Grotto of Our Lady of Fatima.

"The Virgin Mary appeared before shepherd children in Portugal during World War I," Ginger said. "She was said to be as bright as the sun."

But we were losing sun. I hitched my backpack higher up on my shoulder, laced my fingers in Horace's reins. He twitched an ear and shied to the side.

I glanced to our right. I thought I saw movement between the trees.

It's just a deer, I told myself. *This is holy ground.*

Unless it's been defiled. Unless the Darkness has been let in.

"Who runs this place?" I asked. "Who maintains it?"

Oblivious, Ginger walked several paces behind, soaking in the memory. "Nuns. Beyond the chapel are dormitories."

Horace pawed. The sound of his hooves on the brick

caused both Ginger and Alex to turn. I heard the hiss of Ginger's indrawn breath. The moon broke free of the tangle of tree branches, shining down on us.

I saw something out of the corner of my eye, on the left side of the path, flitting between the trees. Something dark. My skin crawled.

"Run," I whispered.

Chapter Ten

Horace needed no urging. My fingers were wrapped in his reins, and he dragged me forward. I cried out as my sore hand struggled to cling to him.

More dark figures moved between the trees, like rotten leaves. I glanced to the cavelike mouth of the Fatima grotto. Shadows slipped out of it, dark as ink, not bright like the apparition of the Virgin Mary. I saw pale faces and hands, framed in robes of black.

"The nuns . . ." Ginger paused. "The sisters are . . ." I could read the shock on her face.

"Run!" Alex insisted. He was ten steps behind me, ten paces ahead of her.

And that was all it took.

The sisters swarmed Ginger. I snatched a stake from Horace's pack, disentangled myself from the reins, and ran back.

"Ginger!"

Alex had turned, and I saw silver flashing in his fist. He slashed at one of the black shadows. It reeled back, hissing.

But one of the blackbird nuns fell upon Ginger. She dropped

to the pavement, shrieking, clawing on the mossy brick. Alex skidded to a halt over her, slashing at the bloodthirsty nun. I thrust my stake ahead of me. It pierced the shadow, and I heard the wet slap of black blood on the brick. White claws grappled around my weapon. I kicked back, shoving the body from the stake like a piece of meat from a stick.

Alex pulled Ginger to her feet and we ran to the chapel. I fumbled in my pocket for my *Himmelsbrief,* stumbling backwards, holding it out at arm's length. The preternaturally pale faces of the nuns hissed at me. Most of them were old women, but I saw the smooth face of a young one, barely older than I was.

"Come to the Lord, little sheep," she whispered.

"The blood is the life."

"You will die, and rise again like Jesus in the Resurrection."

I backed up the steps of the chapel. I heard Alex behind me. The doors crashed open, and Horace's hooves banged on stone. I ducked into the chapel, hoping that I was not walking into deeper Darkness.

The doors slammed shut, blotting out the night. I heard scratching on the door, plaintive cries . . .

. . . but the door held fast against them.

"It's still holy," I whispered, turning to face the inside of the sanctuary. It felt like a miracle that this place was safe. "How?"

"Maybe it's an island . . . like your barn protected by a hex sign when your larger community had been defiled." Alex's voice was disembodied, distracted.

I saw red and blue patches of light on the floor, cast from the moonlight moving through the stained-glass windows.

Depicted in one was Mary, appearing in a cloud before a young woman. I wondered if this was one of the women who'd seen her at Fatima or Lourdes.

"We need light." I heard Alex scrabbling around. There were clicking sounds, and one by one, cylindrical glass votives were illuminated. They must have been battery powered, with metal flames flickering inside. The glass was red, and the light cast was wan. But it was light.

I followed his lead, punching buttons on the top of the votives. There were hundreds. I mashed the buttons, seeing them light up, greedy for the light.

I noticed a metal box beside them with a small sign that read $2.00 DONATION.

"For each candle. For a prayer." Ginger was unsteady on her feet, leaning against the back of a pew. I slipped my arm beneath her, cried out when it came away with warm blood.

Something thumped against the door and giggled. "The blood is the life."

Horace clomped on the slate floor, blowing at the door.

"Take her up front," Alex ordered.

I supported Ginger down the aisle, our footsteps ringing loudly on the slate. Alex charged ahead of us, to the altar, which was surrounded by hundreds more of the lights in their iron holders. He slapped them on, illuminating a fabric-draped altar with gold ornaments and an intricately painted statue of Jesus looking benignly over us.

I helped Ginger lie down on a pew, tugged her coat off. There was blood on her shirt collar, trickling down her sleeve. I unbuttoned her shirt, apologizing as I did so, to examine her shoulder. I couldn't see what had happened—there was too much blood.

I dug through our packs for one of the T-shirts taken from the Animal Farm. I wiped away at the wound, saw that there was a tear in her skin. She cried out when I touched it.

I ran to a stone bowl full of water at the front of the church. I soaked the T-shirt with it and grabbed the small yellow sponge at the bottom. I did my best to wash the wound. Alex hovered over the back of the pew. He and I traded glances in the flickering light.

"Is it a claw mark?" Ginger asked. "Tell me that it's just a claw mark."

If it was a claw mark, she would live. Alex had told us that much, from his time on the Outside before he'd come to us. It was a bite that we had to be fearful of, a bite that would transmit the infection.

I hesitated. It was a surface wound, one that a person would easily survive . . . if it had not been a bite.

"It's a bite," I said quietly.

Alex swore and turned away. Ginger began to sob.

The only thing I could do was hold her as she shook.

———

"How long?"

I couldn't help but ask.

Alex and I stood at the back of the church. I'd bound Ginger's shoulder up as best I could with bits of robes that I'd found in a closet. She was kneeling before the altar, praying. She had been there for hours, still as the statue hanging above her. I had crept halfway up the aisle twice to check the rise and fall of her shoulder, to make sure that she was still breathing. I had seen the glitter of dampness on her cheek.

"Based on what I saw before I came to your village . . . it could be hours. Or a couple of days." His hands tightly gripped the back of the pew, whitening his knuckles. "I suspect that the holy water you used to rinse out the wound may slow the progression somewhat, but there's really no way to know."

I placed my hand on his. "We'll deal with it when the time comes. If it comes. Maybe the holy water will stop it."

"It's my fault," he said in a small voice. "I picked where we were going."

"No," I said. "It's no one's fault. It's just . . ." I struggled to find the right words, to articulate the helplessness that we all felt in the face of this tragedy. "It's just *Gelassenheit*. God's will."

He shook his head. "No. I don't believe that." His hand curled into a fist beneath mine. "No loving God would want this. For any of us."

I slipped away from his fury, walked up the aisle to Ginger. I knelt beside her.

"I'm never . . . never going to see Dan or the kids," Ginger said. Her voice was rough with crying.

I put my arm around her. "You will see them again. In heaven."

A choked sound emanated from her throat. "I wonder if they are already there. It's been . . . years since Dan took communion. My daughter is a practicing Catholic, but my son gave it up when he was a teenager."

"There is no way to know if they will precede you in heaven," I said. "But God would not allow you to be separated."

What I told her was the opposite of what the Amish *Ordnung* said. We believed that unless one was baptized in the Amish church, one wouldn't reach heaven and be reunited with one's loved ones. I hoped that God would not be cruel to those of us who meant well.

Ginger stood suddenly, wiping at her face, disentangling herself from my arms. She walked with purpose to a small closet in the back of the church. She closed the door behind her. I heard a latch scrape on the inside and Ginger's soft voice, whispering.

"What's she doing?" I asked Alex.

"Confessing her sins." He gestured to the little cabinet. "A priest sits on one side of a screen, and the penitent on the other. The penitent confesses in anonymity and the priest grants absolution, assigns a task to carry out to make things right. Usually a bunch of Hail Marys, from what I understand."

I stared at the strange carved box. It seemed scarcely larger than a coffin. Again, a human intercessionary standing between earth and God. But there was no one there. I wondered if Ginger imagined a priest on the other side, if that was some comfort.

The whispers eventually died away, but Ginger did not come out. I waited, sitting in the last pew. I waited for a long time, until fear grew in me. I strained to hear any sound.

I stood and knocked on the door. "Ginger? Are you all right?"

"You're going to leave me here," she said. I heard the fear in her voice. "You should."

I sucked in my breath. I imagined it for a moment: locking

her in the confessional as she began to change into a vampire. Alone. It was a cruel abandonment. Like being buried alive. I imagined the squeak of her fingernails on the wood, her cries to the priest who wasn't there. I wondered if she would be able to escape the holy box, if its power would erode under the onslaught of the evil that gestated within it. I wondered if it would hold and she would starve within it.

I shivered. It disturbed me that I could even think of it.

"No," I said. "We won't leave you here." I reached for the door and wrested it open. A small hook and eye closure inside the frame splintered and gave way.

Ginger sat on a little bench inside, deep in shadow. The ornate cutout pattern of the confessional screen obscured most of her face.

"I don't . . . I don't want to become like them." Her glass blue eyes fixed on me. Whether they were fevered with conviction or infection, I couldn't tell. She reached out, her cold fingers knotting in mine. "Don't let me become like them."

I sucked in a breath, let it out.

"I won't," I said. "I promise."

And that promise hung as heavy on me as stones.

———

We left at dawn, when the dark sisters had retreated to their grottoes. The sun shone brilliantly as we emerged from the shadow of the church.

I had a bit of hope. Hope that the holy water and that our prayers might have helped Ginger, as they had helped me at Pastor Gene's church. But that hope dwindled as I saw her in the growing light of morning. Ginger had grown pale. Dark circles settled beneath her eyes. She refused to eat more than a bite or two of some crab apples I found and turned away from the potato chips from the convenience store.

As the day wore on, we wandered through golden, unharvested fields of wheat. I thought I saw a suspicious ripple of movement in the tall stalks. I glanced at Alex.

He nodded. He'd seen it too.

I squinted. There was the flash of a gray tail.

"I think we're being followed," he said.

As long as it wasn't by vampires, that was all that mattered.

Exhaustion hit Ginger by noon. We'd put her on the horse, but she was nodding asleep over Horace's neck. Alex called a stop so we could rest. We stomped down the stalks of wheat in a broad circle to provide rough bedding.

Ginger and I lay in the golden field, staring up at the shapes that the clouds made in the blue sky. I rested while Alex kept watch, feeling the sun warm on my face and Ginger turning fitfully beside me.

It almost reminded me of home. Of a normal life, feeling earth at my back and sky above me. I remembered sneaking a few naps like this in my father's fields when I was a girl, when my chores were done. I'd wake and look up at the clouds, picking out the shapes of beasts and men, daydreaming about the future. My dogs would doze with me, moving their legs and whimpering as they dreamed of chasing rabbits.

Now I watched Ginger twitch beside me. Her eyes were closed, but a thin gloss of sweat covered her face. Angry red tendrils from the wound at her shoulder had crawled up her neck. A sign of infection. She moaned in her sleep. I wondered what she was dreaming. I wondered if it hurt.

A couple of hours before sunset, we roused ourselves to continue moving. Ginger opened her eyes and blinked at the sunlight. I noticed that there was a small fleck of red in the glass blue of her iris. I took her pulse and laid my hand across her forehead. She had a bit of fever, and her heartbeat was rapid.

"How long?" she said, licking cracked lips.

"I don't know." I smoothed a piece of blond hair out of her eyes. "But you're still with us right now. And that's what matters."

I glanced up at Alex, but he couldn't meet my gaze. He turned away, and his shadow blotted out the sun. But I could see his shoulders shaking in grief.

———

Turning toward Darkness is a gradual process, in all things.

When I was a child, I was taught that evil creeps in stealthily. First there are little things, like coveting a pocket mirror in the sin of vanity. Then lying to one's parents, reading magazines with subversive ideas, drinking beer and smoking. These sins seem small, but they taint the soul and grow larger, become theft and rebellion and turning away from God. Once the seed has taken root, there is no stopping it.

I don't think that I believed that philosophy, then. But I might now, seeing the terrible Darkness of vampirism slowly destroy someone I loved.

Ginger stopped eating that evening. The crab apples had been vomited up in a mess of black blood. She was awake all night. We took the risk of a small fire to make her more comfortable. It was the time of year in which we were beginning to have no choice in making them at night if we wanted to avoid frostbite. But Ginger backed away from it. I saw the fire reflecting in her eyes as she looked out in the darkness.

Somewhere, in the black countryside, something howled.

I wondered if it was one of the wolves from the Animal Farm, or local coyotes. I wondered if he—or they—were following because they were hungry, because they smelled death.

Horace's ears twitched. He'd begun to edge away from Ginger, and the wolves made him nervous.

I sidled up closer to Ginger. "Tell me about your family. What was it like when the kids were little?" I wanted to anchor her as much as I could in her humanity.

She licked her cracked lips. "They were always good kids. Dan and I tried to raise them to be independent. Part of that was me wanting to shield them from being hurt when we moved around so much. Dan would be stationed one place and then another for a year or two at a time. We didn't want them to be crushed when we left their school and their friends."

I couldn't imagine that. I'd lived in one place for my whole life, with the same set of friends. Being under the *Bann*—being kicked out of my community—was the first time that I'd spent the night away from home. I had cried. I don't think that Ginger or Alex heard me. I didn't want them to.

"I did a good job, I think. Tom and Julia both went to college, far away. Julia isn't as rebellious as Tom, that's for sure. I never caught her smoking weed in the basement." Her eyes glistened. "I think that Julia has a bit of natural faith about her, a docility. Tom, he has to learn everything the hard way. I hope that he's not learning it the hard way now.

But maybe . . . maybe Dan can find them."

Ginger had lived alone after her children went off to college. Her husband had reenlisted in the National Guard and was gone for months at a time. I knew that she had gone home every day to an empty house.

"He will," I said soothingly. "He has all the power of the military around him—all the machines and the minds. He will find them."

Her gaze was unfocused. "I just wish that I could have told them goodbye."

I kissed her cheek. "We will tell them."

Her head lowered, and she smiled ruefully. One of the cracks in her lip split open. "It's funny. As I passed fifty, with the house empty . . . I had developed a fear of dying alone. Of having a stroke or a heart attack and lying dead on the kitchen linoleum for days before anyone found me."

I pressed my hand to her cheek. "That won't happen. I promise."

She took my hand. Hers was cold. "Thank you."

It was the least thing I could do for her, but also the hardest.

Alex and I watched as Ginger grew paler and the flecks of red in her eyes grew over the course of the night. Her gums receded, and I could see the teeth growing. Once, when I approached her to offer her water, I startled her and she hissed. She shied away from the sun the next day, sleeping under a tree. She unconsciously rolled and followed the shade in her sleep. I watched as the fingers wound in her coat contorted and twisted, the skin splintering.

"I don't think she's going to last much longer," Alex said.

I nodded. We kept our distance from her for the rest of the day. Horace would no longer graze near her. He stood on the opposite side of this bit of pasture. I rubbed my eyes, hiccupping.

I knew how to destroy vampires. I knew to cut off their heads, stuff their mouths with garlic if we had it, and burn the bodies. I had done it before, to people I knew.

But never someone I loved.

Alex took my hand. "We'll do it together," he said.

"As gently as we can."

"And it should be before dark. While she's still sleeping." He cast her a troubled look. "I think she'll turn then."

I bowed my head.

CHAPTER ELEVEN

We searched the pasture for a rock. Alex found a big chunk of pink jasper, as large as Ginger's head. We wanted her to feel as little pain as possible, and to our thinking, it would be easier if she was unconscious.

I took the rock from him. He was reluctant to let it go.

"I should be the one to do it," I said quietly. In the Plain way, men prepared men for burial, for reasons of modesty. Women cared for the women. This seemed no different. More grisly, but the same.

And yet . . . these conditions seemed too harsh for those old rules to apply. This was not bundling a peaceful grandmother in her favorite dress to be buried. Ginger had been my friend, had been like a second mother to me for many years. I rubbed my dripping nose and sobbed.

Alex embraced me. "I will help you. We will do this together."

"But I . . ."

"You're not going to be alone in this. I promise."

Once I could draw breath without sobbing, we walked back to the tree and stood over her. I don't know if she felt the cool of our shadows on her, in between the sparse shade of the tree. She was drawn in upon herself, like a ball. Her platinum blond head peeked above her coat and her eyes were closed. I gently tugged the coat up over her head, so I didn't have to see her face. The coat moved against her nose with her breath, outlining the profile of her face.

I lifted the stone twice before I was able to bring myself to slam it down onto her head.

Ginger gave a small squeak, like a startled mouse. A soft exhalation disturbed the fabric of the coat. And then there was no more — she lay still.

Tears streamed from my eyes. The rock slipped from my hands and rolled down away from the tree. I staggered back.

What had I done?

"I'm sorry," I sobbed. "I love you, Ginger."

Alex knelt down and turned her over. I could not bring myself to look over his shoulder as he removed the coat. I saw a stain on the dirt that was dark. Not the color of blood, but like molasses. Dark.

"She's gone," he said quietly. He gazed at me with a stricken expression of tenderness.

I saw the silver knife glittering in his left hand and a stake in his right. We knew what had to be done to keep her from rising as a vampire.

I knelt down beside him, shaking. I opened Ginger's coat and the stained and soggy blouse. It took me three tries to work the buttons. Her chest was pale, and I could see that the red tongues of the infection had worked beneath her bra strap and wound around her ribs.

I forced myself to try to take the knife from Alex. His hands were frozen around the hilt.

"No," he said. "I'll do it."

The stake plunged between the upper left two ribs, spilling a dark, viscous fluid on the ground.

I was glad that Alex was here, glad that he was here to take some of this terrible burden from me. The silver glinted in his fist as he brought the blade to her throat. I looked away, away until her head rolled down the little slope to come to rest beside the stone.

I stood there, gasping. The sunshine washed over me, cold and distant. Alex had his back to me. I could see his stained hands, the way his shoulders shook.

I couldn't help myself. My whole spirit buckled and shattered. I pressed my hands to my mouth and let loose a hoarse cry of anguish, like a raven's caw.

———

We used some of the remaining lighter fluid on Ginger's remains and dragged her head and body to the pyre. I stripped her wedding rings from her fingers with the intention of giving them to her family, if we ever saw them. I gently removed her broken glasses from her pocket and tucked them into our pack. We sat upwind of the pyre, feeding the fire with leaves and dried branches. We were covered in blood. I'm sure that if there was something lurking in the countryside, it could smell us. I don't think I cared much, anymore. We were open, exposed, and I felt, deep down, that we deserved whatever came for us. But Alex insisted that we burn our clothes and don the English garments we'd taken from the Animal Farm. I cast my

Plain dress and apron into the fire, watching the remnants of my former life flicker and burn. But I kept the bonnet in the pocket of the loose jeans I wore.

"We can bury her ashes in the morning," I said. I was pressed up against Alex's side. I felt him nod against me. I covered his hand with mine. I had slipped Ginger's rings on my right index finger. There was a simple gold band and a gold ring with a diamond in it. It was the first time in my life I'd ever worn jewelry. It made me feel closer to her.

"She is at peace now," I said, mostly to convince myself. "It is *Gelassenheit*." *Not murder,* I thought. *Please, not murder . . .*

He said nothing.

I tugged at his sleeve, pleading for him to affirm me. "She's at peace . . . God's will . . ." I whispered. It sounded like a question.

He choked and turned his head away. "This isn't *Gelassenheit*. This is a cruel God tormenting us."

"Don't say that," I said. I wanted to believe that what we had done was terrible but necessary. "I was always told that God smiles upon those who do his dirty work."

"Bonnet, I . . . I can't believe in an all-powerful being who would allow this . . . who wants this to happen. Screw your *Gelassenheit*."

I shrank back. I pressed the heels of my hands to my eyes, to try to blot it all out: the fire, the ache in my chest, the rings around my finger. And Alex's anger. I knew that it wasn't directed at me but at the easiest thing to blame. And that was God.

We passed the night without speaking further, watching Ginger burn from a safe distance. I thought I heard howling, and shivered. But I was determined to stay put, to make sure that the fire didn't burn out. I didn't have power over much, but I could ensure that Ginger's remains didn't fall to scavengers.

By silent agreement, we took turns on watch. Alex lay curled up on the ground, his head in my lap. I wore his coat around my shoulders.

I thought of how far I'd come. Not just in terms of miles, but how far I'd fallen from grace. I had given my heart and body to an English man. I had been placed under the *Bann* and cast out of my community. I had learned how to use weapons and how to kill. Except for the bonnet in my pocket, there was no sign of who I had been.

And Ginger was gone. I hoped that I could honor my promise to tell her husband and children goodbye for her. I hoped that the world would be set to rights and that I would be given that chance, to do something good for the woman who had loved me like one of her own children. The woman whom I'd just killed.

I sobbed, scrubbed at my eyes with my sleeve. It wasn't fair. I felt like screaming at God, like demanding answers. But I knew that he wouldn't answer me. He never answered me. He was just as distant and cold as the stars above.

I stared out into the night, and my breath caught in my throat when I saw a pair of glowing eyes staring back at me.

For a moment, I considered closing my eyes. Surrendering

to the Darkness and letting this long nightmare be finished.

But I couldn't. It wasn't just me. I had to protect Alex. He was all I had left.

My hand crept down to the silver knife lying closed on the grass.

The eyes crept closer, and a creature of smoke and sinew came into the touch of the firelight.

Not a vampire. A wolf.

The animal warily approached, watching me with soft golden eyes. I recognized it from the Animal Farm — the smallest one who had just a bit too much gold on its chest, which made me think that there was some domestic dog in it. The one who had stayed behind after the others had left.

My hand moved away from the knife.

"It's all right," I whispered. "I won't hurt you."

I hoped that it wouldn't hurt me. My father had said that wolves were shy of people and the only hazard they posed was to unguarded cattle if they were hungry. But those were different times, and everyone was hungry.

At the very edge of the firelight, the wolf slowly and deliberately lay down. He did not break from my gaze once as he did so. I could see the tension and fear in his body. He didn't look as painfully skinny as he had the last time I'd seen him, and he looked clean.

My fingers snaked to the pack beside me. I found a fruit pie from the truck stop, one of our last ones. I had no appetite. I quietly unwrapped it and tossed it to the wolf.

It was a clumsy throw. The pie landed short, about three feet away from it, and broke apart. The wolf's nose twitched.

Without breaking eye contact with me, he sidled over to the pie, his belly close to the ground.

He gobbled it down and licked the grass for crumbs, reminding me of the dogs I'd owned and bred.

The wolf didn't approach me. He went back to the spot at the edge of the fire and lay down. I saw that some of the tension had drained from his muscles, and he put his head between his paws.

"All right then," I whispered. "You can help me keep watch."

When dawn began to flush the edge of the horizon and the stars began to burn themselves out, the wolf climbed to his feet. He padded away into the tall grass. I wondered if I'd ever see him again. But I was willing to take his visit for what it was —a bit of comfort in the darkness.

Alex woke shortly after, and I didn't mention the wolf. The fire had died down by then, and we went to poke through the ashes with sticks. Ginger's bones were still there, burned black and covered in ash.

We found a couple of flat stones and set to digging a hole. It wasn't a very respectable grave. But I needed to bury her. I set the bones inside the hole with the foot and leg bones facing east, in the Amish fashion.

Alex brought the skull, placed it on top of the burned rib cage and pelvis. I winced when I saw it. The top left portion of it had been caved in, down to the eye socket. And the mouth was slightly open. I could see the sharp teeth inside, and shuddered.

We scraped dirt back into the hole, stomped the fresh earth down to keep the scavengers out. I tied two sticks together in a cross shape with some dry grass and staked it in the top of the disturbed earth. Alex stacked rocks before it in a pillar.

We stood before the makeshift grave. I tried to memorize where it was, how many paces from the tree. Alex carefully marked the area on his map.

Plain people did not eulogize their dead. I didn't know how to begin to do that in the English fashion. So I began in Deitsch:

> *"Unser Vadder im Himmel,*
> *dei Naame loss heilich sei,*
> *Dei Reich loss komme . . ."*

Alex said "Amen" with me at the end of the Lord's Prayer, and I felt a small spark of warmth, that perhaps not all his hope had been lost. He took my hand and we stared at the small grave. In a Plain service, there would be sermons. Someone would give the name of the deceased, her birth and death dates. I was ashamed that I didn't know Ginger's birth year or her middle name.

Instead, I said: "Goodbye, Ginger. We shall see you in the kingdom of heaven."

———

We traveled fast, since there were only two of us. Three, counting Horace.

Four, counting the wolf.

Alex and I rode together on the horse, wrapped in the cloak

of silent mourning. We were mindful not to push Horace too hard, with our combined weight added to the poundage of our dwindling gear. But there was something reassuring to the feel of Alex's arms around me. He was not much of a horseman. I had to show him how to mount and dismount without falling off, how to guide the horse with the reins. But he was gentle with the horse, and Horace knew that.

We traveled across open farmland. Occasionally, Alex would point to where we were on the map. I felt the strength of winter coming and worried over our food supplies. We were down to one bottle of cranberry juice and a bag of potato chips, which we shared before a small fire. It was getting too cold to contemplate night without it. Our lighter fluid was gone, and I managed to start a fire with some dry pine, but I had been lucky to find it.

"We're going to have to consider carrying an ember," I said. "In pine needles or a jar or something. Some way that it can smolder and still get air. I don't know how well I can start one once it's wet." I blew on the tiny orange flame I'd started in the tangle of pine, nursing it as I would a bird fallen from its nest.

"I'll work on it." He shared the last of the juice from the bottle with me and began to carve out a hole in the side with his knife. He stuffed the inside of the bottle with pine needles and unscrewed the cap for a chimney. I could put a spark in it and it would remain live for a long time, able to breathe and smolder.

"That's perfect," I said, warming my hands over the flame. We'd set up camp in an open meadow, where we could see in all directions. This land was a bit higher than some of the flat land we had left, and I could see for miles in the daylight. Now the night was soft and total. I saw no lights. No sign of humans. Only the light of the fire and the stars.

"What are we going to do if we're the last ones?" He opened the bag of potato chips and handed them to me. I took a handful and passed the rest to him.

I shook my head. "We're not. We can't be."

But I wouldn't say that the thought hadn't occurred to me.

"What happens if, under my brilliant leadership, we get to Canada and there's nothing there?" He stared into the tiny blaze.

"Then . . ." I was going to give him a heartfelt platitude about the value of hope or *Gelassenheit*. But that wasn't what he wanted. And, feeling the hollowness of Ginger's death, I wasn't sure that I could say it and mean it. Instead, I said: "Then we will survive there, just as we've managed to survive here, for as long as we can."

"And why the hell are you following me, anyway?"

I blinked at him. I felt a stab of hurt. We'd all come together, and I'd assumed . . . "Where else would I go?"

"That's not what I mean. I mean . . . you just agree to submit to my authority. Is that something that you're doing just because I'm a man? Having a penis doesn't make me infallible." He rubbed his hands through his hair, and I could see his Adam's apple bob as he was trying not to cry. "I got Ginger killed. You *should* question me. Challenge me if I'm making the wrong call. Not follow me out of some biblical edict or cultural force of habit."

I placed my hand on his sleeve. "I'm not following you out

of blind faith. Or love, for that matter. When I follow you, it's because I've thought about it and I agree that what you're doing is right."

He leaned over and kissed me. His lips were warm and he felt alive.

"Thanks, Bonnet. I just . . . I'm not cut out to be any kind of person in charge."

"You're making the right choices." I truly believed that.

"I'm not convinced." Alex licked the salt from the bag. "We are now officially out of food. I don't know how long that's going to be, Bonnet, but . . ."

He stiffened, and his gaze was focused beyond the fire. I felt him reach for his knife at his side, but I put a hand on his arm, stilling him.

Glowing eyes crept to the edge of the campfire. But they were familiar golden ones. The wolf came within the reach of the light. His tail was low and his ears were pressed flat. He carried something in his mouth.

I felt Alex suck in his breath as I murmured, "Our shadow has come back."

The wolf paused at the edge of the fire and laid down his burden. It was a rabbit. He backed away from us, moved to the other side of the fire, and lay down.

Alex crawled forward, on hands and knees. He touched the rabbit. "Is this . . . is this for us?"

The wolf thumped its tail on the ground and whimpered. He looked a bit frightened of us. Horace cast him a dim eye but did not shy away.

"He is too used to being with people," I said.

"Should I chase him off?"

I shook my head. "No. It's his choice whether to follow us or not. Perhaps he wants the fire and the light."

I took the rabbit from Alex and set his knife to it. The wolf watched as I skinned it and drove a stick through its body to roast it. My stomach grumbled as it cooked on the tiny fire and the fat sizzled in the embers.

Alex and I took turns devouring the hot meat. It was the best meal I'd had in days. I was careful not to eat it all. I tossed some scraps and the bones to the wolf. He dragged the bones to where he lay and put them between his paws. He quietly gnawed on them, the sound of his chewing melding with the pop and crackle of the fire.

"Shall we give him a name?" I asked. I was relieved for the wolf's presence. It gave me something to focus on other than Ginger and the lingering cold feeling of that stone in my hands. I wondered if the sensation would ever fade. Plain people were instructed not to dwell on the dead after the funeral. We were not to allow grief to shadow our footsteps, to devour us. We were to have faith that our loved ones were with God. I repeated these things to myself, but my hands were still cold.

"I guess. If he sticks around." Alex seemed to think on this. "What about Fenrir?"

"Another mythological name?" I rubbed my hands on my skirt.

Alex watched me. A little hiccupped sob escaped my lips. He took my hands in his, stilling them.

"Fenrir is a wolf in Norse mythology. He was born as a son to Loki, the god of chaos, and a giantess named Angrboda.

Angrboda was the herald of sorrow. They had three children: Fenrir, the giant wolf; the serpent Jörmungand; and the mistress of death, Hel.

"The gods of Asgard cast a prophecy that said that Fenrir and his children would be responsible for Ragnarök, the end of the world."

"Apparently, the end of the world is not a new fear," I said. But I wanted him to continue, to tell me another story that would take my mind from grief. My hands felt warm in his, and I focused on that feeling and the cadence of his voice.

"No kidding. Ragnarök is 'the Doom of the Gods.' It's the end of the cosmos. It's preceded by Fimbulvetr, the winter of winters that will last a year. Humankind will fight itself to the death.

"Then the wolf Skoll will devour the sun, and his brother Hati will eat the moon. The earth is ruled by Darkness. The stars will vanish from the sky. Then a couple of roosters wake the giants, harass the gods, and raise the dead."

I shuddered. "If we see roosters, we'll know to beware."

"Yes. Beware the roosters. Hmm . . . chicken . . ." He looked distracted. "But back to Fenrir . . . the gods of Asgard caught the wolf as a puppy and put him in a cage. Tyr, the god of war, broke him free and cared for the wolf.

"Fenrir grew freakishly large and strong. The gods chained him, and he broke free. They then got the dwarves to make a magic chain. Tyr reluctantly went along with this. In revenge, Fenrir bit off Tyr's hand.

"The gods chained Fenrir to a rock a mile beneath the earth and put a sword between his teeth to keep him from biting. He waits there until the day of Ragnarök, when an earthquake will free him and he will kill Odin, the king of the gods. And Odin's son is prophesied to kill Fenrir."

"Your myths are always terrible," I told him. "But I think that Fenrir is a fine name."

Fenrir closed his golden eyes and slept. His black lips drew back, and I think he smiled.

Chapter Twelve

Fenrir proved himself to be a mighty hunter.

He was still with us the next morning. He followed behind for some time, ranged away, and would come back. He'd become distracted by pheasants, by rustling leaves, by smells, and would vanish for hours. Then he would return and slink along in our wake.

At dusk, he brought us a chicken. I have no idea where he found it, or if he'd been listening to Alex's story. Alex gently took it from him, and the wolf shied away.

"Thank you," I said.

Alex held up the chicken and turned it to face him. "I'm gonna name you . . . Ragnarök. Because I can't remember any of the names of the magical roosters in Norse mythology."

I grinned. I had not smiled in a long time. It made my face hurt.

"Ragnarök is going to be delicious."

And he was.

But I was beginning to lose a bit of heart. We had seen no more signs of other living people in all our journey north. We saw some of their leavings, like bits of litter blown up against fences. A turned-over mail truck in the middle of a two-lane highway spilled out a gut of letters and parcels that were growing mildewy. But no sign of anything else. No buildings that hadn't burned. There were no vampires, which was comforting, until I thought about what that meant: no food. And that worried me.

I think that's why we veered a bit west, toward a small town that Alex spied on the map. The night had grown cold, cold enough that we saw our breath make ghosts in the air. We couldn't continue sleeping out in the open, exposed. We needed supplies. Alex still wanted to find a car. Or bicycles. And for that, we'd need to venture close to what had once been civilization.

We followed the two-lane highway until it intersected with a large four-lane. The road was empty and abandoned, but a cluster of a town had sprouted up around the freeway exit.

It seemed innocuous enough, in the gray light of afternoon. There was a gas station, three fast food restaurants, and a steakhouse. An electronics store sat back from the road, along with what looked like a strip mall. Rain had begun early in the morning, mixing with sleet. My coat was heavy with ice beginning to form, and I couldn't stop shivering. Even Fenrir kept close for warmth, skulking along the culvert as Alex and I headed into the town.

We walked along the edge of the strip mall parking lot. Broken glass glittered beneath the coating of sleet, and I could see bent traffic signs. Fenrir found a garbage can to dig through, but nothing edible inside. A sandwich wrapper stuck to his paw, and Alex scraped it off. The traffic lights were out, pulled down in a tangle of wire.

"I take that to mean there won't be any power."

We paused before the window of a Chinese restaurant. I peered inside the glass, to see the rotting remains of a buffet. It was likely that any fresh food that hadn't been taken or eaten by survivors had spoiled in the time that had intervened in this disaster. I felt a pang of regret. I had never had Chinese food before. It was one of the things I had looked forward to on *Rumspringa*.

"Hey, look at this."

I heard a thick metallic thump. I looked back to see Alex pounding his fist on a sheet of metal. I squinted at it. It was a large turquoise building, bricked like a fortress. A flexible metal gate covered the front, like a garage door.

"What is it?" I asked.

"A department store. And it looks like Fort Knox." He shoved on the metal, but it did not give.

We circled around it, finding a locked man-size door at the back and another one of the large metal gates on a loading dock. A few bits of graffiti covered the brick. It was too stylized to read, but it certainly seemed to be a frustrated scrawl.

"Doesn't look like anybody figured a way in."

"Not yet," I said. I shivered, staring up at the smooth, seemingly impenetrable façade.

Alex turned up the collar of my jacket against my throat. "Don't worry. We'll figure out a way."

I looked up, and our eyes caught on a slatted vent on the side of the building. It was much too high to reach.

"There's our entrance," he said with determination.

After several jumps, slips on ice, and much swearing, we arrived at a solution. Horace was brought to stand below the vent. Alex and I stood, wobbly, in his saddle, leaning up against the wall. Fenrir watched in an amused fashion from a distance, his tongue hanging out of his mouth in what appeared to be good humor.

"Okay," Alex said. "I'm gonna lift you up. See if you can pry open the edge of that vent with the knife." He put his hands on my waist.

I looked at the vent above dubiously. "About the leadership thing . . ."

He waited. "You want to move on?"

I shook my head. "No. I'll try it."

He lifted me up, and I reached for the corner of the vent. I jammed the knife under the fabricated metal edge and worked to loosen it. There were no screws that I could see. Alex had to set me down twice, when his muscles trembled. Horace snuffled in irritation below us.

I finally pried the cover of the vent open.

"All right," I said. "I think I can reach."

Alex hoisted me up and I grasped the lip of the vent with my hands. The edge was sharp, and I could feel it cutting into my palms. I squeezed between the gap in the vent cover and the lip of the vent. Alex shoved as hard as he could, and I scrambled inside the shaft.

And prayed that there were no vampires inside.

I had an immediate panic when I felt dust and silt shaking

down on me. I feared the sensation of the spider webs that meant one of their nests was close.

I paused, tried to control my breathing. This was an old duct, and there were likely real spiders here. There had been no sign of assault from the outside, I reasoned. And vampires would have no interest in a closed-up store with no food.

Behind me, I reached for the vent covering. I pulled it closed and flush against the side of the building, drawing the seams close to the edge of the wall. If I made a way in, I did not want it to be an obvious place for others to enter. I pulled it tight, in its original position, tucked the bent pieces of metal around the shaft walls. I was sealed in.

Through the grate, I could see Alex down below with the horse. He nodded at me, and I could see the sleet freezing on his jacket.

I turned around to face the darkness.

On my elbows and knees, I crawled forward. My movements made loud thuds on the sheet metal, surely announcing my presence to any awaiting creatures. I could see nothing but pitch black. But I struggled to quell my fear and forced myself to keep moving.

I crawled for what seemed like a hundred feet before I felt something change beneath me. The shaft had sloped downward, and I felt a different texture than dusty metal under my palms. I explored it with my fingers. It felt like a metal grate, a panel with holes. I backed off and pushed down on it.

Nothing happened. I crammed my legs beneath me and

scrunched myself into a sitting position. With all my might, I kicked downward on the pane.

Once.

Twice.

On the third blow, the grate gave away with a ripping sound. I nearly fell into the hole that spilled out from the bottom of the darkness. The air below me was a bit warmer, and it smelled like cinnamon.

But I had no way of knowing for certain how far down the floor was. I could guess, based on what I'd seen outside. The vent had been about twelve feet from the ground. Assuming that it didn't open above a stairwell, that was still a substantial drop. I could break some bones on the descent and die in this place.

I'd be alone. Entirely alone.

I sat for a few moments, cradling my aching hand in my lap. Eventually, the pain and my fear dulled. I turned around, swinging my legs over the edge of the vent. I took a deep breath. I backed out into darkness, lurching into it, keeping my grip firmly on the edge of the vent.

The vent groaned and shrieked under that concentrated weight. I felt my grip slipping, the metal shifting beneath me. The vent collapsed, but I tried to hang on. I heard drywall cracking and felt my arms tangling in metal. I grabbed whatever I could, grappling with the wave of collapsing duct and ceiling until it dumped me out onto a hard floor with a deafening thud that jarred my spine and backside.

I lay still on the floor. Pieces of crumbly drywall rained around me. I felt sore and bruised, but did not feel anything broken. My palms and arms were scraped, but everything seemed intact. I crawled to my feet, wobbly in the cinnamon-scented darkness.

I sucked in a breath.

Something was glowing.

And I was trapped here with it.

This wasn't anything like the glowing of vampire eyes, or even the golden shine of Fenrir's. This was an artificial, dull luminosity. It reminded me of the stars on the ceiling in the boy's bedroom at the Animal Farm.

Cautiously, I stumbled toward it. I jammed my knee against what must have been a display containing glass—it broke and I cried out in startlement. I weaved and bobbed, heading toward that light.

And I paused, uncomprehending. They were glowing human shapes . . . transparent, filled with light. Mannequins, I think they were called. They were perched in what would have been the front window of the store, now shrouded by the metal shutter. There were four of them, posed as if in dance, with translucent wings. The mannequins were wearing gossamer dresses that must have been for sale somewhere in the store. They looked like angels, lit from within from strings of lights like those I'd seen Englishers use for Christmas decorations. I stared up into the empty skulls of the figures. They had no faces. In this way, they were like Amish dolls, blank. We didn't create graven images.

I touched a translucent face. It seemed alien. Unreal. And I was pretty sure I wasn't part of the intended market for the short dresses they wore in varying shades of white sheer fabric. Far too immodest and vain for a Plain girl.

I brushed bits of drywall off my sleeves. But maybe I wasn't a Plain girl anymore. I didn't look like one.

In the dim glow of the mannequins, I searched for a way to bring their light with me. I tried to pull one of the mannequins off the display, but her cord only extended six feet. Once I drew her beyond that, the cord came unplugged from a giant battery beneath the stage, and she went dark. I fumbled around and plugged her back in. I let her lie on the cold marble floor, but she threw enough light for me to be able to see the glass doors of the main entrance and the metal door beyond. I had to get them open somehow.

The glass doors were easy enough. I pried the first set open with my fingers. They gave way under the pressure of my shoulder. I guessed that these were automatically powered doors. The second set was locked, top and bottom, with strong slide bolts.

And the metal segmented door stood between me and the outside. It extended all across the face of the building. I searched at the bottom of it for a handle, for a way to raise and lower it. It seemed to have rolled out of the ceiling, but was connected to the floor by a metal footer. I searched for a way to release it, crawling on my hands and knees, probing with my fingers, until I found a series of release switches. I tripped them all. Taking a deep breath, I slipped my fingers beneath the metal curtain and lifted.

The noisy metal wall rolled up like a roman shade. I'd lifted it no more than three feet when I saw several sets of legs before me: human, horse, and wolf.

And the gray light behind them washed in.

A smile broke on Alex's face.

"Welcome to paradise."

———————

For that brief time in that closed-up store, it was paradise. And more.

Alex led Horace inside, and Fenrir hesitantly followed in their wake. We closed down all the doors, refastened them.

Alex grinned as he locked the last set of doors. "I feel like I'm in a military installation."

"And that's good?"

"Yeah. This is our fortress. Our stronghold against the night."

I blew out a breath. I was beginning to feel safe, for the first time in many weeks.

The first thing to fight was the worry of darkness. Alex brought inside the spark I'd so lovingly ensconced in pine needles in a hollowed-out plastic bottle. The spark seemed very bright after I blew on it. I could see it gleaming in my hands, like an orange star.

"Here," Alex said. "Try this."

He'd found two pillar candles from a holiday display. They smelled strongly of cloves. I gently poured the fire from my ember to the wicks, blew on them until the breath of life stabilized the fire. The candles burned, dripping wax. They were covered in glitter, but they were perfectly functional for what we needed, which was to explore our surroundings.

We passed by the cash registers at the mouth of the store. Money was useless in our new world. We crossed to the candle display, unwrapped more candles, and added light there, to mark our surroundings.

Horace clomped on the marble floors. He nosed past a harvest-themed display of straw bales and scarecrows, reaching up to taste a garland. It was quite lovely, made of corn husks, ears of fancy dried corn, figs, and oranges studded with cloves. I'm sure that someone had worked quite hard to create it, and Horace appreciated the artistic effort involved. He nipped it off as high as he could reach and then bit the head off of one of the scarecrows. The hapless scarecrow head dangled from his mouth, then quickly disappeared.

Fenrir had vanished as soon as he entered the store. I could hear his claws clicking on the floor from a far distance away.

The department store was composed of two levels, split by an escalator. At the foot of the escalator stood a nonfunctioning fountain. The first floor was primarily clothing for men and women. It smelled heavily of perfume. I saw more of the gossamer dresses the mannequins wore, organized on hangers. There were different departments for "misses" and "women." That made no sense to me. Only the young unmarried women wore small sizes and the married women wore the larger ones?

There were warm, dry coats. I fingered the wool and leather with some envy and desire. I walked past the women's formal dresses. These must be the ones that English girls wore to go to dances and weddings. The fabrics shimmered with sequins and lace. I let my hand brush the edge of a large white dress advertised for a bride.

I smiled and shook my head.

"What's so funny?" Alex said.

"A Plain woman wouldn't ever be married in that. It's too vain. And shows too much flesh."

"What do you wear for weddings?"

"Each girl makes herself a new dress. It's usually blue. But very similar to what we wear every other day."

"To avoid the sin of pride," he said.

"*Ja.* A marriage is a union of people in the light of God. It hasn't got much to do with . . ."—I paused to read a tag—"'a self-bustling train with pickups.' Whatever that is." It sounded like a selection of heavy machinery.

I smoothed the surface of the dress and felt a pang. I wondered if Ginger had worn a dress like this at her wedding. I wished that she were here so I could ask her.

We passed by the glittering jewelry counter and the cosmetics counter full of inscrutable jars and bottles. I had worn makeup only once, when Ginger had done it for me. When I put it on, I had felt beautiful. Until Elijah told me that my face was dirty and that I should wash it.

There were some useful things here: perfumed soaps, soft cloths to scrub with, and brushes for hair. And having a watch to tell time might be helpful. I had lost track of which day it was. I hadn't paused to honor the Sabbath—I honestly had forgotten when it was.

"Boots!" Alex shouted happily. He was in the men's department, surrounded by hiking boots.

I grinned, feeling my cold toes squish against the interiors of my ruined shoes. New boots would be a very good thing.

We wandered upstairs, which seemed to be the province of domestic and sporting goods. Furniture of all kinds was on display, with beds dressed in the finest linens. I paused before an ornately carved four-poster bed and rubbed my hands over the embroidered velvet coverlet. The pillows were down, and the sheets were something called Egyptian cotton. I tried not to drip wax on them as I knelt down to examine the tags. Four-hundred-dollar sheets.

"This must be how the rich English live," I said.

"This is how English with credit cards live," he said.

I frowned. "We only use cash."

"That's smart. Credit cards are a way of getting into a hole, really fast. Getting seduced by luxury goods that will take forever to pay for. It's like selling your soul to the bank."

I stroked the velvet coverlet. Was one's soul worth a velvet coverlet? Maybe it depended on the soul.

"Score. Sporting goods!"

I heard Alex whoop from beyond, and I followed him. He smiled broadly in an aisle surrounded by sleeping bags, tackle boxes, battery-powered lanterns, and camping cookware. "Look!" He swung his arm to the top of the aisle and pointed excitedly: "Tents! Fishing poles!"

I uttered a prayer of thanksgiving. No more sleeping out in the elements.

I heard a frustrated whimper. I turned to see that Fenrir had knocked over a box of "gourmet beef jerky for outdoorsmen." He had a plastic-sealed package between his paws and was shredding at it without much success.

"Come here." I knelt, and Fenrir brought his prize to me. I peeled off the plastic and handed the jerky stick to him. He snatched it from my hand and trotted off in happiness.

I paused beside a display of gourmet foods and choco-
lates. There were some dried fruits that would be suitable for
a horse, once he'd finished stripping the garland downstairs.
With a moment's hesitation, I tore into a bag that said it contained "White Peppermint Snowballs." I did not regret it. It
contained cookies coated with peppermint. They were possibly the single most delicious thing I'd ever eaten. I closed my
eyes in sublime happiness.

When I opened them again, there was a wolf snout in the
bag.

I let him have the bag, then stared up at the display of gourmet crockery that my mother never could have imagined. The
tags identified the devices as an electric miniature pie maker, a
panini press, an ice cream maker, and a convection oven. Cop-
per-bottomed pieces of cookware hung from a rack, so shiny
I could see my reflection in them. They were nothing like the
cast iron we used at home. I picked up a five-hundred-dollar
pan and promptly dropped it, shocked at the price and how
light it felt.

"What on earth are we going to do with all of these things?"
I muttered in awe.

"We're going to party, Bonnet." Alex came around the corner. He was wearing a ridiculous fur parka, a pair of sunglasses,
and a broad grin. He held a volleyball. "We're going to party
like it's 1999."

Chapter Thirteen

And party we did.

I felt a momentary stab of guilt at tearing into the luxury goods at the department store. But in the light of our need and the sheer absurdity of the items, that guilt was quickly abandoned.

Alex and I played volleyball across the escalator. We'd found flashlights in the sporting goods department and something called glow sticks in the children's toys. The flexible sticks could be fastened as necklaces and bracelets, and I wore three around my neck as I careened crazily after the ball. Alex was a dismal volleyball player. I served it perfectly off the balcony of the second floor and he missed it entirely. It splashed into the dead fountain, startling poor Horace, who had been noisily taking a drink.

"Damn, Bonnet. You should go pro. Play on the beach." His face was green in the light of the glow sticks.

"We play volleyball a good deal back home," I said. "Often before the Singings, in the summertime, when the youth gather. It's a good sport for both boys and girls to play together."

"You've never seen women's beach volleyball on television, have you?"

I cocked my head. "No."

"Let me show you the uniform." He disappeared into the women's department. I wrinkled my forehead. I hadn't seen any uniforms down there.

I sat down on a bench in the middle of the floor, next to the fountain. We had dragged something called a "fire bowl" down from the "Outdoor Living" section. It was a large copper bowl that held hideously overpriced wood and scented pinecones that one could burn. It was doing a good job of warming up the space, I had to admit. We'd set a couple more around the store for light and warmth. The mannequins around them seemed to twitch in the turning shadows.

"Ta-da!" Alex said. He brought forth a garment on a hanger.

I squinted at it. I guessed from my time surreptitiously leafing through *Cosmopolitan* magazine that it was a bathing suit. Barely.

I picked it up and stared at it. It was two pieces. The top fabric, held together with beaded strings, was barely enough to cover the breasts. The bottoms appeared to be similarly engineered. It was bright pink, and cost eighty dollars.

I raised my eyebrows. "Really?"

"Oh, yes," he said enthusiastically. "The ones that the volleyball players wear don't have the strings, of course. That's not very aerodynamic to have beaded strings slapping your ass as you hammer the heck out of your opponent. But that's the gist of it."

"No thank you," I said primly. I knew that he enjoyed

teasing me about our cultural differences. I took no offense, but I reserved the right to be fascinated or aghast. Or both.

"You know what we should do . . ." He scanned the shadowy realm of the department store.

"What?" I kicked the volleyball across the floor. Fenrir trotted after it and vanished into the men's section, shedding on thousand-dollar suits.

"We should have a date. A real date. With dinner and dancing and stuff."

I was suddenly unsure. "I, um, can't dance."

But he was on to the idea. "I'll show you," he said enthusiastically. "I can find a CD player around here, probably some cheesy elevator music packaged with some potpourri in the gift section."

I looked on him dubiously. "A real date?"

"Yes," he nodded. "Like real people in a real world that hasn't gone to hell. With formal clothes and fancy shoes."

My gaze slid to the sparkling dresses in the shadows of the misses' department. I struggled to find an idea like what he was suggesting. "Like . . . like prom?" I had heard that the English high school girls and boys dressed up for formal dances.

"Yeah. Sure."

I frowned. "We don't really do that. When Plain people are courting . . . it's not so fancy." I blushed. That was an assumption that perhaps I shouldn't make. Courting was serious business in the Plain community. From what I'd observed of the English, dating was casual.

He touched the back of my hand. "Bonnet, you've done a

lot of things that Plain folk don't do. And you'll probably do a lot more. "

I thought of Ginger. I looked away.

"We don't have to," he said. "But I'd encourage you to live just a little. You'll have plenty of time for all that dire stuff later."

I sighed. Perhaps I was taken in by the sparkle of the dresses. Perhaps I had always been enthralled by the idea of *Rumspringa*. Perhaps I was more than a little seduced by Alex.

"All right," I said. "But you have to get Horace's nose out of the fountain so that I can get a proper bath."

He grinned.

"In privacy."

"Okay, okay." He bent down, took my hand, and kissed it. My heart flip-flopped. "I'll meet you at the top of the escalator in two hours, eh?"

I smiled, watching him lead Horace back into the realm of shoes.

Perhaps this was to be my only fairy-tale evening in the world Outside. But I was determined to make the most of it.

Just for one night, I pushed the dark world outside away. I tried to put aside feeling guilty over Ginger, missing my family, and fearing for the future. I tried to imagine what the world might have been like if I'd done as I intended, if I'd gone on *Rumspringa* and experienced the Outside world under normal conditions. I tried to imagine what it would have been like if Alex and I had met under other circumstances.

That thought troubled me. We had been thrown together at the end of the world. I don't know if we would have cared for each other if we had met in a more usual way. There was genuine affection between us. What we had was not the idealized love of English movies, or the bonds of duty that would have been expected of me as a Plain woman. This was . . . something wholly other. And I had no template for how to deal with it.

But just for tonight, I told myself to take it for what it was. That there may be nothing more. This was the last bit of juice I could squeeze out of the withering apple of the world.

I bathed in the tepid water of the fountain with a plethora of products from the cosmetics counter, including a body wash that was purported to smell like pomegranates. I had never smelled a pomegranate, but the fragrance was pleasing. I found some shampoo that was supposed to "rehydrate and restructure damaged hair." It lathered up in a wonderful way. I even indulged in a conditioner in a black bottle that was supposed to be made of "hydrolized keratin protein and fresh acai berry." It smelled like dessert.

I toweled off with some extraordinarily plush towels, then slathered a mint and rosemary body cream over my skin. It smelled close enough to real food that Fenrir came by for a sniff. I wrapped the towel around myself. I glanced upstairs, at the sporting goods department. I could hear Alex digging around up there, but I didn't know what he was up to. As long as he gave me some privacy, I was fine with that.

I shrugged into a soft robe. Carrying a candle and leaving damp footprints behind me on the marble floor, I began to think about a dress.

Here I was out of my element. I knew about Plain clothes. I knew how they were constructed, knew exactly what was expected in terms of hemlines and seam allowances and reinforced stitching. These English garments seemed flimsy and needlessly complicated, covered in shiny bits of beads and zippers and buttons.

And the sizing made no sense to me whatsoever. I'd used store-bought fabric patterns, and I knew exactly what size I was from those measurements. A twelve. I was a slender girl, and a twelve fit me well for modesty's sake—no clinging. A dress was made to work in. But there was no similarity in these misses' garments. A size twelve seemed too large.

I reminded myself that I was not searching for a dress to work in. This would likely be the only fancy dress I ever had on my body in my life. All that was required was that it cover me decently and that I could sit down and walk in it.

My fingers trailed over fabrics that were foreign to me —stretchy, sheer, and metallic. I picked up one, then another. Eventually, with an armload of dresses, I ducked into a mirror-lined area called the "fitting room."

The first dress made me laugh out loud. It was a dark red and floor-length with no sleeves or straps. It reminded me of my mother's red velvet cake. It had a curved neckline and some sort of stiff scaffolding inside it, but I simply didn't have enough bosom to fill it out. I turned my upper body and the dress stayed in place, facing front.

Next was a metallic turquoise dress that reminded me of fish scales. It was made of a stretchy material that clung tightly to my body. I blinked when I saw myself in it. I looked like a full-grown glamorous woman from a magazine. The neckline was low and left little to the imagination.

Interesting, I thought. But not at all appropriate.

I stepped in and out of dresses, trying them on and twirling in the mirror. I had discovered that I was a size four, more or less, based on English sizing. Sometimes a two, sometimes a six. Once, I was startled to see that a dress marked a size zero fit. That seemed to make no sense whatsoever. I flipped through the tags. Some of these gowns cost hundreds of dollars. I was amazed, wondering how much wear an English girl got out of one of these dresses. Could she wear it to more than one prom?

But this was fun, I secretly admitted to myself. The dresses accumulated in a heap on the floor of the fitting room, and I had to step over them to get to the mirror.

I even tried on a bridal dress. Against my better judgment.

I think that I was fascinated because it was white. I'd never worn a white dress. It seemed very shiny and eye-catching. Vain. Prideful. All those things that were against how I'd been raised. When I pulled it on over my head, I got lost for a moment in all that white frothiness and had a moment of panic as I struggled to find the top. I found the opening of it and wriggled through.

I pulled the laces closed at the back and stood in the mirror, regarding myself. It felt like something out of a dream. An illusion. The white reflected in the candlelight off my skin, making it seem like I was more luminous than I could ever hope to be. My hair hung unbound over my shoulder, and my blistered feet were hidden. I stood up straight and moved my callused hands behind my back.

For a moment, I had a glimpse of what I would have been like if I had lived another life.

Not that I wanted to be married. Elijah had asked me and I'd said no. Plain unions were made of duty and solemnity. Submission to God and one's husband. A pragmatic statement of commitment before the community. I had always felt that there was a bit of resignation to it. But this dress and what it represented seemed something apart from that, a fairy tale made of spun sugar.

For now, no one was watching, and I sank into that illusion, reveling in it. I tried to memorize every bit of it, from the weight of the skirt to the feeling of satin against my skin. I gave a twirl, and the skirt moved as if it had a life of its own. Maybe that was the idea.

But the illusion was too heavy. I struggled to get the dress off, feeling as if it had devoured me, was smothering me. I fought through layers of lace until I could breathe again.

In the end, I picked a dark blue dress for my date with Alex. It was the one I felt most comfortable in. I had no idea if it was considered stylish or not. It was made of a softly draping column of fabric, pooling at the neckline and sweeping over my waist and hips. The hemline reached the tops of my feet, where a good Plain dress should. However, it exposed much more than a Plain dress: my arms and collarbone were bare, and it dipped low in the back. But it looked like the night sky, and that was something I was familiar with.

I took a pass through the undergarments section of the department store and picked out some that I thought would work with the dress. I tucked the *Himmelsbrief* into my bra. Experience had taught me never to be without it. Everything they had was much fancier and more complicated than what I was used to. The same for the shoes. I tried walking up and down an aisle in a pair of high heels, but stumbled and nearly turned my ankle. I didn't know how English women did this —it must have involved years of practice. I settled for a pair of silver flat sandals that tied at the ankle.

I had saved the cosmetics counter for last. I felt a pang of sadness, again remembering Ginger applying makeup to my face when she had been alive. My fingers slid over the golden tubes and mirrored compacts.

I gathered some items at random, then pulled a stool up to the counter and leaned in toward a mirror. I played with the pots of color, dumping one across the counter and dropping a lipstick on the floor with a sharp crack that shattered the tube. I applied the paints and peered at myself in the mirror.

I looked like a caricature of myself, as if a child had drawn me in crayon. I wiped most of it off, leaving behind only the stubborn waterproof mascara and sheer pink lipstick. Better. I still looked like myself, only slightly more glowy.

With more than a bit of nervousness, I walked past the fountain to climb the escalator stairs. Horace whickered at me. I think it was because I smelled like perfume and not sweat. I gripped my candle tightly and watched my feet, mindful not to trip.

A low whistle emanated from above.

I looked up. Alex stood at the top of the steps. He was leaning against the rail, dressed in a tuxedo. His hair was damp and combed back from his face. He looked . . . really amazing. And so unlike himself.

I blushed, looked down to pick up my skirt from the hip to climb the stairs. When I reached the top, he took my hand and kissed it.

"You look gorgeous," he said, against my knuckles.

I felt my face flush more deeply, and was glad that I'd not left on any of the cosmetic blush. Alex's fingers brushed the shoulder of my dress.

"I like this," he said. "Very Grecian. It suits you."

I looked up and found my voice. "You look nice too."

He offered me his elbow. I stared at it until he folded my fingers into the crook.

"Dinner awaits," he said, leading me to a grouping of patio furniture that he'd arranged around one of the fire bowls. Fenrir curled around the bottom pedestal of the bowl, drowsing. Heavy china plates were set on the wrought-iron surface, and I fingered the brocade cloth napkins.

"This is lovely," I said.

He pulled my chair out for me. The iron squeaked on the marble floor, and he winced. "Wait until you try the popcorn."

I grinned.

Dinner was the richest meal I'd ever eaten—and the most eccentric. Alex fed me chocolate-covered cranberries, hot chocolate, and camping entrees.

"They're MREs," he said, around a mouthful of something that purported to be beef stew. "The military makes them. But they're also supposed to be popular among campers and survivalists."

"It's delicious," I said, twisting the pepper mill to deliver six kinds of gourmet pepper onto my MRE. I meant it—hot food without fear of contamination was something to be treasured.

A pop sounded from the fire, and I jumped, nearly knocking over my hot cocoa. The pop was followed by a flurry of others, like hail on a metal roof.

"Popcorn's ready," Alex said. He turned toward the fire bowl to pick out our foil packages of gourmet popcorn. He dropped one in front of me with a pair of tongs and tore it open. I took a hot morsel and dropped it into my mouth.

"It's good." I grinned.

"It ought to be," he said, around a mouthful of his own. "It's supposed to include French cheese."

"I don't think I've ever had French cheese before."

"And we may never have it again." He raised his mug, which was a ridiculously dainty cup shaped to look like a cupped leaf. "Cheers."

"Cheers," I said.

"To beauty. Yours."

My cup stilled in my raised hand. I wasn't sure that I could toast that. It felt vain. But anything seemed possible tonight. My uncertainty must have showed.

"You really are lovely," he said. Sincerity shone in his eyes.

My fingers crept self-consciously to my unbound hair. I was unaccustomed to thinking of myself in that way. "Am I beautiful when I'm dressed as an Englisher?" I asked. I was only partially teasing. I wanted to know the truth of what he thought.

"Nope. You're beautiful when you're covered up to your neck in Plain clothes. You're beautiful when you're plucking a chicken. You're beautiful when you're caked with mud. You're beautiful when you're praying. When you're soaking wet. And when you're lying awake, fretting, thinking no one is watching."

I lifted my fingers to his lips to still them, but he went on: "You're beautiful when you're powerful. And especially when you let your guard down. When you trust."

I lifted my eyebrows. "Are you sure that's not just because I could be the last woman on earth?"

He reached out to touch my cheek with the backs of his fingers. "Bonnet, you'd still be the most beautiful woman on earth if you were one of seven billion."

I smiled. He was much more eloquent than I would ever be. Eloquence was not really something Plain people valued. But Alex's words and his deeds were consistent. And that was important.

When the fire had died down and Fenrir began to snore, Alex took my hand. He pulled me to my feet and kissed me. He smelled like some kind of artificial aftershave, but tasted like hot chocolate.

He turned on a battery-powered CD player and grimaced at the sound. "Barry Manilow was all I could find."

"I don't know Barry Manilow."

"For the best."

He placed my hands around his neck and settled his around my waist. He swayed to the music, and I tried to follow, feeling self-conscious. I stepped on his feet twice. I think that I was supposed to be letting him lead, but I lacked the experience to follow well. Meanwhile, Barry Manilow was singing about a girl named Mandy, who Alex said he used to believe was Barry's dog, but then he saw a television program that said that was just a myth.

After Barry Manilow fell silent, I let Alex draw me behind him, away from the fire to the part of the department store that held the four-poster bed with the velvet coverlet. He had turned down the covers, added some blankets, and ringed the bed with candles.

"This is beautiful," I said.

"I thought we both deserved a little romance."

He cupped my face in his hands, kissed me. I put my arms around his neck, feeling the kiss deepen. His hands slid so that his thumbs rested on my collarbone, and I shivered to feel that touch in such a leisured, unhurried fashion. His body was warm against mine.

I suspended thoughts of love for now. I didn't know what love really was. I was still sorting that out for myself. Whatever Alex and I had negotiated between ourselves suited us, and I resisted the idea of putting a label, an obligation, on it. I felt like the boundaries of my morality were growing more fluid, and that was both good and bad.

One of his arms slid around my back. He leaned back against the bed, taking me with him.

The *Himmelsbrief* fluttered out of the neckline of my dress. In another time, another place, we might have let it lie there on the floor.

But he paused to pick it up, to tuck it under the pillow.

And it was that amount of care that showed me what we had was a different sort of love.

Not perfect. It was, at times, clumsy and bumpy. Driven by outside forces and circumstances.

But it was unselfish.

And that was what mattered to me.

Chapter Fourteen

One of the most enduring lessons I had learned on this journey was that nothing ever stays the same. Not for long. That was in direct opposition to what I'd been taught as a child: to preserve order and to value the predictability of day-to-day life. This new world was constantly in flux, and we moved with it, as if pushed by a great and terrible river.

But sometimes we found ourselves washed up on a tiny island. Times like these were precious. But they had to end. We always had to jump from the safety of the island back into the river again.

At the department store, we had loved, slept, eaten, and gathered provisions. We stripped the camping department bare. We had found a tent, warm boots, a camp stove, a fancy metal stone that sparked fire, and a nesting set of camp dishes and cutlery. There were flashlights and batteries and even a radio. It never captured anything but static while we were in the store, but Alex assured me that it might be different elsewhere. I pretended to believe him and carefully read the cold rating systems for the sleeping bags. Fenrir was helping me; he had tunneled into one and installed himself as an immovable lump in the bottom. Horace had dismembered all of the scarecrows on the lower level, and his sides felt firm and round as he digested their limbs.

When we were ready to go, when Horace was packed up and the backpacks were full and propped beside the glowing mannequins, I came to Alex. He had dressed himself in the warmest coat he'd found, which he called his pimp coat. It was a long black leather coat with a bizarre gray and black furry lining.

"It's like *Blade* meets *Jersey Shore*," Alex said.

"I have no idea what you're talking about."

"It would take too long to explain and would reduce your faith in humanity."

"*Ja,* thanks, then."

I had dug through the women's department and found a long dark gray coat. It was lined in velvet and possibly the warmest garment I'd ever seen. I'd picked out some tall warm boots without heels and plenty of traction, and gloves and warm leggings.

I had found myself a dress that was as close as possible to an Amish dress. It was dark purple, and long-sleeved, reaching nearly to the tops of my boots. The neck was fancy, with ruffles that reached up to my chin. And there were ruffles on the cuffs. But it was, by and large, plain. I put my bonnet on and walked out to meet Alex and the animals.

He nodded in approval at me. "You look beautiful, Bonnet."

"Thank you," I said. The idea still seemed unfamiliar.

He reached down to unlatch the metal grate. I squinted. It

had been too long since I'd seen full daylight. I'd grown accustomed to the faint half-light of candles and the softly glowing luminescence of the mannequins. I shaded my eyes with my hand.

"Oh," I breathed.

It had begun to snow. The ground was coated in a thin layer of white.

And there were not any other footprints. Not for miles.

I saw only the sketchy tracks of sparrows as we walked away from the town. There was a certain safety in that. But it also confirmed that we walked in an empty world.

I buried my face in my hood. I had wanted to be away from any threats. Part of me even wanted to be a coward, to stay at the department store until the caramel popcorn ran out. But it seemed the farther we moved away from threats of Darkness, the closer we moved to threats from nature.

Fenrir relished the snow, bounding like a puppy. It stopped falling around midmorning, allowing the cold eye of the sun to burn through pearly clouds. But until then, the wolf skidded after it, and bit at the white flakes. Alex made him a snowball and tossed it far. Fenrir tried to maul it to death, but it broke apart on impact. He wound up only rolling in the snow. Horace gave him a pained snort.

"Wolves are supposed to love snow," I said.

"Why's that?"

"The rest of their prey is starved. Weak. They can spot it easily in the snow. Winter is their harvest season."

"That's damned cheerful, Bonnet."

I held up my gloved hands. "It's the truth!"

If any one of us were to survive the end of the world, it would be Fenrir. He found two rabbits before the afternoon. The first one he gave to us. The second one he devoured on his own. I figured he was probably tired of jerky and gourmet popcorn.

We moved north, along a freeway. Alex said that if it was safe, we could follow it west and north to Canada through Michigan and hopefully reach Saulte Ste. Marie without being molested by city vampires.

And it seemed safe. There were no human tracks this far. We appeared to have God on our side.

Especially when we found the fireworks factory.

Alex paused at a guardrail at the edge of the road, staring at a boxy metal building. The rotted and frozen remains of a produce stand stood outside in a gravel lot. There were no cars.

The last time we'd come upon a structure like this, Alex had steered us away. I asked why.

"It's an adult bookstore," he'd said. I could swear that he blushed.

"Aren't most bookstores for adults?" I was familiar with libraries. Unbeknownst to my parents, I had frequented the one in the town near our home. Most of the books there were for adults, but some had been for children. I supposed that, in the English world, perhaps there were separate bookstores for adults and children.

"*Nnnnoooo.* This is a euphemism. For pornography. Magazines with naked women and videos of men and women in the act. In a lot of acts, really. Sometimes men and men. Women and women. Doing stuff that you really can't imagine. With props." He pinched the bridge of his nose. "Trust me, it would blow your mind. Maybe . . . if you really want to, we'll go on the way back after the end of the world is finished."

"Oh." My brows drew together, and I looked back over my shoulder. I was curious, but not curious enough to risk entering a den of vampires who had been slavering over pictures of naked people. And whatever else was in there.

But Alex was quite keen on this building. The cartoon figure of a superhero was painted on the side, sporting a cape and shooting magical blue fire from his hands. The sign read CAPTAIN BLOWTORCH'S FIREWORKS.

I squinted at it. "I saw fireworks every year on the Fourth of July. They set them off in the nearby town. They were pretty."

"And also highly flammable. And probably better than any other weapon we could find against the vampires . . . if the place hasn't been cleaned out."

"It's worth checking," I agreed.

We walked down the exit ramp to the store. Fenrir sniffed vigorously along the side of the building. He caught a vole and swallowed it in two bites.

There were no windows in the small metal building. That made me a little nervous. Alex tugged on the front door. It was locked with a padlock. I supposed that was a good sign. Nothing had gotten in—or out—in a long time. And there were no tracks but ours in the dusting of snow.

"Locked. But not for long." He produced one of the tools from the camping aisle: a flexible cable saw. He tugged it through the hasp of the lock, back and forth, until it fell in pieces and metal dust on the ground.

He rubbed his hands together. "Let's see what we've got in here to fight the vampire apocalypse, eh?"

I lifted my flashlight as he opened the door.

The fireworks factory was nothing more than a pole barn set up on a gravel floor. Picnic tables were arranged on the gravel, and they were stacked high with wooden boxes and brightly colored cardboard bins. I swept the light beam around, up into the rafters, into corners, searching for vampires. I saw only an opossum with its babies scuttling along the floor.

Alex let loose a low whistle as he peered into a box labeled NUCLEAR GLITTER MELTDOWN. He held up red white and blue colored boxes in two fists. There were eagles printed on them and a backwash of fire. "Jackpot."

"What is that?"

"Not sure. But if we follow the instructions and set fire to it, it promises a 'blaze of wrath.' Also plenty of 'glittery after-trails.'"

I picked up a stick labeled MORTAR FURY CANNON. "This looks promising."

"Swweeeeeet."

Alex and I did some quick calculations about the amount of additional weight that we could carry. Horace was saddled up with almost a hundred pounds of gear, and we didn't want him to break a leg now that there was danger of ice. We decided that each one of us could carry an extra bag of anti-vampire weaponry if we committed to walk on foot with fifty additional pounds for the horse.

"I don't know how to use these," I said.

"Set fire to the fuse end," Alex said. "Throw it. And then I think we run."

We walked out into the gloom of the evening, our arms and pockets full of artillery. The sun had set, and shadows gathered thick around us. I felt irrationally cheerful at pulling off the fireworks heist . . .

. . . until we stepped out onto the parking lot. A siren sounded, and blue and red strobe lights flashed. I squinted. I could make out the shape of a police car, one that said HIGH-WAY PATROL. A figure stood before it.

My heart plummeted into my gut and bounced into my throat. It plunged at the thought of being caught stealing, but soared to think that there was someone human here. That there was law and order in the world.

The silhouette walked toward us. He wore a broad-brimmed hat. His boots crunched in the gravel, and I saw him rest his thumbs in his gun belt as he approached.

"You two wouldn't be disturbing the peace, would you?" he said. He pulled his gun from his holster. "Breaking and entering?"

I stared down at our cache of weapons. We were caught. But better a night in jail than a night out here.

"Officer, are we glad to see you," Alex said.

"Not nearly as glad as I am to see you." He lifted his head and smiled.

In the flash of red and blue light, I saw fangs glint.

"Damn it," Alex said.

I was rooted in place. I didn't know which I was more afraid of: the teeth or the gun.

A low growling emanated from our left. The trooper turned, aiming his weapon toward Fenrir.

"No!" I shouted.

Alex threw his box of fireworks at the trooper. It knocked him off balance, and the gun went off with a deafening *crack*. The bullet sparked on the gravel. Fenrir lunged for the cop's gun arm, and the vampire hissed.

The gun clattered away. Unthinking, I lunged for it. It came up in my hands, feeling heavy and cold.

The vampire flung Fenrir across the hood of the car. The wolf yelped and rage boiled in me.

"Leave him alone," I said.

I held the gun on the trooper. I was not unfamiliar with guns; my father had owned a hunting rifle. I assumed that this followed the same principle. But I had been taught never, never to aim a gun toward a person. Never to cause harm. Always to turn the other cheek. My finger sweated on the trigger. Through all the violence I had committed, this seemed like a strange new method. One that I knew I could master.

The trooper snarled. His hat had been knocked off, and he advanced toward Alex.

"Don't," I said.

I squeezed my eyes shut and pulled the trigger.

The gun bucked up and over my head, flinging my arms with it. I opened my eyes to see that the bullet had struck the vampire in the shoulder. A black ooze emanated from below his shiny metal epaulets.

He just smiled at me, unfazed. "That's a felony, girlie. Assault on a police officer will put you away for a long time. Maybe even forever."

Fear lanced through me. I didn't know if the vampire cop understood what had happened to him. Was he just fulfilling his pre-death programming of enforcing the law? Or was this part of some sadistic cruelty I didn't understand?

It didn't matter.

I pulled the trigger again.

And again.

The gun bucked in my hands, but I forced it down, kept firing. I think I hit the car; I saw glass break. One of the hot casings struck me in the cheek. I couldn't hear anything else over the roar of the gunshots.

But the vampire kept coming. He had turned away from Alex toward me, his mouth open in a dark leer. The bullets would push him back a step, but he would recover and gain traction.

I wrenched down on the trigger again, flinched, but nothing happened.

I was out of bullets.

The trooper grabbed my arm, hauled me toward the car. I kicked and struggled. The roar had receded in my ears, and I could hear the pounding of my own blood. He slammed me against the back door of the car, lifting me so that my feet didn't touch the ground. I reached into my pocket for my *Himmelsbrief.* I got the paper half out of the pocket, and the trooper snarled, dropping me.

"Hey, Smokey!"

I heard Alex's voice above the ringing. Alex hauled back the trooper's collar and stuffed a flaming firework down the back of his shirt.

The vampire hissed and dropped me. He reached behind himself, trying to claw the back of his shirt, which was sparkling with an unnatural blue fire.

I ran to the horse. Horace was backing away, ears flattened. Alex grabbed his reins, tossed me up into the saddle. From the corner of my eye, I saw Fenrir slink out from behind the police car. Alex swung clumsily into the saddle behind me.

The trooper clawed at his back, ripping his shirt out of his belt. I turned Horace toward the exit ramp, away. Fenrir loped after us.

The firework exploded in a shower of blue sparks. I heard hissing and growling.

"What was that?" I shouted.

"Blue Victory."

I turned back in the saddle. "Not victorious enough . . ."

The smoldering cop was missing an arm, but he climbed behind the wheel of the cruiser. The car spun out in the lot and turned to pursue.

"We can't outrun him," I said. "We should go off the road . . ."

"No," Alex said. "Go to the bridge."

He pointed ahead of me, away from the freeway. An old covered bridge useless for heavy traffic crossed a river.

"He can still follow us," I protested.

"Cross the bridge!"

I bit my lip and dug my heels into Horace's sides.

The horse ran as fast as he could toward the bridge. Flecks of spittle came back to strike me in the face. Fenrir was a gray blur at the side of the road, struggling to keep up. I flinched, seeing our shadows driven before us by headlights and hearing the rev of an engine. Stray snowflakes shimmered in the darkness.

"Go, Horace," I whispered into the horse's flattened ear. "Go!"

The horse's hooves slammed onto the wood floorboards, and we plunged into the total darkness of the covered bridge. The headlights grew more distant behind us, like stars.

I turned back.

The police car was stopped at the edge of the bridge.

"Why isn't he following?" I shouted.

"I don't think he *can*."

We thundered across the bridge, onto a dirt road beyond. I pulled Horace up, looked over the black water at the still headlights.

"There's an old myth that vampires can't cross running water," Alex said. "I didn't know if it was true, if it would apply in this case, but . . . it seems to have stopped him."

Fenrir paced to the riverbank, howling softly. It was a high, mournful keening. Whether it was in victory or warning, I couldn't tell.

But no one answered him.

––––––––––

We followed the track of the river the rest of the way north. It was slow going, and there frequently was no road.

Fenrir stuck closer to us. He had allowed Alex to touch him after the fight with the trooper. He seemed bruised, nothing broken, as near as we could tell. When Alex and I slept in our tent, we found him curled at our feet in the morning. He didn't look apologetic in the slightest, and even allowed us to pet him. I knew that he liked me, but he had a special bond with Alex. Maybe, to Fenrir's way of thinking, Alex was his pack leader.

Funny to imagine animals working with *Gelassenheit,* in their fashion.

I could tell we were getting close to Lake Erie when there was a change in the air. It smelled and moved differently. Alex said that was often the way of things around large bodies of water. The wind was sharper, stronger, more cutting, slicing through long strands of plants Alex called "sea oats." We passed over some marshland laced by vacant highway. Herons continued to fish in the gray landscape, the water a mirror to the sky. I saw a pair of white swans swimming. I had never seen swans before. I wasn't sure that Fenrir had, either, but they honked at him before taking flight, leaving him forlorn on the bank.

"They're wild, the farther you go up north," Alex said. I could tell he was homesick, the way his eye kept wandering to the horizon.

We passed by boat docks and mini–storage facilities perched on fingers of the river. I felt uncomfortable being this close to civilization, but there was nowhere else to go to move north. According to Alex's maps, we had to find the turnpike and follow it toward Canada. Maybe many others had tried before us. I wasn't so sure that anyone else had made it.

We walked along the shoulder of the road. Snow had begun in earnest, and had accumulated about two inches. It showed no signs of abating, and slowed our progress. Alex had wanted to make it farther before dark, but I felt the night fast upon us again.

I was weary of the dark. I was weary of jumping at shadows, of the terrible things that hunted in it. Part of me was ready for God to simply take us, to sweep us off the face of the earth and wait for the end to come, whether in ice or in blood. I wanted this suffering to be over.

Maybe God heard me.

There was a sudden revving of engines in the distance, muffled by snow and mud and the hissing trickle of water in the drainage ditches.

Alex and I exchanged glances.

"Do you think it's the trooper?"

"Not unless he's got friends. That's a lot of engines. Smaller ones."

A thin, tinny scream sounded.

I grimaced. "I hope that's not what I think it is."

We crept to the edge of an overpass, stared down into the darkness. I could see more than a dozen lights, like headlights, but trained on a patch of the road where a car had stopped. The tiny car had slid sideways in the slush.

"Bikers," Alex said. His fingers tightened on the rail. "And it looks like they've got supper."

Men were climbing off their motorcycles, descending upon the car. They were dressed in leather, their hair as long as

Samson's in the Bible. The chrome on their bikes gleamed in the low light. So did their eyes.

I saw people moving inside of the vehicle. The engine choked, struggled.

"They will kill them!" I said.

"I don't think that there's much we can do to stop it," Alex said.

Horace's ears twitched, and Fenrir's tail slapped my skirt.

"We can't let it happen." I reached into my right pocket for the *Himmelsbrief.* I pinned it to my coat breast with shaking hands. I reached into my left pocket for one of the fireworks.

"We're gonna get killed," Alex said, gripping my elbow. "I don't want that to happen."

A shriek echoed below, and I heard glass breaking.

He knew what I knew. "We can't lose our humanity in this," I told him.

I stood up on tiptoes to kiss him.

He sighed in resignation. "There's a saying in rock-and-roll. 'Better to burn out than to fade away.'"

He released me and reached into his pocket for a lighter. He shared the flame with me, and I lit the fuse on my firework.

We hurled the fireworks down to the underpass. The bikers turned from their task of rocking the car and tearing out the broken windshield, startled by the fire that slipped down from the sky like falling stars. Gleaming red eyes turned to us.

We threw the fireworks overhand in glittering arcs. Sparks cascaded down upon the gathered knot of Darkness, exploding in brilliant arrays of yellow, red, and blue. It was beautiful, the whistle and the flash and the sizzle. More than one shadow ignited and ran hissing into the blackness. One redoubled his effort to peel open the car like a can. Others climbed on their bikes, gunned the engines, and turned onto the road.

Coming for us.

I reached for more fireworks and one of my makeshift stakes. We had only a few left. Not enough to battle the dozen men moving toward us in the cacophony of engines and head-lights. The army of night had come for us at last.

Alex peeled off his coat and his shirt. His breath steamed, and I could see his gooseflesh under the tattoos. His silver knife glinted in one hand, a firework in the other. I stood beside him, holding one of the last gleaming fireworks in one fist and a sharpened tree branch in the other. Fenrir growled beside us.

One of the bikers gunned the engine. They bore down on us, spooking Horace. I forced myself to hold my ground. I lobbed the firework at one of the bikes. It swerved. I jammed my stake into the chest of one of the bikers that passed. It snapped off—I wasn't sure if I caught meat or just spokes. Something ripped, and I cried out when I discovered that it was the *Himmelsbrief,* tearing away from my coat.

My firework whistled and exploded. It was a beautiful gold, the color of sunshine drizzling across the pavement. It was too close. It nearly blinded me.

I heard growling beside me, Fenrir gnawing on a biker writhing on the ground. A line of bikes gathered opposite us for another pass, a deafening game of Red Rover. Alex threw his last firework at them. Red. With some kind of corkscrew spiral that caused them to hiss.

I stood up straight. My hands were open. I was without weapons. I could see the Darkness converging, coming for us, passing before their headlights, past the fire and the light.

I thought I was ready. Ready for the end.

I lifted my chin. The last scrap of my *Himmelsbrief* scraped under my chin in the cold breeze.

I saw, beyond the Darkness, something in the hillside. Something that glowed like the mannequins in the department store. My brow wrinkled before I could resolve what they were, both in my eyes and in my brain.

People. People that shone with a green light like foxfire. I could see their outlines coming over the hills.

My indrawn breath scraped my throat, and I whispered:

"Angels."

Chapter Fifteen

The angels came down from on high to fight the Darkness.

This truly was the end of days.

The vampires hissed at the sight of them, at their light and their loveliness. They moved to attack the angels, seething toward them. But the vampires could not touch them. Their skin smoked and singed where they tried to lay hands on the angels.

The angels held out their hands to drive them back.

And one of them had a gun.

I think it was what is called a flare gun. It shot a lurid red light across the air and embedded itself, burning, in the chest of the vampire nearest me. The creature fell to his knees and tried to tear it out, but the red light scorched his hands so badly that he could not grasp it. He howled like a piteous beast.

The angel reloaded the flare gun and fired again, at a vampire astride a motorcycle. The red light slammed him off the bike, and the motorcycle careened across the road, sliding into the concrete berm with a crash.

The others began to flee as the flares arced into the air.

I saw Alex pick himself off the pavement and hurl a broken headlight after them.

Trembling, I fell to my knees. I laced my hands together and prayed. Tears of gratitude streamed from my eyes. Salvation was at hand.

The pale green glow stopped before me. I could not look up. I was too overwhelmed.

An angel reached down for me. "Honey, get up."

The angel had a peculiar drawl. I had heard a southern accent once before, from a tourist near the town where I used to live. I blinked and looked up.

I gazed into the face of a softly glowing woman. She shone as if there was a light pulsing beneath her skin. I could see it moving, in the veins and capillaries of her face, even in the vessels of her eyes. It was utterly inhuman, alien, but also strangely beautiful.

"Are you . . . Mary?" I asked, in the tiniest voice I could muster. "Or Gabriel?"

Her brow creased, and she said, "My name's Judy."

"Are you an angel?" I squeaked.

She threw back her head and laughed. "No, sweetie. I'm the farthest thing on earth from an angel."

She pulled me to my feet. I could see that she wore English clothing—jeans and a sweater. The glow of her skin pushed through the knit of the fabric to glimmer in the light. Her ears were pierced multiple times, glittering under short hair.

"I don't understand," I said.

She pushed a string of hair away from my face. "Don't worry, hon. Come with us, and you will."

Numbly, I gathered Horace. Fenrir had glued himself to Alex's side. The shining people circled us and we followed them to the water.

I could hear the lake before we saw it. I had never seen a body of water larger than a river before. But when we walked down the paved and darkened street of the little town, a great expanse of water came into view. The lake was as black as the sky, and pieces of moon were broken up in it, like shards of glass. The waves rushed in and crashed up against the rocks. I couldn't see the horizon. Viciously cold wind scraped over us, and I tied a double knot in my bonnet strings with shaking fingers to keep the cap from being torn from my skull. It took me three tries, but I got it done.

The only light other than the moon came from our guides. As I looked more closely, they seemed like ordinary English people, except for the glow. There were two teenagers, three middle-aged men, and two women. They had left behind their coats when they'd come to rescue us, and the light dimmed as they put their coats back on, like a shade over a lantern. That reminded me a bit of Alex and his tattoos. They incandesced softly as we walked, and I checked to make sure that their feet made contact with the ground. They had also gathered the two young women attacked in the car. They had been cut badly with the glass. Bleeding, they walked with us, arms wrapped around each other.

Alex had initially been stunned as I was. But his intellectual curiosity seemed to propel him to speak. "How did you find us?"

One of the men jabbed a thumb over his shoulder. "None of us have seen fireworks since July. That was a nice bit of improvisation, by the way."

"Um, thanks," Alex said.

"We just use these." He lifted the flare gun.

"It's effective."

"Very. As long as you don't run out of ammo."

"Where are we going?" I whispered to Judy.

"We're going someplace safe," she said.

And I believed her.

We walked down a paved street, past a retirement village and a dock, to a gate. The gate was a simple one, just a steel arm. It reminded me of the ones that we used to rotate cattle in and out of fields back home. A sign with a large cross on it read WELCOME TO WATER'S EDGE.

We climbed over the low gate without opening it.

"The vampires . . ." I said.

"They can't get in here," Judy said. "This little town, all fifteen square blocks of it, was founded as a Methodist colony in the nineteenth century."

"It's holy ground?"

"Yes. Still. The tourists that came here for the religious conferences and the contemplation are still here."

"But the vampires can be invited in . . ." I began, remembering the shrine and the nuns.

Judy shook her head. "Everyone at Water's Edge has been altered. The glamour doesn't work on us."

I cocked my head. "'Altered'?"

"Matt will tell you all about it. He can explain the science much better than I can."

Science. I bit my lip and traded sidelong glances with Alex.

As soon as we passed through the gate, the luminous members of the group visibly relaxed. Their knot around us loosened, and we moved down tiny narrow streets bounded by small, pretty cottages. Frozen flower beds and hanging arrangements surrounded concrete yard ornaments. There was no grass to speak of, as the houses were built right up to the sidewalk, as if land was at a premium. You could literally reach from the upstairs window of one house to another. The shadows of cats flitted in the tiny alleyways. I wound my fingers in Fenrir's ruff to keep him from chasing them.

Most of the houses were shuttered. But many of them held light. I was amazed to see it. It wasn't the cold light of electricity but the yellow, uneven glow of oil lamps like the ones used by the Amish that I recognized.

We walked down the main street, past a shuttered ice cream parlor and a pizza restaurant, to a paved path that dipped along the lake. A dock with a flagpole reached into the lake behind us, the U.S. flag tearing in the wind. The bluster drove waves up over the rocks, soaking the paths. Many of the houses facing the lake were covered with storm shutters, but there was one that was open: a large grand house facing the black water with nearly every window lit with warm yellow light.

"Here," Judy said. "This is Matt's house."

We walked up a brick path to the back porch. I wasn't sure

what to do with Horace. One of the men rubbed his nose. "He's a nice horse. Where'd you get him?"

I took a deep breath. "He came to my village without his rider." I omitted the part about finding a human foot in the stirrup.

"He looks like he's a Sabino white."

"You know horses?"

"A little. I used to work for a veterinarian. I can take him to the park to graze. There's still a bit of grass there. I'll take off his saddle, rub him down, and get him a blanket." He moved to take the reins from me. "I'll bring your gear back."

Horace seemed placid around the glowing people. I clutched the reins. I was more worried about Horace than the gear. "Will he be safe?"

"It's on the property. He'll be as safe as any of us."

I nodded and handed the reins over. "His name is Horace."

The man clucked to the horse. "Tell the others that he went with Keene. They'll know where to find me."

I watched Keene and Horace strike off through a gap between the houses, up the main street.

The man with the flare gun led us past patio furniture covered in tarps. The back door was unlocked. In fact, there was no lock on it at all. It reminded me a bit of Amish houses in that way. He opened the back storm door to a parlor that smelled of lemon soap. We clustered awkwardly in the light of an oil lamp perched on a table. Books were strewn on the table and on the formal, overstuffed chairs.

I noticed that the glow of our "'angels" had dimmed once

we entered the presence of artificial light. Judy, standing closest to the lantern, had stopped incandescing entirely. She looked like a normal woman: blond hair, blue eyes, freckled skin. Unangelic.

"Matt!" the man shouted. "Hey, we need a doctor."

My gaze slid to the two young women. Their hands were knotted together. They were probably only a year or two older than I was. They looked like sisters, with the same long black hair and pale gold skin. But there was blood splashed on their faces. One of them held a hand over her eye. What I thought was snow on their clothes didn't melt—it was glass glittering.

"If you're looking for a doctor, you've come to the wrong place."

A man entered the parlor, wiping his hands with a dishtowel. I guessed him to be in his middle forties. Gray was beginning to streak his brown hair on the left temple, and his hazel eyes were lined with humor. He was dressed in jeans and a sweatshirt. I liked him immediately.

He looked at us, and then at the girls. "What happened?"

The man with the flare gun nodded at us. I saw that his name was Peter—It was embroidered on his coveralls. "We saw the fireworks, went to look."

"It could have been a vamp trick."

"It wasn't. These two"—he pointed at me and Alex—"were trying to distract the vamps from taking the girls out of their car."

"We weren't trying to distract them, actually," Alex said. "We were trying to kill them by hitting them with the fireworks. But we weren't very effective."

Peter grinned. "Good idea. Need better aim."

Matt wasn't listening to us. He went to the girls. He was talking softly to them, persuading the one with the wounded eye to take her hand away. I couldn't see what he saw, but I thought it was bad because Peter looked away.

The girls nodded, but spoke back in another language that I didn't understand. I wished I could know what they thought, but there was an invisible wall between us. I wondered if the English felt that way when we spoke Deitsch around them.

"Anybody get bitten?" Matt asked.

"No," Judy said. "We asked before we brought them in."

I wondered what they would have done if one of us had been bitten . . . would they have done as we did for—or to —Ginger? I hoped so. But I still shuddered to think of it, and a pang of grief twitched in my stomach.

"Let's get them to the kitchen. I think we need some towels. And tweezers. See if someone can find Cora. She'll be able to tell better than I can."

Peter unhooked a walkie-talkie from his belt, pressed down the button. "This is Waterfront House. Looking for Cora. Over."

The radio crackled back. "This is Summer House. Cora's here. Over."

"Send her to Waterfront, with supplies. We've got two girls we found on the road, cut up pretty bad. Over."

"We'll wake her and send her right over. Over."

"Roger Dodger. Copy. Waterfront out."

I gaped in amazement at the walkie-talkies. I had not heard an artificial human voice in months.

Peter clipped it back on his belt. "Each occupied house has one. I'm the maintenance guy, so it seemed like a good idea, as long as the batteries hold out."

"Aren't you a doctor?" Alex asked Matt.

Matt gave a short bark of laughter, shook his head. "Not a medical doctor. I'm a biologist. But I'm hell with a pair of tweezers. Cora's coming, though. She used to be a nurse."

Judy ushered the girls to the back of the house. "I'll see if there are any wounds we missed." She traded an inscrutable glance with Matt and disappeared.

Matt glanced down at Fenrir. I didn't know if animals were allowed in the house. I should have asked.

"He's beautiful," Matt said. "Looks like mostly timber wolf. With a bit of shepherd mixed in."

Alex knelt beside him, scrubbed his ears. "Fenrir's harmless. Don't worry."

Matt extended a hand to him, at nose level. Fenrir sniffed at him. He shied away when Matt tried to touch him, slipping back behind my skirt.

"So . . . you're not aliens. Not that I would believe that now," Alex said. "What the hell are you, other than biologists, nurses, and maintenance men?"

Matt spread his hands out. The sides facing the lamp looked normal. Human. The palms turned toward us, in shadow, glowed softly. "We're human. Don't worry. We've just found a way to adapt to the vampires."

Steps clomped on the back step.

"That's Cora." Peter let a woman in her sixties inside. She had tightly permed gray hair that was flat on one side, and was dressed in a pink sweatsuit. I was envious of the imprint of a pillow seam on her cheek. A raincoat was thrown over the sweatsuit, and she clutched a first-aid kit.

"What did you find?" Her eyes were wide and bright.

"Two girls . . . They're speaking Vietnamese. I think. Judy has them in the back. Cut up with glass. One of them has a pretty bad-looking eye."

"I'll take a look." She bustled to the back.

"You guys will have to excuse me," Matt said. "I think I might be needed to hold a tray while Cora picks glass out of those wounds. But I will come up to talk with you later. I promise." He nodded to Peter. "Set them up in one of the guest rooms."

Peter glanced at my bonnet. "Not to be too prying, but . . . would you like a separate room, miss?"

I swallowed and shook my head. I edged closer to Alex. He put his arm around me. "Thank you. *Ja,* that is very thoughtful of you. But after all that has happened . . . where he goes, I go."

"All right, then. Follow me."

Peter led us up the back staircase. He didn't light a candle or bring a flashlight. Perhaps he'd had much time getting used to glowing in the dark.

Alex started whistling. It was a song that I didn't recognize.

"What's the song?" I asked.

"'Stairway to Heaven.'"

I stifled a shiver.

CHAPTER SIXTEEN

I couldn't sleep in the House of Angels.

I had learned to sleep in the open, on the cold ground, in darkness, in daylight. But I couldn't sleep in this warm, soft bed with Alex beside me. Not after I'd been fed ham and cheese sandwiches with milk. Not with only a useless scrap of my precious *Himmelsbrief* remaining, knowing I was spiritually defenseless. And not with the knowledge that there were glowing beings in the house. I still wasn't certain that they were quite human.

And I couldn't sleep with the screams.

From the floor below, I could hear the dull murmur of voices, trying to be soothing. I guessed that the sobbing girl's injuries were more serious than we thought. I didn't know if they were pulling glass from her eye . . . or taking the eye itself.

I cuddled close to Alex. "It sounds like they're hurting her."

"I think that all we've got left is primitive medicine," he said. "And I'm betting that there's no alcohol allowed on the premises of a Methodist colony."

Alex slipped out of bed. He went for the door, rattled the doorknob.

Locked.

"They may not be sure about us yet. Not that I blame them," he said. "We could be incubating vampirism from some hidden bite. We could be thieves."

My fingers chewed the blanket. "Or we could be prisoners."

He came back to bed. I buried my head in his shoulder. Fenrir crawled into bed, burrowed under the covers, and whimpered.

We were dressed and sitting on the edge of the bed when the door opened the next morning. It was Judy, and she had brought a silver breakfast tray of bread and fruit. She didn't glow in sunlight.

"I'm sorry for that," she said, placing her hand on the knob. Dark circles had spread under her eyes. "Matt wants the two of you to either submit to a thorough search or agree to quarantine for three days."

Alex and I exchanged glances.

"That's a reasonable request," he said. "As long as we get answers."

"What happened to the girls?" I asked.

Judy stared down at the tray. "Linh lost an eye. It wasn't good. Yen . . . we're not sure about Yen."

Alex's eyes narrowed. "What do you mean?"

"We missed what could have been a bite. She was pretty

bloody last night. We're going to watch her closely for the next few hours. If she shows evidence of vampirism . . ." Judy's hand tightened on the doorknob. "We'll have to send her outside. Before she turns. Otherwise, the holiness of the ground will be compromised. Vamps will have the run of the place." I could see the deep worry mark on her forehead, the fear of losing their sanctuary.

The hair on the back of my neck stood up. That sounded a lot like what had happened to us, when we were cast out of my community. And there was a certain resoluteness to her actions that seemed familiar—reminiscent of both the actions of the Elders that I'd despised, and my own when I had killed Ginger.

One of the things that I was beginning to learn was that kindness is often brutal. And that there was blood on all the survivors' hands.

Alex said, "I don't mind being searched. But Bonnet's got a different religious sensibility than I do."

I lifted my chin. "I could be searched by a woman. No men."

Judy let out a breath. It was clear that she'd been expecting resistance. "That can be arranged. We're just . . ." She rubbed her forehead. "We haven't found any survivors before. And we should have been more thorough."

"It's okay," Alex said. "We weren't doing so hot out there on the freeway."

"We are grateful that you saved us," I said.

"It was the human thing to do." Judy smiled at me. "Come on . . . I'll give you the once-over in the bathroom, and I'll send one of the guys up to check out Alex. And then you can talk with Matt over breakfast, downstairs."

I followed Judy down a short hallway to the bathroom. She awkwardly turned her back while I untied my bonnet.

"So you're Mennonite?" she said, making conversation. "Amish?"

"*Ja,* I'm Amish," I said as I undressed. "From south of here. Near Torch."

"I know vaguely where that is. I think my parents went there to buy furniture once."

"*Ja,* we have exceptional carpenters." I folded my dress, placed it on the back of the toilet, and began to strip out of my leggings and underclothes.

"Why did you leave?"

"We were forced to leave," I said. "Vampires had gotten inside. Some of us wanted to fight it, but . . . the Elders were not listening."

"And you were a dissenter?"

"*Ja.* I was placed under the *Bann*—shunned—for harboring Alex. We were sent out along with an English friend who was staying with us."

"That's harsh." I could hear the disapproval in Judy's voice. But she didn't ask what happened to Ginger. For that I was glad.

"The *Ordnung* is not to be argued with," I said. I stood on the cold tile in the nude, my toes curling. "I am ready."

"I'll try to make this fast," Judy said.

She did try, but she was very thorough. She examined my scalp, as if checking for lice, peered at every mole on my back, asked me to lift my arms. I blushed furiously as she examined every inch of flesh, even between my toes.

She paused when she saw my hand. Her fingers were cool on the scabbed flesh. "What's that?"

"It was a snakebite."

"You were lucky to survive that."

"It was something of . . . a miracle."

She turned my hand right and left. "It looks like it's healing. Not like a vampire bite. Those have black and red runners, and they are always open. They never scab up."

"I know," I said quietly.

"The English friend you were traveling with?" she guessed.

"*Ja.*"

She didn't push further. "I'll let you get dressed. You can meet us downstairs, in the kitchen. And Matt will tell you about us."

I gathered my dress to my chest to cover myself, and she left the bathroom. I dressed quickly and crept slowly down the staircase, like a child eavesdropping on her parents.

Alex was already there. He was holding a cup of coffee, sitting in a ladder-back chair in a sunny breakfast nook with chintz curtains. Matt was sitting beside him, and Judy had brought the fruit tray down. There was no sign of the Vietnamese girls.

"Good morning," Matt said. Like Judy, he seemed tired. "Please join us."

"Good morning," I answered. I slipped behind the table into an open chair. There was a window behind us that showed the shore. The sky was brilliant blue, and the lake shimmered beyond it. I saw the dark outline of what must be an island. I longed to walk down and touch the water, to see if it felt as cold as it looked. I could feel the pull of it through the glass.

But now was not the time for such things.

Alex stared over the rim of his mug at Matt. "Not to put too fine a point on it, but . . . what the hell are you guys?"

"We're human. Sort of. Like the vamps, we started out that way. I guess it's a long story, but I'll start at the beginning.

"Initially, we heard that a contagion was affecting the East Coast. I was up here on sabbatical, doing some research on late-season algal blooms affecting the Great Lakes. Tourist season was over, and it was a great time to get some peace and quiet. There are only a few straggler tourists here after Labor Day, those and the locals. Plenty of time and space for me to collect samples, set up in the house, play with sequencing DNA of algae species. I brought a truckload of equipment. I meant to stay here for a couple of months, and then return to Case Western—where I teach—by December. Write a paper, get some grant funding—the usual academic stuff.

"But then . . . this thing happened. I saw reports on TV and in the newspaper about a plague on the East Coast, then popping up all over the world. I called my colleagues at Case Western. They had some theories. They thought that a germ had somehow gotten tangled up with a novel strain of rabies. Someone else pointed out that a meteor shower had hit us a few days before the first reports and suspected an extraterrestrial bacterial influence. There was a popular theory that something nasty had crawled out of Chernobyl or Fukushima. And a dirty bomb detonating in Washington days before didn't help speculation much either. The most plausible theory I encountered seemed to suggest a widespread mutation in antibiotic-resistant anaerobic bacteria. That's where I'd put my money, if I still had any.

"But by then it was too late for any of our theories to matter. The military was rolling out. There was talk of nuking entire cities. I lost contact with the other folks at the university. Television went out, then the radio. There was a lot of talk about vampires." He shook his head and stared into his cup.

"You didn't believe that?" I asked.

"No. Not at first. I'm a scientist. I'm not supposed to believe in things that go bump in the night." His mouth flattened into a self-deprecating line. "But after I saw . . . I went out beyond the gate of Water's Edge to get some food. And I saw a man being eaten alive by a pack of fishermen. Fishermen with teeth, with red eyes . . ." He shook his head. "I began to believe that there was something to the myths. And when we discovered that we were safe here, at Water's Edge, for no demonstrable reason other than it's holy ground . . . I sure began to reexamine my ideas.

"I mean . . . I can scientifically explain the idea that a contagion caused this. It's transmitted through saliva, and works as fast as necrotizing fasciitis—flesh-eating bacteria. I can rationalize these things. I can guess that anaerobic bacteria—bacteria that don't need oxygen to survive—shrivel in sunlight. But I couldn't explain why a vampire can't cross into Water's Edge without an invitation. I couldn't explain how they can entrance their victims.

"Not at first. I had to get out of the box. I remembered

reading about this guy in Japan who did experiments with water. Masaru Emoto." Matt leaned forward, his fingers laced together, as if trying very hard to capture an idea. "He had a theory that water, when exposed to human thought, changes. If it's exposed to positive thoughts, like love and hope, the molecules become more orderly and form ice crystals that can be photographed. Similarly, water that's exposed to negative thoughts and words will not form crystals, becoming disorganized and chaotic."

Alex interrupted. "That sounds like total crap."

Matt spread his hands. "That's what I thought, too. Way too new-agey for my taste. Nobody in the scientific community really took him seriously. But I began to wonder . . . what if human consciousness, the changes that occur to human brain waves during prayer and meditation—really a perfect alpha state—affect the physical world?

"So I started to run some experiments. I used some of the water here at Water's Edge, compared it to water I collected from outside the settlement. Now get this: The water here forms unusually organized crystals. And that's not just the lake water. Even the tap water here is much more molecularly organized than tap water coming from just outside the gate." Matt pointed to the refrigerator. I saw pictures of what appeared to be snowflakes tacked up on it.

I pushed away from the table and crossed to the refrigerator to get a better look. Some of the crystals were breathtakingly beautiful. Each one was labeled in felt-tip marker. The ones marked "Water's Edge" were gorgeously symmetrical and glistening white with bits of rainbow gleaming in them.

Not all of them were beautiful. I saw several that looked like broken rings, like black holes, uneven and stained. These were labeled with other locations: "Tap water from gas station west of town." "Culvert one block west of Water's Edge." The blackness inside seemed to reach forever.

"So, I started thinking about humans and how we affect our environments," Matt was saying. "What if there was something to it? What if human consciousness can organize the molecules of water, minerals in the earth, or what-have-you in a way that the creatures find intolerable? True 'holy water' or 'sacred ground.' I'm guessing that this is especially pronounced when many people are praying over a finite area with clear boundaries. Even the symbols or rituals that have been used by many people over time, whether man-made or natural, could be vectors that organize this mental energy.

"And once the holiness becomes molecularly disorganized or degrades, evil finds a way in. 'Evil' being shorthand for destructive forces. If I expose some of this water to negative stuff . . . even if I tell a glass of tap water here that it's stupid every day for a week, the crystals break down and the molecular structure becomes chaotic. Maybe, someday, with enough experiments, that could be something I could prove . . . but for now that's just conjecture."

I touched a photograph of a crystal. But it was beautiful conjecture.

"Is that what happened here?" Alex said. "An experiment in positive thinking? You thought yourselves glowy? Or is this the part where aliens show up and rescue humankind?"

Matt put his hands before him, about a foot apart, and shook them. He leaned forward, and in a slow, dramatic voice said: *"Aliens."*

Alex mimicked him. *"Aliens."*

I swallowed. If aliens existed . . . My worldview wasn't ready to be expanded that far. I was pretty sure it was going to burst at the seams. "Aliens?"

Both men dissolved into laughter.

"It's an Internet thing," Alex said. It was clear that this was some pop culture reference I didn't understand. "Mad scientists. Sorry."

"No aliens. At least, not unless the extraterrestrial bacteria theory is proven to hold any water." Matt shook his head and wiped his eyes. "And what we're doing is an experiment, but not one in positive thinking. I figured that if this was a catastrophic evolutionary event, we'd have to do *something* to survive. My colleagues, before I lost contact with them, were trying to figure out ways to destroy the vampires. Weapons systems using flamethrowers, concentrated UV light, that kind of thing.

"But this is larger than that. There are more of them than there are of us. Last reports indicated that two-thirds of the world's population is gone. That there are pockets of survivors, on submarines and cruise ships and at holy sites around the globe."

"I heard that too," I said. "My friend's husband was in the military. He said that there were people safe in very unusual places."

"Right. Mount Fuji, mosques, synagogues, Jerusalem. But this is a global catastrophe. There simply aren't enough of us to fight them. Not anymore."

Alex's jaw hardened. "We can't just wait for them to kill us. Lie down and die."

"No. No, we can't. And we can't win. Which is why I proposed that we adapt." Matt steepled his fingers in front of himself. "I watched the vampires. I knew that they were afraid of sunlight, of fire. But not artificial light. I knew that there had to be something about natural light that bothered them. I observed that they only are interested in fresh flesh, whether from humans or animals. Meat that's starting to rot is of no interest to them. There are particular bacteria that multiply in room-temperature meat. If you leave a chicken out for a couple of days, it will start to glow in the dark. Faintly. People have been noticing this since the time of the Civil War, when wounded soldiers had glowing wounds when there was no antiseptic."

"Bizarre," Alex said.

"Those bacteria thrive on oxygen, though. And doctors during the Civil War observed that wounds that glowed healed better than those that didn't—the bacteria removed dead tissue. And I noticed that the vampires hate foxfire. It's a fungus, but it's still producing natural light."

I nodded. "We sometimes use it to light haylofts in the winter."

"I found a little bit of it in some rotted wood at the park. I smeared it out on the street, beyond the gate, and watched with binoculars from a nearby house. They wouldn't cross that line."

"That's really . . . really cool," Alex said.

"Bioluminescence is cool stuff. Cold light is created when you have three things: something called a luciferin, a luciferase, and oxygen. They react together to create cold light."

I frowned. "Lucifer?"

"It's Latin for 'light-bearer'—a chemical not affected by heat. And a luciferase is an enzyme destroyed by heat. It's a catalyst. Add oxygen, and . . . there's glow.

"I study bioluminescent algae. Scientists have had a lot of success in recent years with altering the DNA of various creatures to make them bioluminescent. Injecting jellyfish proteins into cat and mice ova, for example."

"I've seen that," Alex said. "It's been all over the Internet. Glow-in-the-dark kittens."

"Right. It's not too terribly useful. But it got me thinking . . . what if we could do that to people? Would that help protect us from vampires?" Matt rubbed his temple. "I've been around and around the issues of faith. Frankly, I'm not qualified to assess that.

"But the cold light—that's something I could understand. I took the gene from the algae I'm studying and introduced it to my body."

"How does that work? Isn't genetic manipulation usually done in vitro?"

"I used a virus. A variant of the common cold was handy, and I don't have access to much else here. I have a decent lab set up, but not anything I can use to do anything more delicate than the crude gene-splicing I did. It was a gamble, and the results were . . . imperfect."

"What do you mean?"

"The virus takes over the body the way a virus usually does. Only this is more painful. There's a lot of algal junk I wasn't able to isolate. I was pretty sure I'd done myself in. And Cora called me an idiot. But within a few days, I started to recover. And I could see cold light spreading throughout my body.

"Once I felt strong enough, I went outside after dark. The others didn't want me to do it, but I had to know if it worked or if I'd just screwed up my body with a bunch of genetic garbage.

"I held my breath. A vampire approached me. He called me Lucifer. He tried to grab me, but my skin on his . . . it burned him. He went away, searching for better prey." Matt fiddled with the spoon in his mug. His coffee must have long since grown tepid. "The others at Water's Edge tried it, one by one. And nobody's died yet. I have no idea what the long-term effects are on abnormal cell growth, reproduction, aging. It could be a long-term poison."

"But it's a short-term defense," Alex said.

"Exactly. We became something other— '*Homo luciferus.*' And it is, for what I can do, the least of the evils."

———

"I'm not sure about that."

"About what?"

Alex and I walked along a paved path to the dock, Fenrir at our heels. The sun shone in a cold blue sky. A small beach with pale sand spread out on our right, and the dock was on a poured concrete foundation, reaching out into the lake. Small boats were moored at a pier to the west, bobbing against the steel gray waves. A solitary gray heron fished along the edge of the dock. Seagulls spun in the air overhead, keeping low against the wind. Keene walked Horace along the edge of the beach, likely more for our peace of mind than any benefit to the horse. The flagpole rope slapped against the pole in a regular rhythm, like a clock ticking away the seconds.

"About what they're doing to themselves being the least of the evils," I said.

Waves crashed against the dock, and I pulled my coat closer around me. We paused at a bench that had been bolted to the concrete and sat down, facing north. An island with dark trees was just ahead of us. To the far west, I could see a spidery industrial apparatus that extended out into the lake. Judy had said that was part of a marble quarry from the next town over.

"You think of it as evil?" Alex asked. He leaned forward, bracing his arms on his knees. "I'm thinking that this looks like the best thing since sliced bread."

I sank into my coat. The wind tore tendrils of hair away from my bonnet. "Plain people don't even believe in dying our hair. Piercing our bodies. Or tattoos. It's tampering with the vessel God created. This is surely violation of *Gelassenheit* on the highest order."

"These are different times, Bonnet." He scratched his tattoos under his coat. "Beliefs have to evolve."

I shook my head. "I don't know. It seems like the further we move away from the old ways, the more trouble we are in. I don't know that I believe Matt's explanation about . . . about vampires being the product of a bacteria."

"It's as good a theory as any. It makes sense."

I shook my head. "No, no it doesn't. It doesn't explain why the vampires can't cross into holy ground. Why your tattoos and my *Himmelsbrief* deterred them. He's stretching to try to explain it with this business about water crystals and human consciousness affecting the physical world. I don't . . . I don't believe that this is a scientific evil. It has to be a spiritual one."

"You think Ginger succumbed to spiritual evil?"

I stared down at my shoes. "She wasn't evil. I know that. But the science doesn't explain everything. There is something of pure evil at work here . . . and also God. I have to respect that."

Alex stared down at his hands. "I've seen Matt's experiment work. For me, the proof is in the pudding. And it would give us another chance to live to see tomorrow. Objectively."

"It will change us. Make us something else. Something not human. And if we are no longer human . . . what are we?"

"I don't know, Bonnet. I don't know what the human race is becoming. But it needs to survive, in some form. Even if that form glows in the dark."

"It is too . . . I don't know that I can. It is turning away from everything I believe in. It is accepting modern technology . . . embracing it on a terrifying level. This is beyond using a cell phone or wearing britches. This is . . ." I struggled to find the words. "This is something irreversible. Something that I fear would destroy my soul."

"And that's the thing that scares you the most, isn't it?"

"*Ja*. Before . . . when I was at home, I didn't feel ready to be baptized. I was not really afraid of being caught out. It didn't seem real. Now . . ." Tears filled my eyes. "Now that I have been separated from my family, I don't want it to be forever. I know that I will likely not see them again on earth. But I want to know them in heaven."

Alex stared out at the lake. "There's nothing I can say that will change your mind on that, Bonnet. It's an article of faith. And I respect that."

"But you don't feel that way," I said slowly.

"No. I don't. I don't know the condition of my immortal soul, if I have one. But I'm pretty sure that the gods won't mind if I do the best I can to preserve the life I've been given."

"I understand." But a pain in my chest began to flower.

"I'm going to ask Matt if he will give me the algae juice … whatever it is."

He reached over and squeezed my hand. The waves washed hypnotically toward me, singing their exotic siren call. He stood up and walked back down the dock. Fenrir followed him. They left me alone to stare out at the lake and contemplate the ache in my chest.

CHAPTER SEVENTEEN

The way I placed my faith in God, Alex placed his in science.

And there was no middle ground in these things, whether our paths led us to the same place or to vastly different ends.

Linh's sister Yen was infected. We could all see it, in her pallor and the flecks of red growing in her eyes. Linh had been told, and she wailed like a banshee. I wondered if the tears burned her ruined eye socket. She wore a bandage over that eye, seeping red. Her sister gazed at that stain hungrily.

Peter and the rest of the men came to take Yen away. Peter carried a rifle, his mouth set in a grim line. Linh followed in their wake, her face swollen, and seeming strangely silent.

Alex and I followed at a respectful distance. I don't know if we watched because we wanted to measure the character of this group of people we'd fallen in with, or because we wanted to make sure that the dirty work was done. I pulled my coat close around me and shuddered.

When Yen saw that they were dragging her to the gate, she howled and writhed in the men's grip. They were wearing heavy gloves, but she hissed and spat. She didn't yet have the full strength of a vampire, but she was strong. She kicked one of the men in the gut, knocking the wind from him. Peter stood back, holding the rifle at his shoulder. He couldn't get a clear shot at her as she thrashed.

I covered my mouth with my hand. I had hoped that he would not have to shoot her. That she would surrender and go quietly. I glanced at her sister. Linh watched with a dull glaze in her good eye, her hands slack at her sides.

The men flung Yen outside the gate. Like the gate in my community, this gate seemed so symbolic, only an arm and nothing to keep anyone in or out. Just faith.

Yen sprawled on the ground. She turned, snarling, her hair in her mouth. She crawled back but could not cross over. It was as if an invisible wall kept her from moving beyond, and she bloodied her fingers on the pavement, scrabbling at the edge of it, with a high-pitched keening.

"Your science cannot explain that," I said to Alex.

He was silent. The men, panting, had backed off. Peter lowered the rifle, let it dangle by the strap from his hands.

But Linh moved forward, slowly, as if sleepwalking. At first, I thought she was following her sister. Then I thought that perhaps she'd been glamoured, that she felt the pull of Yen's need through the gate.

In a burst of speed, she snatched the rifle from Peter's grasp. She lifted it to her shoulder, advanced upon the gate.

The men began to pursue her.

"No," Peter said. "Let her go."

Linh moved the slide back on the rifle, held it to her good

eye. She looked down the barrel at her sister, hissing, on the street. I didn't understand the language that they spoke, but I knew that Yen was pleading by her tone, knew that Linh said something soothing.

And then the loud crack of a rifle shot obliterated her soft words.

Yen fell backward on the pavement, her forehead blossomed in a red smear. Linh held the rifle out to her side, her gaze fixed on her sister, her back turned to us. Peter snatched the rifle away.

Linh stood there at the gate for a long time after, unmoving.

It was done.

"This is irreversible," Matt said.

"It's what I want," Alex said. "It's my only hope of getting north in one piece."

The two men stood in the kitchen. Matt was sterilizing metal syringes in a pot of boiling water. I stood in the shadows, watching.

"I don't know what it will do to you, long term," Matt warned. "It could make you sterile. Give you cancer, or worse."

"Nothing is worse than that." Alex jabbed a thumb over his shoulder at Outside.

"If you're willing, then, I want to try something different." Matt went to the refrigerator and pulled out a dish of something that looked like mold. He unfolded plastic wrap on the top.

"Is that . . . the algae?" Alex asked. It looked faintly grayish green, floating on a pool of clear liquid.

"This isn't the original culture . . . it's a colony of it. I want to see if we can create separate colonies that can thrive, if we can perhaps take the cultures beyond the gate. Give the immunity to vampirism to other people."

Alex nodded. "And I get to be your guinea pig. I figured that you guys had a motivation for letting us in."

Matt shook his head. "Well, we try to be good Samaritans, but I wouldn't pass up a chance to see if we can go beyond what we've done."

I found my voice. "I don't like the idea of you being part of an experiment."

Alex reached out to me, took my hand. "I know, Bonnet. But I gotta try."

I lowered my head. I had no choice but to accept this. He let my hand go.

"What can I expect?" Alex asked, rolling up his sleeve.

Matt fished a syringe out of the boiling water with a pair of tongs. "Well, it sucks, to be honest. I won't lie to you. It's painful. The algae and recombinant virus DNA will invade your cells. It will hurt like nothing you've ever felt. You'll vomit, shake. It's a lot like going through drug withdrawal."

I could see Alex hesitate. He rocked back and forth on his toes as Matt drew up some of the fluid from the bottom of the dish with the syringe.

"Still want it?" he asked.

Alex stuck his arm out. "Yeah. Load me up, doc."

The bright silver needle slipped underneath his skin. I heard Alex hiss in pain. The contents of the syringe disappeared slowly.

Matt nodded, withdrew the needle. "It's done."

Alex rubbed his arm, flexed his elbow.

I looked away. There was no going back.

———

Becoming an angel is not like I pictured it.

The Bible told me that angels are luminous shining beings, sitting at the foot of God. I believed that they bask in the direct love of God. There is no need for them to prove themselves. They have eternal love and eternal life.

Humans are not that fortunate.

Alex went to bed with a fever and stayed there.

I sat beside him with a bowl of cool water and a sponge. I bathed his hot face as he tossed and turned. I watched as cramps racked his body, stroked his hair as he retched into a bucket. He grew pale and his eyes sunken. Water would not stay down.

"You know, Bonnet," he said. "I thought about forcing you to take the serum."

My brow narrowed. "You wouldn't—all that talk of respecting strength and self-determination?"

His sweaty hand crept toward mine like a spider. "But all that seems like nothing when you're considering life and death. I want you to live."

"I want you to live too." And I wasn't so sure that he was going to.

Three days later, he was still suffering. His skin was loose, and sweat plastered his hair to his forehead. He was freezing, teeth chattering. He'd grown delirious, babbling about bonnets and vampires and Dracula when his eyes were open. When his eyes were shut, his breathing was faint and shallow. His pulse was light and thready. Once or twice in the night, I thought he'd stopped breathing, only to hear him start again with a rasp.

I looked over his head at Matt standing in the doorway.

"Is this normal?" I demanded of him.

"Nothing's normal around here," he said. "But . . . it hasn't been this bad before."

"Do something!" I insisted.

"There's nothing to do. Just wait . . . and hope he survives it."

Furious, I lay next to Alex in bed. Fenrir was draped across his feet, watching him with worried eyes. I closed my eyes and prayed in the darkness, prayed that Alex would survive, even though he had turned his back on God's plan for his human form.

I was pretty sure that even if he did survive, God would not accept him into heaven, no matter how much he might repent for it later. The only lifetime he would have was this one, here on earth.

And that made me angry. Angry that he would leave me. That he had somehow pushed me aside.

I drowsed, listening to his breathing. I slept with my hand on his chest, feeling his heart and rib cage move.

I dreamed strange dreams of glowing, wingless angels with

sharp teeth that could sever bone. No matter how far I ran, I couldn't escape them. They followed me wherever I fled, in darkness, in daylight, on ground sacred and profane.

Perhaps it was the sudden stillness that jolted me awake.

I opened my eyes to stare at Alex. I could see tiny blood vessels shining a phosphorescent green, a fine and blotchy webbing beneath his skin.

His breath shuddered under my fingers, and I saw the artery in his neck push light from his chest to his head. The light had spread beneath his tattoos, sharpening their black outlines in the darkness.

I pulled my hand away. He seemed alien to me. Unreal. Tainted.

His eyes opened. They glowed in the darkness.

Not so different from vampire eyes.

———

Alex had emerged from the grip of the serum. Alive, but changed.

He and I sat on the bench at the end of the dock, watching the gulls wheel overhead in the cold sunshine. The sky was clear and blue and the lake calm. Black ducks bobbed and fished in the rills of waves. A blue heron paced along the edge of the dock, opening his wings to the sun.

Alex and I sat at opposite ends of the bench. Fenrir sat on the ground between us, though he leaned against Alex's leg. I knit my hands together. I felt that everything was leaving me. Without Alex, there was nothing left.

"What's it like?" I asked at last.

He shrugged, the movement constricted by his hands in his pockets. "No different from how I felt before, now that I'm past the assimilation sickness."

I glanced sidelong at him. "Really?"

He squinted at the distant horizon, and I could tell he was thinking. He took a hand out of his pocket and wiggled his fingers, examining them as if he hadn't really looked at them before. I didn't think that he would lie to me.

"It's subtle. But I feel a bit lighter. A bit more at peace. I think that probably has to do more with the decision being done than any actual biological effects. But I feel . . . hopeful. Hopeful that some of us might survive this. That there might actually be a future." He blew out his breath. "But it's gonna be hard. It's going to be beyond what any of us expected. Something completely crazy happened. But this might allow us to continue to exist."

"You would take the serum north?"

He nodded into his coat. "Yeah. Matt says that the daughter cultures will grow all on their own. They just need cool temperatures and darkness. If there's a chance that I could bring this to my parents, or, or . . . whoever's left . . . I feel like I have to."

"I understand." But I also understood that I couldn't go with him, not like I was now. Vulnerable. I had lost the *Himmelsbrief,* and I was just meat now. I had no choice but to stay here.

"A bunch of the others are going to take cultures, go out, try to find others and give them the serum."

"It sounds like missionary work." Plain people didn't do such work. We believed in conducting life according to God's will, according to the *Ordnung,* and teaching only by example.

"In some way, yeah. Perhaps, eventually, there will be enough of us to survive as a species."

I looked down at my hands. I didn't want to never see Alex again.

"You could do that too, you know. Take the serum back to your community."

I can't say that I hadn't thought of that, but I figured it would be a useless errand. "It's against every belief we have. It's tampering with God's creation. Railing against God's will."

"There's a myth from ancient Egypt about how the souls of the dead are judged by Ma'at, the goddess of justice. The heart of a deceased person is weighed against a feather. If the heart is pure, lighter than the feather, then its owner is allowed to enter the afterlife."

"That's a lovely story." I felt my jaw tighten. "But I don't think it's Ma'at who will be judging me."

He shrugged. "The whole game has changed, Bonnet. Dogma's gonna change. You can't say that things weren't changing when you were placed under the *Bann.*"

I frowned. "The Elders were acting . . . beyond the *Ordnung.*"

"To put it mildly. They tried to kill me. They imprisoned your Hexenmeister, denied the evil when it was on your doorstep. In the crucible of a crisis, Bonnet, power corrupts."

I could not argue with that. "But I have been sent away. If

I came back, under the *Bann,* no one would speak to me or open their doors to me."

"Even if you had the only means of survival?"

My voice was small as I spoke aloud a dark thought, my worst fear that had begun to grow deep in my chest, chewing into my lungs with black roots: "If there is anyone left."

"They may refuse it," Alex said. "But you could offer them a choice."

I thought of my parents. Of my little sister. And the incredible possibility of having the power to save them all.

It was too seductive.

CHAPTER EIGHTEEN

I had prayed to God for guidance.

I went to the little church in the center of Water's Edge to see if perhaps God would hear me more there. The building was cold, empty. My breath made ghosts in the air as I knelt before a wooden altar, as I had seen Ginger do. A carved wood cross cast a shadow down upon me.

"Please," I said. "I know that I've been selfish and willful. And that I have no right to answers, to question your divine will. But please . . . tell me what I should do. Give me a sign."

Sunshine burned through high windows. I watched the dust motes stir. Doves warbled in the rafters above.

There was no answer.

I knew that I was safe here. I could stay here at Water's Edge, eat down the stores of food in the household pantries with the rest of the inhabitants. I could listen to the lake, lose myself in that roar. I could spend the rest of my days here, on my knees, asking for forgiveness from God and hoping that my soul would be saved. I could wait for the finality of the end of the world, for God to say "Enough" and bring the kingdom of heaven to earth.

Or I could fight.

My knees ached when I climbed to my feet. I felt anger. I had devoted my life to God but had received no answers. I felt betrayed. That anger scorched my throat as I whispered, "How could you let this happen?" And that damning whisper echoed incredibly loud in that bitter, vacant space. I felt tears dripping down my chin, and my fingernails pressed into my palms. "How could you let this happen if you loved us?"

Doubt overtook me. What if Matt was right? What if all our safe places and holy relics only held some molecular evidence of our beliefs, and there was nothing behind them? No God, nothing but atoms and molecules aligning in crystalline forms?

I left the silent church without an answer from God. But I had an answer from within.

I asked Matt for the serum.

I rationalized it, told myself that it was no different from getting an immunization. Many of the children in the Amish community received immunizations when they were available. But I knew an immunization would not change me in the way that this shot would.

I was a coward about it, looking away when the needle slipped beneath my skin. I felt a hot burn of metal and something spreading within my veins. It scalded like the snake's venom, and I feared I had made the wrong decision. Maybe it was the right one, but I had come to it from the wrong source, from rage and anger. Either way, I would have to live with it.

Alex took me upstairs to bed. He murmured soothing words, scraped my hair out of my face as I vomited. When my fever grew high, he shoveled me into the shower and turned the frigid water on. He wrapped me in blankets and told me it would be over soon. I felt Cora's cool hands on my forehead and the murmuring of Matt and Judy.

And I dreamed. I dreamed, in my delirium, that I had returned home, under a thick and leaden winter sky. I had come back to houses razed by fire, to blackened and hollow barns. I searched for my home and found it still standing.

The old Hexenmeister stood at the door. He was nearly translucent in his paleness.

"Herr Stoltz," I said. "What has happened?"

The old man's rheumy eyes filled with tears. "The Darkness came. And I could not root it out alone."

I reached out to steady him. I could see that he was too frail to fight now. His hand shook on a cane, and I knew that it was too palsied to write, to script another *Himmelsbrief* or paint another hex sign.

My hand seemed very strong beside his. Young. Powerful.

"My family?" I choked.

"Go see."

I walked into my house. The screen door slammed behind me. I could see the Darkness moving inside.

And also light. I saw the green glow of foxfire, seething within.

Only the green glow wore the faces of my family members. It was an eerie incandescence, uneven under mottled skin and fading into my mother's and sister's hair and my father's beard. I felt no heat from them, nothing but the pale light of their hands.

I reached for them, expecting them to be as solid as the people I'd met at Water's Edge. They had been convinced to take the serum. I had saved them. I felt my heart sing in happiness at seeing them whole and alive, no matter their form.

But my hands passed through them, and I realized that they were no longer alive. They were just apparitions. Ghosts. Dead and gone.

The light faded, and I was in darkness.

Alone.

I stared up at the ceiling, awake, knowing that I had made a terrible mistake. I heard the ticking of a clock, heard the thin roar of waves outside and the sound of voices downstairs in the kitchen.

I sat up in bed. Alex was gone. I thought I heard his voice downstairs.

I looked down at my hands.

They glowed. I could see tiny pulses of light in my palms, pushing blood and light from my wrists to my fingertips in a smear of phosphorescence. I rubbed my palms together, but the light wouldn't rub off.

With dread, I crept to the mirror above the dresser. I lifted my hands to my face. My skin shone with a dull luminescence. My eyes were like stars and each faint freckle part of a constellation. My jaw fell open and the interior of my mouth shone, backlighting my teeth, light leaking around the edge of my lips, as if I'd just eaten a handful of bright berries.

I felt dizzy, my weight shifting from foot to foot and heart hammering. I was not myself.

I was incandescent.

I was beautiful.

I snatched up my coat and slipped it on over my nightdress, jammed my feet into my boots. I fled down the steps and out the back door before anyone could stop me, into the darkness that I had feared for so long. The wind lashed at my legs, and I instinctively ran to the water.

Shivering, I stood on the rocks and stared up at the sky. I knew that I shone brighter than the full moon. My fractured green reflection in the waves was more luminous. I felt terrified. But not numb. Every nerve ending felt abraded and open. My frozen breath even reflected the green gloaming.

I stumbled down the jagged rocks to the edge of the water to press my hands to its shocking coldness. I wanted to scrub the light away. I wanted to reassure myself that I was still human, could still feel.

I waded into the water. I sucked in my breath as the cold invaded my boots. My nightdress floated around my knees, my coat opening like a black wing. I knelt down, reached for my reflection in the water.

"Bonnet."

I whirled. Alex approached me, Fenrir at his side. The wolf ran into the lake and began to whimper. My wet hand strayed into the soft fur between his ears.

Alex glowed like I did. The planes of his face were illuminated in odd angles. Like something terrible, other than human. I was reminded of Eve's awful choice in the Bible, of being tempted by the serpent and the knowledge of good and evil. I wondered if she thought she could protect Adam from it by knowing it.

Alex sloshed into the water. He wrapped his arms around me, and I sobbed into his shoulder.

"What have I done?"

"Shhh. It'll be all right, Bonnet," he said.

But I didn't believe him.

Something had moved between us.

I think it was more than just one thing. It was this . . . evolution into something else, something more than human. Matt called us *"Homo luciferus."* It made me shudder every time I heard him say it.

It was also the knowledge that we were going to be apart. Alex was going north, to his family. And I, having done all that I had done, felt that I had no choice but to go south. To try to see what was left of my home, to see if I could save anyone.

And it was also time that moved between us.

We lay in darkness, in silence. I closed my eyes when we made love, against the light and the idea of the humanity we'd lost. I could not bear the idea of losing him, of letting go.

"I love you," he said. His forehead rested heavy on mine.

"And I love you." My palm rested on his cheek.

But there was nothing to be done for it. I rationalized it: We came from different worlds. It would not have lasted, under even ideal conditions. But a part of me wanted it to. A large part, larger than I wanted to admit.

When the time came to leave, maps were spread out on the kitchen table. All the people who were young and healthy traced their routes out on the maps and packed their bags. Matt would stay here, it was decided, nursing the mother algae culture. Cora and a few of the others would stay with him. Cora had carefully sectioned off pieces of the mother culture into plastic bottles for us to carry, and Matt was cleaning and writing out instructions on sterilizing needles and dividing the daughter colonies to provide cultures to the people we'd hopefully meet along the way.

Peter and Judy were among those who were leaving. I saw Judy lacing up her snow boots.

"Where will you go?" I asked.

She nodded to the map. "South. I have family in Tennessee. I expect that it will be hard, but"—she double-knotted her boot laces—"I think that there must be some survivors."

"And you?" I asked Peter.

"West. He put his hands in the pockets of his tan coveralls and grinned. "I always wanted to see Colorado. Maybe I'll get that far."

"Katie, the best way for you to get back to your community is by water," Matt said.

I wrinkled my brow. I had been practicing a bit, with the small boats at the edge of the lake. It seemed simple enough when I was within sight of shore. My concern must have shown.

"Don't worry. It's easy. The water shouldn't freeze for another few weeks." Matt pointed to a blue line on the map. "You can follow the water south and east, mostly downstream. We'll send a map with you, and you can cross off the bridges as checkpoints to see where you are."

I nodded. The idea of navigating a river alone frightened

me. But I didn't want to say I was afraid. There were others heading off by themselves, on boats, on foot, in twos and threes. We had an elixir to save the world. My fear didn't matter.

"What about Horace?" I asked.

"I'll take Horace," Alex said quietly. "North."

I knew the horse would be in good hands. But it hurt me to hear Alex say that they weren't coming with me. I blinked back tears and stared down at my boots.

The handful of men and women leaving by water gathered down at the dock. Cora had given me a plastic bottle and a package of needles with instructions to keep the culture cold and dark. Judy armed me with a fishing pole and a kiss on the cheek.

I gathered my supplies into the boat as Alex handed them down to me. Other boats slipped away, down a narrow stream to the marshlands Alex and I had seen when we walked here.

I had hoped Fenrir would accompany me. But he whimpered and stayed on the dock, afraid of the water. Or perhaps he loved Alex more.

Alex held my hand. Neither one of us wanted to let go. I could feel it in the way our cold fingers laced together.

"Be safe, Bonnet."

And he let me go, out into the water and into the world alone.

———

The light I'd been given provided no warmth.

Cold radiated from the water through the bottom of the aluminum boat, soaking into my cramped legs and feet. Wind pushed at my back, and I huddled down in the seat. I paddled hard against the current, making slow progress until the river turned into a new watershed basin. Then I followed the fast current of the little rivers south, dipping the oars into the water to keep the boat from nearing the banks, where trees reached in with long brown branch fingers. They trailed into the frigid water, providing haven for cold-sluggish fish.

I ate from the supplies I carried with me and the fishing pole Judy had given me. I let the line trail behind me with a hook made from part of a floating pop can top. My success was small. Every night, I dragged the boat up to the edge of the bank, built a fire, and slept alone.

Mostly, I lay in the bottom of the boat, tangled in my sleeping bag, staring up at the sky. I had traveled far from home, farther than I could imagine. I had gained a great deal and lost much. I expected that they would turn me away when I reached home. But I would know that I had tried, that I had attempted to bring this terrible temptation of survival to their doorstep.

I would bring them the choice.

I thought of what Alex had said in his delirium and his honesty, that he had thought of forcing the serum on me. I vacillated on that. Perhaps it would be easier if he had. There would have been no element of free will, no choice. God would not blame me for being a victim.

But Alex respected me. He let me choose.

And that was part of why I think I loved him so much. No one else in my life had really given me choices. My parents had given me some latitude, but I always felt the weight of their expectations upon me: that I would grow up, be baptized in the church, continue living life on the same land and in the same way that they had. I also had felt the weight of Elijah's expectations on me: that he assumed that I would marry him, become a certain kind of wife. And the expectations of the Elders: that I would obey them and their interpretation of the *Ordnung* without question.

I had even resented God. I had doubted his existence, in a dark moment. But I came to realize that it was not he who was placing these expectations upon me. It was other people. In many ways, he had blessed me. Kept me safe, when others perished. In some strange way, I could see that I had his favor.

Maybe it was the light moving in my veins, but I also felt the stirring of faith.

And I saw life around me. The seagulls receded the farther south I drifted, replaced by starlings and sparrows. The river, a living thing, broadened into the flat floodplain of the fields. Squirrels warred along the trees beside the bank, scurrying with walnuts in their mouths. A red-tailed hawk perched in a tree, searching for rodents along the ground. At dusk, the deer came to the water's edge to drink, warily eyeing my shining reflection. A great stag watched me, noble and majestic, his eyes as dark as sloes.

Not human life, but aspects of God's creation. Being Plain, I was largely accustomed to these things in a way that the English were not. I grew up with my hands always in the dirt, and my eyes always overhead, noting the time and the season. I thought that this was the way that things should be. And after all my time in the Outside world, I was ever more certain of it.

And as terrible as it was, I thought that perhaps this catastrophe was just part of God's plan. The world looked much more beautiful from the cold river, without cars and noise and electricity.

And even if we humans did not survive as a species, I was comforted by the idea that life would go on. There would be plants that would sprout up under the concrete and split it apart. There would be animals that grazed in sunshine who were too fast for the vampires to capture. Birds would continue to sing.

All of God's kingdom on earth was not lost.

I only wished that I had someone to talk to about this. I wished that Alex were here to challenge me, to give voice to my fears. He was a good teacher that way.

I supposed that now I would have to do that for myself.

At dusk, I felt scraping at the bottom of my boat. I sat upright, thinking that I'd drifted too close to shore and scudded over a felled tree.

It was debris, but not the kind I expected. Up ahead, I could make out a blockage in the river. Fallen trees, it looked like, their leaves gone brown and sodden in the water. It didn't have the organized shape of a beaver dam; I'd seen those before, and this water was too deep for their liking.

My boat bumped along the branches. There were three trees, two reaching from one side of the river. I prodded them with the oar, searching for a way past, but found no opening.

I sighed. I would have to drag the boat ashore and take it around. The branches scraped the side of my rowboat as I pushed it toward the bank. I didn't relish the feel of frigid water on my feet, so I searched for the shallowest spot I could find.

I paddled up into the mud and anchored the boat among the tree branches and debris and tucked the oars into the bottom. With the tow rope in my fist, I leaped lightly onto the bank. My boots slipped and smeared in the mud. I dragged the boat forward a few feet, searching among the weeds for a smooth path to haul it ashore.

It was then that I realized that something was wrong. By the dim light of the moon, I could make out a flaccid outline along the bank. It was the deflated remains of a raft, tangled in the tree roots and cattails.

I looked up. The trees on this side of the bank had not fallen jaggedly, as if from a wind or the char of a lightning strike. These were smooth, clean cuts, from a saw.

The hair on the back of my neck lifted. I knew of traps that the vampires could lay. Alex had told me of a roadblock that he'd encountered before we met, dead deer in the road. He'd nearly wrecked his motorcycle trying to avoid them, and the vampires had fallen on him. It was then he had lost his girlfriend, Cassia.

Something clattered overhead. I stared up, expecting to see the waning moon tangled in the branches. I saw it, gleaming through the stripped trees.

And also bones. Pale, stripped bones jammed and dangling

from the maples like Christmas ornaments: the cage of ribs, a femur, the broken socket of a skull . . .

With a certainty that reached from the top of my scalp down to the frozen soles of my feet, I knew it was a trap.

CHAPTER NINETEEN

I reached behind me for an oar. If I could get back to the water, I could wait night out, cross during the day . . .

But I was too late. A dark shape knocked me off my feet, pressed me into the cold mud. Fetid breath raked over my face. I saw glowing red eyes and felt the weight of the creature against me.

"Come here, fishy."

Claws raked the hood of my coat, tearing it aside. My hands scrabbled in the mud behind me, searching for a stick to use as a weapon.

"Little fish, stop struggling."

The vampire ripped my hood away and cried out as light from my face spilled out into its eyes. It flinched back.

I thrust my hands before me, full of blotchy light.

It growled and got off me, backing away.

"You're no fish!" it cried out.

I felt the light surge up and sing in me. I scrambled to my feet, opening my heavy coat. Light shone through the thinner fabric of my dress, like a candle flame behind a curtain. It reflected in the water and confused birds roosting overhead, who took off in a dark flurry of wing shadows.

"You can't touch me," I whispered.

I felt powerful, more powerful than ever before in my life.

I moved toward the vampire. It slipped and scrambled in the mud, caught between me and the moving water. I realized that it had once been an old man. A backwoodsman, I guessed. He wore rubber hip waders and a shirt that was rotting out from under his arms. His stubbled face was contorted in horror.

Of me. Of the light I brought.

I reached down for a stick. The stick was attached to a root. I tugged at it awkwardly, but the mud wouldn't release it.

The vampire snatched a piece of driftwood and clubbed me with it. It struck me in the shoulder, knocking me back to the mud.

He stood over me, swinging with the piece of soft, dripping wood.

"I may not be able to eat you, glowfish. But I can kill you and hang you in that tree until the glowing flesh drips from your bones. Then I'll suck the marrow out."

And I saw in his hot red eyes that he would do his best to bludgeon me to death. Not for survival, but for pure evil.

Suddenly, a growl emanated from my left. A blur of gray fur slammed into the vampire, knocking him into the river. The water churned around the creature's screaming, flailing form.

I scrambled to my feet, watching wet fur and vampire flesh splash in the thick water.

"Fenrir?" I gasped. My heart burst at the idea that he had followed me.

"Bonnet!"

I heard a voice up the bank from me. I turned, catching sight of a green shining form, gleaming flesh behind intricate black tattoos.

My filthy face split into a grin. "Alex!"

"Here." He tossed me a broken-off sapling.

I caught it, waded into the water. My coat flared out behind me, dragging at my steps. Fenrir backed off, leaving the thrashing creature in the water.

I brought the sapling down into that dead flesh, like staking a slippery fish. The body was pinned underwater. Its legs kicked up in a spray, making me gasp, and its fingers broke the surface. But I had the head and chest pinned to the silt below. I leaned forward, pressing all my weight against it, until a black stain was released into the water.

I waited for the dark water to dissipate and the thrashing to subside. Fenrir danced in the shallows, growling and snapping at the feet.

When Fenrir stopped growling, I released the stake and backed away.

Alex stood on the bank, gazing at me with glowing approval.

"I missed you, Bonnet."

I ran to him and pressed my cheek to his cold and luminous chest. "I . . . I thought you went north," I stammered.

He wrapped his arms around me, and I felt a sigh deep in his chest.

"My place is with you."

And that was all he would say. I could feel the lump in his throat, and I didn't force him to say anything further.

I knew that it had cost Alex greatly to follow me. I knew what it meant. It meant giving up hope of seeing his family again on earth, likely any hope of ever seeing his home again. But my heart swelled to see him, to hold him in my arms.

Fenrir whimpered and washed my face with his tongue when I knelt to pet him. He was certainly a dog and not a wolf —he smelled like wet dog.

And I was glad to see Horace, to rub his nose and tell him that he was a good horse. Working silently, we salvaged my gear from the boat and moved away from the river. I shivered as we walked down a dirt road for a couple of miles, hoping we didn't encounter any other vampires.

When we stopped, Alex built a fire using the steel spark tool from the department store. I stripped out of my wet clothes and into my only dry set, wormed into a sleeping bag. Under the uneven glow of my skin, I couldn't tell if my toes had grown black with frostbite. They began to burn as they warmed, so I knew that it wasn't serious. Alex rubbed Fenrir down with a dry sweatshirt and then spread the wet clothes out on the ground near the fire, propped up with sticks.

I watched him feed the fire. From behind, in shadow, he glowed like an alien being. From the front, in the light of the fire, he looked human. Like the Alex I'd grown to love.

"Why did you follow me?"

He didn't answer me for a long while, just stirred the fire.

"I just couldn't leave you alone. I love my family, but . . ." He blew out his breath. "I did some ruthless, ugly math in my head."

I waited for him to continue. Fenrir plopped down beside me, in the curve of my belly. I reached down to rub his ears.

"My folks are old," he blurted. "They're academic types. They're soft and theoretical. They're wonderful people. Good people. Loving people. They collect books and have a beautiful garden. My mom makes really nice afghans, and my dad plays guitar."

I watched the flame and shadow flicker across his face. "Bluntly, there's no way that they were going to survive." His hands knotted around the stick he was using to prod the fire. "My father couldn't kill wasps that got in the house. He'd gather them up in a jar and set them free outside, even though my mother was allergic to bees. Goddamn bees. My mom habitually runs the car out of gas and has to call for my dad to bring her some. Dad is an insulin-dependent diabetic. Neither one of them can figure out how to change a tire without help."

I shrank back from the harshness of what he said. I felt his pain and my own guilt at drawing him away from people who needed him.

He rubbed his eyebrow. "I was hoping . . . maybe I was kidding myself. I wanted to believe that things weren't as bad as they seemed. But . . . I can't see my parents fighting off one vampire, much less a neighborhood of them.

"I think I had hope up until the time that I started off

north by myself. I'd built a fantasy that home was safe, untouched. But then I saw fire in the distance. I knew that this was everywhere. Matt had told me, but I didn't want to believe. And I realized that all I've got left in this life is a horse, a wolf who thinks he's a dog, and you. All I have is what I can see and touch—right now."

He stared into the fire. It hissed and popped.

I wriggled my hand out of the sleeping bag to reach for him. "Thank you." The words seemed tiny and insignificant in the face of his loss, but they were all I could give.

He kicked off his shoes and snuggled into the sleeping bag behind me. I savored that warmth, but I pretended to sleep so that he wouldn't know that I knew he was crying.

———

"They say you can never go home again, Bonnet."

I believed him.

I expected to see dirt roads lacing around pastoral fields, small houses and pockets of forest dotting the land where I'd grown up. I expected the earth to smell clean and cold as it did every winter, with a touch of manure from the cattle grazing behind wooden fences. I expected to see Plain men and women working their chores: hauling wood in wagons, carrying water, carrying buckets of grain to the animals. I expected to feel comforted by the way things had remained unchanged for hundreds of years. I wanted to be immersed in that history again, to be lost in that vast, unchanging stretch of time.

But a plume of black smoke rose from the horizon, staining the blue sky. The lump in my throat grew with each step

I took toward home. By the time we reached the gate to the single road into my community, it had grown into a cold stone of dread in my chest.

The gate stood twisted, wide open, the metal wadded up like aluminum foil.

I began to run toward the dark smoke, the frozen earth jarring against my heels. I ran from the dirt road into a field of unharvested blond wheat, stirring in the wind. My first thought had been to find the Hexenmeister, to learn what had happened.

But a barn was burning, and instinct drove me toward it. Orange flames blistered white paint, reaching toward the sky. The barn belonged to one of my neighbors. Most often, barns burned as a result of lightning or accident, when someone accidentally kicked over an oil lantern.

But this blaze was no accident. The doors to the barn were nailed shut with two-by-fours, and it was ringed by men in green uniforms. Soldiers. They held guns, and one of them was coating the base of the barn with gasoline. Sparks and ash blew in the wind. I could smell the acrid gasoline and sweet straw burning.

I skidded to a halt, shocked. I heard hoofbeats behind me, sensed Alex's shadow on my back.

"That doesn't look good." His voice was tight.

"What are they doing here?" I gasped.

"There's an army reserve base about a hundred miles from here . . . maybe they're from there. The base certainly isn't holy ground, so maybe they had to run, find a place to regroup."

A human-shaped form climbed out from a shuttered window in the barn. It shrieked and writhed in the fire, hissing.

A soldier walked up to the vampire and shot it in the head. Alex and I were too far away to hear voices, but the reports of three sharp gunshots echoed across the field. I jammed my fist in my mouth.

That had no doubt been someone I knew.

"They're trying to burn the Darkness out."

I whirled, hearing a faint familiar voice. The Hexenmeister stumped over to us, hunched over a cane. I flung myself into his arms. His beard had grown thin, and the old man seemed incredibly fragile. He smelled of eucalyptus, of medicine. I could feel a tremor in his chest when I hugged him. His face crumpled into a smile when he saw me, and he patted my cheek with a shaking hand. The left side of his face seemed oddly rubbery, and it did not move when he smiled.

"Herr Stoltz!" I cried out, my words tumbling over each other. "You're free! What's happened? How is my family? What are the soldiers doing here?"

"Come with me," he said, his voice thin. "I will tell you everything."

We followed the Hexenmeister back to his little whitewashed cottage at the edge of our settlement. It looked sadder than it had when I had left, the paint peeling and the fence across the front yard missing a few pickets. A muddy paddock in back held two black horses chewing at a hay bale.

It looked the same except for the tank parked on the road.

I shuddered. Fenrir whined and hid behind my skirt.

The Hexenmeister ushered us inside. There, I could see that things had changed, changed much for the worse.

"I'll make you something to eat," he said, stumping away to the kitchen.

Clutter was strewn on the unswept floors: bags of potatoes growing roots through the burlap, uneven stacks of firewood, a spilled tinderbox. But those didn't disturb me as much as the old man's worktable.

The Hexenmeister was responsible for creating the hex signs that adorned the barns and houses in our community. We had once believed that they were merely pretty designs, a relic from the old country. But Herr Stoltz had constructed these and the *Himmelsbriefen* he'd made me with a purpose: to ward off the Darkness. No other Plain communities that I knew of allowed such decoration. But the men in Herr Stoltz's line had been Hexenmeisters since the time of our people's emigration from Germany. The old man had kept this tradition alive, and the supernatural defenses it provided.

I paused at the edge of his worktable. Where I was accustomed to seeing precise calligraphy and flawless geometric patterns, I saw illegible scribbling and brush marks that didn't fall between the lines. It was as if a child had been painting.

I looked at Herr Stoltz. He was reaching up into a kitchen cupboard. His hand shook too much to remove a can from the shelf. Alex took the can from him, and we exchanged glances over the man's head.

"Herr Stoltz . . ." I began. "Are you all right?"

He stared at the can of cocoa powder in Alex's hands. "No,

Katie. I suppose that I'm not. Shortly after you left, I went out to feed the horses, fell . . . lay there for an hour before I could get back up."

Tears prickled my eyes.

"The military medic said it was . . . a blood clot in the brain."

"A stroke," Alex breathed.

"*Ja,*" he sighed. "That was what he called it. A stroke. The Elders no longer saw me as a threat. They simply say that I am a crazy old man, not worth locking up. I cannot even write my own name. Like a child." He made a face and turned away.

I stared at the ruined paintings. The Hexenmeister's magic was gone.

Alex led him to the kitchen table, and I automatically set about putting the kettle on. These things felt familiar, and I focused on boiling the water to keep from blinking back tears.

"My family," I said. "Are they all right?"

I was afraid of the answer, but I had to know.

"*Ja.* Your sister and mother and father are alive. Though their house is swarming with soldiers."

I said a prayer of thanksgiving under my breath.

"How did they end up here?" Alex asked.

The Hexenmeister leaned forward in his chair and braced himself with elbows on the table. His watery eyes were unfocused on the blank wall. "After you left, there were more killings. The Wagler and Lapp houses were set upon by vampires."

I closed my eyes. I knew the daughters of both of those houses well. We went to school together.

"The Elders were forced to admit that the Darkness was

upon us. Around that time, the soldiers came. They said that they would try to fight it back, and the Elders had no choice but to agree. We gave them food and lodging for patrolling the night."

"You told them what you knew about the vampires?"

He nodded and rubbed his swollen knuckles. "*Ja*. I told them that this was a spiritual evil grown out of control."

Alex gathered mugs from a cupboard. "We met a man. A scientist. He believes it's a contagion."

Herr Stoltz made a dismissive gesture. "The Darkness has been present since the time of Judas."

"Since biblical times?" Alex asked.

"*Ja*. Judas Iscariot betrayed Jesus for thirty pieces of silver. He felt remorse, tried to give it back, but it was too late. He hanged himself."

"I remember," I said softly. It was a familiar part of the Bible.

"What was not told was that Judas hung himself at the heckling of the angel of death, Azrael. Azrael was one of the fallen angels, who lured Judas to his death and not true repentance. Azrael blocked his path to hell. Unable to go to heaven, Judas rose in Darkness."

"He became a vampire?" Alex asked.

"*Ja*. He would never walk in Jesus' light again."

"How do you know this?" I asked. I struggled with reconciling the science I had seen with the Hexenmeister's story. I knew that what we had seen was pure, spiritual evil. And I wanted to know the root of it.

"It has been passed down. For generations. Even Solomon

knew of this, before Judas. Much of what he learned about keeping Darkness at bay we still use today."

Alex walked to the ruined hex sign on the table. "The sacred geometry," he murmured, tracing a line with a finger.

"What do you mean?" I asked, pouring water from the kettle into the mugs.

"There were several seals tenuously attributed to Solomon. Figures that served various purposes of binding demons and warding off evils spirits. These have . . . some of the same shapes."

Herr Stoltz nodded. "The old ways endure." He stared down at his trembling hands. "Endured. But I am afraid that all that is now lost, and what we have will soon burn."

"No," I said. "We found an answer."

His bushy eyebrows drew together. "A way to defeat them?"

I clasped his hands and drew him to his feet. I led him beneath the stairwell, where no sunshine could reach. I wanted him to see me as I now was, glowing in that darkness.

The old man took a step back, stumbled, nearly fell.

His voice was soft and wondering. "Now it is your turn to tell me what happened."

———

We told him all of it, in bits and pieces punctuated with chewing stale bread and reheating hot cocoa. The Hexenmeister listened in wonderment, occasionally taking my hand to squint at it in sunlight and then moving it into shadow.

"This elixir," he said. "You brought it with you?"

"*Ja,*" I said. I pulled my jar out of my backpack, and Alex brought his from his coat pocket. We set them on the kitchen table and stared at them.

"Do you think that they will accept it? Or will the Elders deny it?" I asked.

The Hexenmeister shook his head. "I do not know. But we should do our best to protect it." He lifted one of the jars and took it to a shelf. He tucked it behind a half-empty jar of white paint, placed a tin bucket over it, and nodded to himself. "No one will think to look for it there."

I held the remaining jar between my hands. Light from the setting sun passed through the window and illuminated the cloudy fluid. "Herr Stoltz, do you want the elixir?"

He stared at the jar, then at us. "I can't rightly say now, one way or the other. I need to pray upon it. The soldiers, I think, will be very interested in what you have. And that is probably for the best."

I lifted my chin. "I want to see my family."

"*Ja,* I will take you to them. You are still under the *Bann,* remember. They may not speak to you. But know that you will meet the soldiers before you will see them. And you will have to explain what you have done to yourselves to all of them."

I nodded. I was ready to take the consequences of my decisions, for good or for ill.

I pulled my hood over my face as we headed outside. The light was fast draining from the day, and I wanted not to be recognized. Herr Stoltz had taken Horace to the pen with his own horses. Fenrir insisted upon following us, ducking under fences and inhaling the strange new scents of the place.

The land looked much the same as I remembered: thick furrows in fields, simple houses and barns. There were a few green army vehicles dotting the landscape, and I saw soldiers gathered outside, drying their clothes on my neighbors' clotheslines.

"Being forced to quarter soldiers is unconstitutional," Alex muttered. "They got rid of that with the British."

"Times are more desperate now," the Hexenmeister reminded us. "I suspect that most of the Plain folk view this as simple hospitality."

"But how will they view it when the food runs out?"

"I think that the Elders hope that the soldiers will move on before then. They are desperate for any protection that can be offered, but have no solution or even any leverage to ask."

"*Gelassenheit,*" I said darkly.

"*Ja, Gelassenheit.*"

We approached my house and my heart soared. I could see lights in the windows, replacing the glow of setting sun. For the first time in many months, I had the sense that everything was going to be all right if I could just reach the light.

My pace increased and I began to run. I felt a smile spread across my face, and I couldn't wait to feel my family in my arms again. Surely they would be happy to see me and would not enforce the *Bann*. Everything else had gone to pieces. I couldn't imagine them following a rule for a time long past.

"Bonnet!" I heard Alex shout. I ignored him, running toward my silhouette of a house. My hood fell from my shoulders and my breath grew fast in my throat.

"Katie." I heard a voice that wasn't Alex's, and the ominous click of a rifle.

I slowed, breathing hard.

I turned around, face-to-face with the barrel of a gun.

And Elijah.

CHAPTER TWENTY

Elijah stared down the barrel of the rifle at me, his eyes large and round. His jaw flexed before he spoke again:

"Katie. What are you doing here?"

"I'm home. And I've brought a way to fight the Darkness." I lifted my head. This was just as much my home as his. I would not allow him to take it from me.

"Stay where you are." His eyes narrowed.

"I'm not a vampire," I insisted.

The last of the light drained from the sky, and I know that he saw. I could feel the light rising in my face, see the green glow reflected in a skiff of ice at my feet.

"What are you?" he breathed.

I swallowed. I didn't know how to explain it to him. "I'm just . . . changed."

"Not human." His finger flexed on the trigger.

A bright glowing shape lurched across my peripheral vision, accompanied by gray fur. A shot rang out, and Elijah was sprawling on the ground beneath Alex, with Fenrir growling at him, teeth bared.

"Are you all right?" Alex asked me.

I ran my hands over my body, checking for holes, shaking. I found none. I could not believe that Elijah would shoot me. I gritted my teeth down on the contempt I felt for him. He was my Judas. It was prideful to think that, but I felt in my gut that it was the truth. "I'm all right."

"Stop struggling, boy." The Hexenmeister stooped down to pick up the rifle. "You don't understand what's happening here."

I heard the clomp of boots. Soldiers were streaming from my house, guns at the ready, shouting.

Alex raised his hands in the air, and I imitated him. "I guess we're going to have to start explaining. Yesterday."

The Hexenmeister toddled out in front of us, waving his arms. "Don't shoot!" The soldiers swarmed around him, snatched the gun from him, and had him down on his creaking knees before I could blink.

I was shoved to the ground amid furious shouting. I screamed at Fenrir to run away. I saw the blur of his fur in my peripheral vision, hoped that he would melt away into the darkness before someone shot him.

A face in a helmet appeared before mine, and a flashlight shone in my eyes. "Identify yourself!"

My voice was thin and bruised. "I'm Katie. I live here." I made sure to show him my teeth.

I was hauled back on my knees, facing the soldier. He wore more metal decorations on his jacket than the others. A patch on his breast read CAPT. SIMMONDS.

"Somebody get a Geiger counter over here!" he shouted. He turned back to me. "Are you radioactive? Do you know what that is? Did you get bitten by a vampire?"

"No," I said, spitting dirt out on the ground. "I brought an elixir. A vaccine."

Simmonds rocked back on his heels. "A vaccine?"

"Ja." I slowly pulled back my hood and rolled back my sleeves to show him my glowing flesh. "The vampires cannot harm us."

Simmonds stared at me for a long minute. "Get her up and bring her to the barn for interrogation. And somebody get me a goddamn Geiger counter."

Under the *Bann und Meidung,* a person would simply be ignored by their community. Shunned. No offers of help or food or shelter or familial warmth. I always thought that the *Bann* was a terrible thing, one of the worst things that a human can do to another.

But there was no malicious intent to harm under the *Bann.* This was much, much worse.

The soldiers took Alex and me back to the barn that I'd used to kennel dogs. There were no dogs there now. I could only hope that they had been taken to the house. The hex sign that Herr Stoltz had painstakingly painted above the barn door had peeled away. There was only the shadow of stylized doves remaining. My heart sank knowing that he could never repaint it and restore the protection that it had offered.

Green trucks were parked in the barn, covered with tarps.

And another tank. The place no longer smelled of sweet straw and dog food; it smelled of gasoline and gunpowder. Green boxes with stenciled letters were piled up along the walls, with guns leaning against them.

The soldiers separated Alex and me. I craned my neck to watch them take him to a stall in the far corner of the barn. They put me in a different stall at the front with a grim-faced guard.

These men all looked the same to me in their green uniforms. I wondered if we Amish all looked the same to the English in our dark clothes, bonnets, and white shirts. I wrapped my arms around myself, waiting for them to decide what to do with us. Waiting to explain. I could hear the Hexenmeister's low voice as he spoke to Simmonds just out of my line of vision. I heard Alex arguing in the back.

I sank down and sat on a bale of hay. In the dim shade, I was conscious that my hands glowed. I caught the guard looking and deliberately stuffed them in my pockets.

And I waited.

The man, Simmonds, finally came back. This time, he brought a man in a plastic suit and white hood who was holding a machine that clicked more quickly than a clock. "Stand up," he ordered.

I complied. He ran the wand of the machine over me. I flinched away from the staticky noise, but it didn't hurt.

The man with the machine took off his hood. "She's not hot."

"What does that mean?" I asked.

They ignored me. "Go check the man," Simmonds said.

I remained standing for a few minutes, because no one had told me that I could sit. Simmonds stood before me, regarding me.

And he splashed an open canteen of water at me. The cold water hit me like a slap. I sputtered and turned away, wiped my eyes.

I turned back to him. "What was that?"

Simmonds watched my face. I felt like a mouse caught in a trap under his steely gaze. "Holy water."

"I'm not a vampire," I repeated. "I have a way to stop the vampires."

His eyes narrowed. "What is it?"

I reached into my pocket. I saw that his thumb reflexively came to rest on the butt of the pistol holstered on his waist.

I pulled out the plastic jar of algae. "This. It's a . . . a glowing algae. A scientist at Lake Erie discovered that it repels vampires."

I offered him the plastic vessel with clear liquid and grayish culture swishing at the top. He looked hard at it. I could see that he wanted to hope. His fingers flexed, and he snatched it from my palm like a greedy squirrel. He took a flashlight from his belt, shone it through the frosted plastic.

"How?" he said.

"It's injected. Under the skin," I said. I knew that Alex could explain it better. But I could hear him shouting and some thumping going on in the back. It didn't sound like rational discourse.

"Please don't hurt him," I begged.

Simmonds flicked his gaze to me and back to the bottle. He made no promises. "Tell me about this."

"It causes flu symptoms. Really bad. For a few days. But at the end . . ." I spread open my hands. "They can still fight against me, but they cannot bite my flesh."

His eyes narrowed. His hands closed over the bottle. "We'll see about that."

He gestured to a man with shiny silver handcuffs. The man tore my coat off me and handcuffed me to a rusty piece of rail over my head. I was left standing there in the dark, incandescing, aching.

And listening to the sound of fists on flesh in the far corner of the barn.

I closed my eyes and prayed. Something about being home made me feel stiller, more passive. I could hear it in how the volume of my voice lowered, in how I averted my eyes. I wasn't sure that remembering who I once was would serve me well now.

After some time, my hands and arms went numb. I tried to flex blood into my fingers by wiggling them, but it just made them hurt more. I noticed that the glow in my fingertips dimmed as the blood drained out.

"Why are you doing this?" I whispered to the guard. "There's nothing we wouldn't tell you. We want to help."

He refused to make eye contact. Perhaps he had too many warnings of vampire glamour. He looked to be my age. Young. His hair was cut so short, I could see his scalp through it, including a pink scar above his ear. The name PVT. TOBIAS was embroidered on his jacket.

"Ma'am, we don't know what you are. Until proven other-wise, you're a threat."

"But we haven't done anything!"

"You could be contagious. You could be a form of vampire we haven't seen yet. Captain says you stay here."

"My family is here," I said. "In the white house across the meadow. Can you at least tell them I'm here?"

"Ma'am . . . I'm not in any position to grant any favors to you. We all do as the captain says."

"I would too if he would just tell me what he wants." A tear dripped down my nose. I felt that I had just given the soldiers everything they needed to save the world.

And they were torturing us for it.

"Can you at least tell me if there are others out there?" I pleaded. "Other survivors?"

He hesitated a long time before he answered me. I could see that he was weighing how much to tell. "Our satellite phones haven't worked for weeks. I honestly don't know, ma'am."

And he turned away, refusing to answer any more of my questions.

I hung like meat on a hook for hours, on my tiptoes. I heard Alex shouting and then silent, shouting and then silent at the edge of the barn. I caught bits and pieces of what he said, but never anything that Simmonds said. He spoke too low. But Alex I could hear loud and clear:

"We brought you the damn vaccine on a silver platter."

"Where's Katie?"

"You fascist pigs! There's this thing in the law against false imprisonment, you know."

But at least I knew that he was still alive. If he was irate, I knew that he was fine.

Simmonds eventually returned. I saw that his knuckle was cut and bloodied. He looked me full in the face.

"I'm sorry to have to do this," he said. "But we need to know if what you're telling us is the truth. And I'm not about to sacrifice any of my men to find out."

I looked at him levelly. "I am not lying to you."

"I hope not." I could see despair clouding the circles under his eyes. "I really hope to hell that you're not."

I heard hissing and snarling. The hair stood up beneath the edge of my bonnet, and I struggled against the cuffs.

I knew that sound. It was a vampire.

Five men dragged a creature in through the dust. It was a man in Amish dress, girdled in heavy chicken fence and barbed wire. I saw thin ribbons of something shinier—maybe silver —surrounding him. Simple wooden crucifixes rattled against the metal. Black blood oozed through his white shirt.

I sucked in my breath. I knew him. He was a deacon. One of the Elders.

And here he was, chalky, snarling, trussed up like a ham. He was emaciated, writhing against the wire with bony wrists and fingers.

The soldiers dragged him into my stall. They pulled the crucifixes away, as if they were removing garland from a Christmas tree.

I twisted to face Simmonds. "What are you doing?"

His mouth was a grim slash. "Feeding you to the vampire."

I struggled against the metal cuffs, writhing and kicking

as the vampire tore through the chicken wire. The Deacon lurched toward me, his red eyes inhuman and ravenous, his hands clawing the air. The paddock door was slammed behind me, and I was trapped with this hollow shell of evil.

I cried out and turned away. I felt hot breath on my face. It smelled like blood that had been drained out of a slaughtered pig and forgotten in a bucket.

And it receded.

I opened my slitted eyes. The vampire was fixated on me, slavering, his clawlike hands twitching under his filthy shirt cuffs.

We stared at each other, a strange stalemate of faith and science. I knew this man. I had even feared him. He had turned me out of our land, to certain death. He had denied the truth that Darkness had befallen our community. And now he had fallen victim to it.

I felt a stab of pity. I wondered for a moment if he would go to hell. Or if he would live forever in this unloving state.

But I knew that he could not touch me.

He turned and lunged at the soldiers. His body slammed against the door of the stall, shaking silt from the rafters and splintering the wood. The old door rattled on its hinges, split.

The soldiers were ready for him. I saw a sharpened stake thrusting through the gap between the door and the jamb.

But the Deacon had not lost all his intelligence in his hunger. He leaped up and gripped the supports that held the walls of the barn. Like a spider fleeing a child's flyswatter, he scrambled up into a rafter, where he hissed at us, bobbing, with red eyes.

A shot rang out, then another.

I shielded my eyes. Dirt and splinters rained down on me. I heard the barn creak and sag, this wonderful building that had been the refuge of my dreams since I was a little girl. I prayed under my breath to God that they wouldn't burn it like they had the other barn. Not with me and Alex inside it.

A volley of shots echoed. Men shouted and screamed. Something heavy fell from the rafters and landed with a crash on the dirt floor.

I opened my eyes, my ears ringing.

Men circled the vampire, kicking it. A sharp stake was driven through its chest, leaking black ooze. A soldier was on the ground, cradling an arm turned at an unnatural angle. Another had a bloodied shoulder. He was the same one who had been my guard. Tobias. He looked younger and more frightened, swimming in his gear.

Simmonds advanced on me. I flinched, thinking he meant to strike me. But instead, he reached up and unlocked my handcuffs. I fell, wobbly, to the floor in a puddle. Feeling came roaring back into my arms, but I couldn't stop staring at the body of what had been the Deacon.

The captain crouched down beside me, and his gaze pierced me. "I'm sorry. But I had to know that you were telling the truth."

I nodded. It was hard to accept his apology. But I had a choice to make. I could decide to be angry and small. Or I could choose to be more than that. To be human.

I swallowed twice before I could say it: "I forgive you."

I forgave him not only because it was my true nature to do so, but because it was part of the *Ordnung* that I still believed in. And I was home. That knowledge seeped deep within me, like sunshine warming cold grass.

Chapter Twenty-One

Home felt so very close but was so infuriatingly far away. It was an alteration not only of distance, but of time. Things had changed since I'd been exiled. I wondered if the people I'd always known and loved had changed too. I wanted to see for myself, run into the house at the far side of the field . . .

But we were still prisoners. Alex had been placed in my stall, and I went to him, pressing my numb hands over the cuts and bruises swelling on his face and chest. He sat on the straw floor, leaned back with his head resting against the rough wood wall. A spider drawled down and began to investigate a fleck of blood on his shirt that looked suspiciously like a fly. I brushed it away.

"How badly are you hurt?" My fingers traced over every laceration.

He shook his head. "Mostly, just my pride." He stared down at a cut on his knuckle, rubbed it as if he could wipe it away. I didn't ask him who'd thrown the first blow. It didn't matter.

He reached for my hands, and his thumbs massaged the raw marks the handcuffs had dug into my wrists.

"They hurt you," he said, and his eyes were as still and dark as cold black glass.

I shook my head. "No. I'm all right."

The door to the stall opened and a man came in carrying a plastic box and a gas lantern. He was dressed as the other soldiers were, in blotches of green and brown, but he bore a white band with a red cross on his sleeve.

"I'm Corporal Jasper," he said. He knelt down at a respectful distance from us, and set down the box and the lantern. I could see that his hands were soft, unstained by gunpowder. "You must be the survivors from Outside."

I didn't feel like an Outsider. I'd grown up here my entire life. But I nodded. *"Ja."*

He rested his hands on the box. He spoke to us softly, gently, as if we were feral animals who could shy away at any moment. I'm not sure where we could have run to, but I appreciated his respectful demeanor. "I'm not here to hurt you. I'm a medic. I usually just treat injuries until we can get people to hospitals, but . . ." I saw a bit of frustration in the downturn of his mouth. "I'm all we have. Myself and Frau Gerlach."

My heart lifted, and a dark shadow slipped into the stall, carrying a bundle. An elderly Plain woman with ramrod-straight posture broke into an uncharacteristically broad smile when she saw me.

I flung myself into her arms. She stroked my head and muttered soothingly at me, tucking my hair away from my cheek and into my bonnet.

"Herr Stoltz said you were alive." Her eyes shone, and I

could feel the tenderness in her rough fingers. These were fingers that helped birth babies and gathered up the dead in our community. Frau Gerlach had always told me that "God smiles upon those who do his dirty work." And she always did so, with silence and humility. "I came as soon as I could."

I nodded. "*Ja*. We survived. And we found a vaccine."

Her eyes slid back to the entrance, where I could see the Deacon's black shoes, unmoving in the straw. "Too late for him," she said firmly.

"*Ja*." I ducked my head.

"I will need to run some tests. Well, as many as we can do here in the field," Jasper said, opening his box. I could see the shiny steel of instruments inside, and clean gauze and bandages. He pulled on some latex gloves.

"Then can I see my family?" I asked.

"I will ask," the medic said. "Please understand, that's all I can do."

Alex grunted in displeasure. I glanced at Frau Gerlach. She nodded, placed a calming hand on my shoulder. She seemed resigned to this occupation of soldiers. But it appeared that she had been working closely with Jasper. He handed her a pair of gloves and she wordlessly began to open plastic packages containing instruments.

"What do you intend to do?" Alex asked. "Not that we have any say in it, but just out of idle curiosity."

"Fair enough," Jasper said. "We want to do a physical exam. Check for bite marks. Measure your pulse and respiration. Take blood, skin, and hair samples."

"We're not contagious," Alex said. "The bioluminescence is generated by a DNA mutation. An injection of the serum that we gave to your captain."

"We just want to be sure," he said.

I lowered my head. This would be the least of the indignities I'd suffered today. The medic led Alex out of the paddock for privacy while I got undressed for Frau Gerlach. The midwife had seen more nudity than any other person in my community, but I still felt blisteringly exposed under her gaze. She hung the gas lantern from the same spot in the ceiling where I had dangled for the vampire like a piece of meat. As Judy had at Water's Edge, she combed through my hair, ran her fingers over my face and neck, had me lift my arms. The silence was heavy as she worked, reminding me of what I might yet face.

"Do you think that my parents will speak to me?" I asked.

I heard her breath come out in an exhalation. "You're under the *Bann und Meidung* still, for certain."

"But you're talking to me." I crossed my arms over my chest and shivered.

I heard a thin smile in her voice. "No one Plain can see me talking to you, dear."

I frowned. Frau Gerlach had always obeyed the *Ordnung* assiduously. I didn't know what bothered me more: that she was breaking the rules, or that she wouldn't admit to breaking them. "The *Ordnung* is still being followed?"

She snorted as she made me pick up my feet to look at the soles, as if I were a horse that had thrown a shoe. "There is much picking and choosing, that is certain. Some of the young men have been off playing soldier with the military men. Neighbors are turning against neighbor, accusing each other of harboring Darkness and summoning the soldiers to ransack their homes for petty grudges. This is a bad time for faith."

My heart sank to hear it.

"This vaccine you bring . . . what does it do?" I heard the curiosity in her voice.

"It changes people. It makes us . . . inedible to the Darkness. It changes our biology."

I reached for the lantern, shuttered it. Only a thin crack of light trickled around the seams. Perhaps Frau Gerlach thought that I was only preserving my modesty. But my naked skin glowed, glowed like foxfire in the semidark. Without the clothes, I was brighter than I had been before. My hands twitched to cover myself, but I stilled them to face Frau Gerlach's judgment.

The midwife looked at me, unafraid. I knew that she had seen many more terrible things than this, especially since the Darkness had entered our community. She was always the one called in at the beginnings of life, to bring babies into the world, and at deaths, to prepare the dead. She had seen everything in between.

"Hnh. The Elders will not like that," she said. She said it in such a matter-of-fact way that it brought a smile to my face. It was as if I stood before her with a full face of makeup, holding a cell phone, not a genetically altered woman who might no longer be considered human under their rules.

"They did not listen to the Hexenmeister when he told them how to stop the Darkness," I reminded her. "Why would they listen to me now?"

"What is done is done," she said with her quiet pragmatism. "We must look to the future."

She uncovered the lantern, looked me over from head to toe. Her fingers were cool and did not tremble. She nodded. "Get dressed."

I reached for my clothes.

"No. Take these." She handed me the bundle she'd brought with her.

Tied in an apron were Plain clothes, like the kind I'd left the village in: a simple black cotton dress, apron, bonnet, underclothes, and shoes. They weren't mine.

"They should fit you, though the shoes might be a bit large," Frau Gerlach said. "My feet are bigger than yours."

"Thank you," I said, stepping into the dress. I fastened it with a clutch of straight pins that had been tucked into the seams. After the luxury of buttons as fasteners, my fingers were clumsy on the pins. I stabbed myself once and popped my finger into my mouth.

"Your parents have not seen you yet," Frau Gerlach said, tying the apron behind me. "Better that they see you exactly as they remember you."

My eyes welled with tears. "Did you tell them that I've come back?"

She shook her head. "No. And Herr Stoltz won't either."

There was a knock at the paddock, and Frau Gerlach told the medic to come in. He was holding some plastic vials.

She held my hands, and there was a ghost of sadness on her face. "You will have to tell them yourself. Tell them, and the Elders, and hope for the best."

───────

The medic was kind to us, as kind as he could be. He listened to my heart and looked at my tonsils. He asked me to take deep breaths while pressing a metal stethoscope against my back. He took my temperature and plucked out a strand of my hair to put in a vial. He scraped a bit of skin from my arm and clipped a piece of my nail. He swabbed the inside of my mouth and took blood from the crease of my arm with a syringe.

I looked away as he did it, feeling dizzy. It was odd. I'd seen so much blood and violence, but this small thing made me squeamish. It was almost as if I'd walked back into the life of an ordinary girl when I'd stepped into Frau Gerlach's clothes.

When we were released from our separate paddocks, Alex asked, "Are we through here?"

"I'm through with you," Jasper said. "For now. But I suspect that these fellows will want to keep an eye on you."

Simmonds stood between us and the door, flanked by two soldiers.

"Are we free to go? Or under arrest?" Alex's hands balled into fists.

Simmonds shook his head. "You're not under arrest. But please understand that I can't let you run around unescorted."

"But this is my home," I said quietly.

"That may have been true," Simmonds said. "But not anymore. This is just as much for your own protection as ours."

"C'mon, Bonnet. Let's go." Alex grabbed my hand and led me by the hand past Simmonds, past the soldiers and the tank. The two men fell into step behind us. I could hear their boots clomping in the straw.

He dragged open the barn door and I stepped out into the night.

I could see a distant light burning on the first floor of my house.

Home.

I picked up my skirt and began to wade through the tall grass toward the light.

I was conscious of a sliver of moon overhead, of the chill slicing through the sleeves of my borrowed dress, of the soldiers and Alex behind me. I was aware of the dim glow I cast, brighter than the moon, as I sailed over familiar ruts and rills, startling a rabbit from its hiding place. I turned at the edge of the vegetable garden, dodged between bits of laundry on the line, barely registering that there were both Plain and military pants hanging out. I rushed up to the back step, my breath burning in the back of my throat and my heart knocking against my rib cage.

I hesitated. Part of me wanted to rip open the door and plunge into the warmth that I knew was inside, to bask in that firelight I could see just through the window.

But another part of me knew that I might not be welcome.

I knocked on the screen door. It was a feeble, rattling sound, like bird bones in a can.

I waited, shifting from one foot to the other. I heard scraping inside, and the front door opened. I held my breath.

My mother's silhouette appeared. She opened the screen door. In a flash, I saw her as she was now: gaunt, with a taut, worried expression on her face. Her eyes widened in horror. The door fell back with a hiss, and slammed against the frame.

I reached out to snatch the door handle. "Mother. Mother, it's me."

My gaze fell on my hand, glowing green in the darkness. I knew that she was afraid. The look on her face was the most heartbreaking thing I'd ever seen. In that instant, I don't know what it was that she saw, whether she thought that I was an angel, as I had thought of Matt's people. Did she think that I was something terrible come to her doorstep? Or, most horrifyingly, did she think that I was simply myself?

But I couldn't step back and turn away. I couldn't.

I wrenched the door handle back and lunged into the house after her. My mother backpedaled across the kitchen floor. She slammed against the table, knocking a bowl against the floor and shattering it.

"Mother, it's me!"

Barking echoed, and I heard the clatter of dog claws on the hardwood floors. Two golden retrievers tackled me, and I stumbled backwards. Warm tongues washed my face, and I scrubbed my hands through their fur.

"Copper! Sunny!" I buried my face in Sunny's ruff. Around my feet, smaller dogs milled. Her puppies, who had just been born when I'd been turned out, were now knee-high balls of russet fur with legs.

"Katie?" my mother whispered.

I disentangled myself from the dogs and stepped into the

light of a gas lamp. I opened my arms. My eyes stung, fearful with the idea that she didn't want me anymore.

She looked me up and down. In this light, I knew that my eyes no longer glowed. They looked like hers—gray like winter clouds. My skin had become opaque and milky. I was ordinary.

She reached toward me, choking on a sob. Her arms wrapped around me fiercely, so tight that I couldn't breathe. My hands clasped her hard, and I felt her shoulders shake.

"Katie . . . is it really you?"

"Yes, Mother."

And for that moment, everything was all right in my world. I was home. My mother was holding me, and I was weeping into her shoulder. I was five years old again, safe and secure.

"How is this possible, *liewe*?" she whispered, using her pet name for me—"dear." She pulled back and pressed her hands to my cheeks. "Is it as they said . . . that the dead have risen up and that Christ is coming?"

I looked into her naked, open face, full of hope. And then I looked past her. My father was standing at the foot of the stairs, staring at me as if I were a ghost.

And then I understood. They had thought I was dead. They had thought that I had stepped Outside, been devoured. I felt a pang of grief at that, that they grieved for me. I took a step toward my father. "Father . . ."

He remained rooted in place, his eyes round and his lips unmoving.

A small figure scurried down the stairs, shoved past him, shrieking, with bonnet strings flying: "Katie, Katie!"

I fell to my knees and hugged Sarah. Her arms were tight around my neck, and she babbled into my shoulder, "Mother said that you had gone to heaven." I felt her doll slapping against my back.

I shot a glance at my mother, in shock. That was a lie. I would not have gone to heaven if I were dead. I would simply have been caught out, become nothing, suspended between heaven and hell.

And that's how I felt now.

My mother bit her lip and looked away. I felt the weight of my father's gaze on all of us.

"Where have you been?" Sarah asked.

I kissed her cheek. "I went Outside."

"On *Rumspringa*?" She frowned. "They said it's dangerous Outside."

"Yes. On *Rumspringa*." I had to lie to her. If my parents hadn't told her the truth of what had happened, I couldn't bring myself to say it to her. "Seeing the Outside world."

"Are there cars and trains and airplanes?"

"Not as many as you might think."

"Sarah," my father said. "Please go to your room for a little while. We have to talk to Katie." His voice was constricted, as if it held unshed tears.

I clasped my little sister in my arms again, and then she reluctantly unwound herself from me. She solemnly handed me her rag doll. I remembered when my mother and I had made it for her, wound the yarn into the head and hand-sewn the now threadbare dress. We made it in the Amish fashion — with no face. No graven images.

I clutched the doll to my chest and watched Sarah climb the stairs.

We waited until the door slammed upstairs. My father glanced out the screen door. I knew that he could see the soldiers there. And Alex, glowing. One of them had offered him a cigarette. I had never seen him smoke before. It seemed odd seeing an angel smoke.

My mother drew me to the kitchen table, pulled out a chair for me. The dogs followed and sat down on the floor beside us. "Tell us what happened."

I placed the doll in my lap. I took a deep breath and told her the story, from the time I'd set foot Outside, through the snakebite and losing Ginger, up through our time at the lake. I glossed over many of the violent details. But I think that she guessed, as she squeezed my hand during the pauses in my tale, when I could not find words.

"And we brought it with us. This . . . elixir that causes us to shine in the dark."

I lapsed into silence at last, running my finger over an uneven seam I'd made in Sarah's doll, along the arm. Copper had rolled over on my feet, warming them. He was snoring.

"You're alive," my mother said. "That's all that matters."

I felt my father's shadow over me. I looked up, desperately craving his approval. I wanted him to say that he loved me, that I could go upstairs to my room and sleep under my old quilt.

He bent down and gave me a hug. I heard a tremor in his chest, felt the prickliness of his beard against my cheek. He kissed my forehead.

He looked me levelly in the eyes. "I love you, my beloved

daughter. And I always will. You have no idea how joyful that you being here makes me. But the *Bann* is still in place."

I swallowed. I felt the bile of resentment rising in the back of my throat. I wanted my parents to welcome me with open arms, to forget the *Bann*.

But I remembered that they had turned me out. That they had not defied the Elders for me. That they had stood behind the gate and watched as Alex, Ginger, and I walked into the dangerous unknown. I knew that they loved me, but love only went so far in the light of faith.

I wanted them to love me more than God.

It was a selfish desire. Evil. But I still wanted that, more than anything. God felt so remote, after all I'd seen. I was *here,* standing in the kitchen before them. Alive and wanting them to accept me and forgive me for all the hard choices I'd made.

My father stepped away. He turned his back to me. I thought I saw a tremor in his shoulder.

"Father . . ." I began.

But he didn't answer me. He simply disappeared into the darkness of the stairwell.

I rose to my feet, Sarah's doll slipping from my lap. My eyes blurred with tears. My mother came to me. I felt her arms around me, felt her sobbing.

"Mother."

She kissed my cheek. I clung to her arms, but she too pulled away and disappeared into the darkness at the heart of the house.

I stood in the pool of light in the kitchen, sobbing. I reached down for Sarah's doll, hugged it. The muslin felt wet under my cheek. I sat it upright in the chair I'd occupied, scrubbed my sleeve across my eyes.

The dogs looked up at me, their brown eyes uncomprehending. I knelt to throw my arms around them. They didn't pull away. They didn't understand the *Bann* or human *Ordnung*. I kissed Sunny's forehead and rubbed Copper's ears. Sunny whined, her tail slapping against the back of my legs.

Hiccupping, I straightened and reached for the door handle. I knew that Alex would hold me, that he would offer me some comfort. But it wouldn't be the same.

And Alex wasn't alone with the soldiers. There were black shadows there, circling them like birds. Shadows I recognized.

The Elders.

CHAPTER TWENTY-TWO

I paused on the threshold, half in the house and half out. The Bishop's gaze fell heavy upon me. He could be kindly. I knew this, saw it in the crinkling around his eyes. But it had been a long time since he had showed me any kindness.

I could hear uncertain muttering among the Elders.

The Bishop's gaze flicked from me to shining Alex and then to the dim soldiers. "These two are under the *Bann*. They have been shunned by us."

The soldier shook his head, his hand resting on the holstered pistol at his waist. "Sir, with all due respect, we're not concerned with your religious practices."

"They are not to be here. They have been exiled from the community."

Alex started forward. I rushed down the steps and caught his sleeve.

The soldier glanced at us. "Did they commit a crime?"

"They violated the rules of the *Ordnung*. They defied our authority. The girl brought an Outsider in, and they burned a house . . ."

"Which seems to be happening pretty damn frequently," Alex spat.

The Bishop glared at him and appealed to the soldiers again. "They are subversive elements. They are not welcome here."

I could feel the coldness emanating from the holy man. "Hey—" Alex started. But I knew he could not fight the Bishop with logic. I wound my fingers in his sleeve.

"Don't," I said. I lifted my chin. "We'll leave."

The other soldier rattled his rifle. "That's not going to happen. We've got orders to keep them under guard."

"They are not welcome," the Bishop said. Murmurs of assent echoed behind him. "They must leave."

Alex hooked a thumb over his shoulder at the soldiers. "So, these guys are guests, and we get the boot. Nice. Is it that they bring bullets and some pretty damn good protection? Or that you can't say no to a bunch of armed guys with tanks?"

I could see red burning on the Bishop's cheeks. "They are not like us . . . not human. No longer God's creatures. Look at them."

I closed my eyes. My eyelids glowed green, and I could feel the shade of my eyelashes on my cheeks.

"She risked everything to come back to you," Alex argued. "To come back with a way to stop the vampires . . ."

I heard clicks from the soldiers' rifles. "They come with us."

I let Alex and the soldiers lead me away into the field. Behind me, I could see the light from my house, outlining the silhouettes of the Elders. I could feel their gaze on us as we retreated.

My heart breaking, I plunged into the dark, shining, casting no shadow.

———————

The soldiers trusted us just as much as my own people did, but in a different way. Where the Plain people trusted in the invisible God, the soldiers believed only in what they could see and feel and measure.

And what they could watch.

They took us back to the stall where I'd been imprisoned. They brought us food, water, and blankets. Alex and I lay huddled together in the straw, much as we'd done before we'd been placed under the *Bann,* months ago. But back then, we didn't have a guard posted outside the door. I fussed with a weak board at the bottom of the stall around which cold air leaked. I was certain that we could escape, if we wanted to. But there was nowhere to go.

"I'm sorry, Bonnet," Alex said, putting his arms around me. I wondered what would be easier—to know as he did that his parents were likely dead, or to be dead to one's own.

I cast my eyes down. "I didn't . . . I didn't not expect it."

"It still sucks." I could hear the anger in his voice, anger on my behalf.

"There's a story that is told often by Plain people," I began. "It's from the Book of Tobit."

"I don't know that one."

"It's not part of the traditional canon," I said. "It is not . . . official. It is part of our Bible, but I don't think that it survived to more modern ones."

"Apocryphal, then. Lost or cast out."

I nodded. I didn't know what that word meant until he told me, but it seemed to fit. "The book starts out talking about a righteous man, Tobit. Tobit's calling was to give proper burial to murdered Israelites. He carried out this task the Lord had given him many midnights, and in secret. For that, his property was stripped from him by the king and he was exiled. A sparrow's nest fell from the sky and blinded him."

"Hnh." I could feel his breath against my hair.

Emboldened, I continued. Alex had told me many of his stories. Now it was my turn to tell him one of mine. "Meanwhile, there was a woman, Sarah, who had lost seven husbands to a demon in Media. God charged the archangel Raphael with two tasks: healing Tobit and freeing Sarah from the demon.

"Tobit had a son, Tobias. Tobias had been charged by his father to go to Media and collect the money owed to Tobit by Sarah's father. Raphael, disguised as a man, came to Tobias and told him of Sarah's plight. Tobias was instructed by Raphael on how to drive the demon away. Then Tobias and Sarah were married."

"Does that method apply to vampires?" Alex asked.

"I doubt it. It involved burning the liver of a fish. The gall-bladder of the fish was used to restore Tobit's eyesight. Raphael revealed himself and disappeared into heaven."

Silence hung in the semidarkness, and I traced a glowing vein on the back of Alex's hand with my finger. "The story is beloved by the Amish for its example of faithfulness and servitude to God. For perseverance in the face of overwhelming odds."

He didn't argue with me. He didn't tell me that my people were showing poor faith, or that I had broken mine.

Instead, he just held me.

And that was enough for me for that moment. Not always, I knew. But for that moment.

The soldiers seemed not to sleep. They bustled around us. I drowsed against Alex's shoulder, conscious of voices and discussion. At dawn, a sharp rap came at our stall door. A formality, but one I appreciated. I rubbed my eyes against the light leaking in from the chinks in the barn slats. I was, as always, relieved to survive to see morning, even if it was cold and I could smell frost.

"Come in."

Simmonds came inside with Jasper the medic and one of the young soldiers who had guarded us. Jasper was holding the jar we'd brought with us.

Simmonds crouched down before us. There was an odd humility to that gesture. He pointed to the jar. "Will you tell us how to use that?"

Alex nodded and pulled himself out of the straw. "You have clean syringes?" he asked.

The medic held up plastic packages of needles. "And we have a volunteer." His gaze flicked to the young solider. "Tobias."

I sucked in a breath. I didn't believe in omens. But it chilled me.

The young man stood before us, his posture ramrod straight and his hands behind his back, feet spread apart. I wasn't sure if that was for our benefit or for Simmonds's.

"It's not an easy process," Alex said. "You'll get sick. Really sick. It feels like the flu times ten. It lasts for days."

The man didn't meet our eyes. He looked at the wall.

Simmonds nodded at him. "I understand, sirs, ma'am."

Tobias extended his arm and Jasper opened the jar. He ripped open one of the packets and withdrew a shiny plastic syringe. He drew a bit of the culture into the syringe. "More?"

"A little bit. About one cc from the clear fluid on the bottom," Alex told him.

The liquid looked innocuous in the growing light. Tobias didn't flinch when the needle was jabbed into his arm and the fluid drained away. The medic dabbed at the puncture site with gauze.

"Now you wait." Alex nodded at him. "And make sure to get a bucket."

I was eager to leave the barn. But also afraid.

I was no longer afraid of the vampires, or even of the soldiers. I was afraid of the shunning of my people.

But I steeled myself. I needed to see this. I had seen the good parts of Amish life, how we cared for one another as brothers and sisters in faith. I had seen the bad, how the Bishop had abused his power. Now I wanted to see my community as an Outsider. As a ghost.

And that is precisely what I was.

Alex and I followed a team of soldiers on patrol. We promised Simmonds that we would not stray from the group. He seemed at odds with himself about our leaving the barn, but in the end he took my word. My word seemed worth more than it had been last night.

And I was not sure that he could spare the men simply to babysit us. Various squads were busily casting crude ammunition from scrap metals and attempting to capture radio signals with antennae perched on top of the barn. Others had gone into the forest to hunt. Two of them had dragged back a doe that very morning.

"At least they seem to be earning their keep," Alex muttered.

I shot him a warning glance. Whatever uneasy peace these men had developed with our community, I was loath to disturb it. We were outsiders among all, and I knew all too well how easily the majority could turn against the minority.

We climbed aboard a truck painted green and brown. It was open to the weather, like a courting buggy. The driver and one man sat up front behind a partition, and up to eight sat in benchlike seats in the back, facing each other. Alex shuffled me around to sit between him and the partition. It was clear that he did not fully trust the soldiers.

And he trusted the rest of our party even less. Two young Amish men climbed aboard, holding their hunting rifles. One was a young man I'd known all my life, Seth Beller. I was surprised to see him there. I opened my mouth to speak to him.

But he looked away, down at his hands. As if I didn't exist.

Elijah climbed into the back of the truck beside him, carrying his own gun and a green military-style pouch that jingled like bullets. Elijah met my gaze, but I turned away. I could feel Alex pressing against my side, glaring at him.

"Is there a problem, folks?" one of the soldiers asked.

Alex gestured at him with his chin. "Other than that he tried to kill us, not much of one."

Elijah shook his head. "No, sir. No problem."

That response infuriated Alex and mollified the soldier. The truck started up, and we bounced over the rutted field.

Home looked much the same, but I felt as if I didn't really exist in it. I saw many of my friends and neighbors outside, caring for their animals, doing laundry, carrying water from their wells. But they would not look at me. My next-door neighbor, upon recognizing me, turned her back and pinned a sheet on her clothesline. The woman who had once been my teacher in our one-room schoolhouse, the woman who had taught me to read and looked the other way when a library card fell out of my pocket, similarly looked away from me as we rolled past. The blacksmith, setting up buckets outside his forge, set down his tongs beside the bellows and turned his broad back to me. Frau Gerlach was feeding her chickens when we passed. I glanced at her but she just chattered to her chickens and pretended not to notice.

We passed a house that made me ache. I saw Elijah's best friend, Sam, cutting wood. My best friend, Hannah, was gathering the pieces in the yard. Elijah and I had intended to go on *Rumspringa* with Sam and Hannah, before the end of the world happened. Instead, Sam and Hannah had gotten baptized at the same time Elijah had, and were to be married. It appeared they had already done so; Sam was no longer clean-shaven. He was wearing the stubble of a beard around his chin, as married men did.

I couldn't help myself. I called out to her. "Hannah!"

She glanced up at me in startlement. Shock crossed her face, and her mouth opened. She took a step toward me.

But Sam had set down his ax. He gripped her elbow and led her back to the house.

I cast my eyes down, feeling bereft and foolish.

I was not the only thing missing from the landscape. Two houses were no longer standing. They were reduced to piles of charred beams and ash, burned down to the foundations.

"Vampires?" Alex asked the soldier at his elbow.

The soldier nodded. "We discovered 'em too late at that address. We chased them until morning, then burned them out at dawn."

I swallowed. Alex and Ginger and I had killed the first vampires that had been unwittingly invited into our community by Elijah. He had thought they were his brothers, but they were not human any longer. There were either more vampires here than we had realized . . . or the land was no longer sacred, allowing any evil to cross in uninvited. I shuddered at that thought.

The soldiers had a list of houses to stop at, like mailmen along their route. At each stop, a soldier knocked at the door, asked for a headcount. He took a brief census of everyone in the house, asked if anyone was ill, and went on to the next.

They had to make a stop at the graveyard, too. The graveyard was larger than I remembered, with disturbed earth. There were fresh markers and at least a dozen hills of unsettled soil.

The truck stopped and we clambered out. I traded sidelong glances with Alex. He and I had followed the Hexenmeister's prescriptions for dealing with the dead: staking, then cutting off the heads and burning the bodies. If garlic was handy, that was a bonus.

"You're still burying the dead?" Alex asked.

"The regular dead, yes. But we check on them. Make sure they're well and truly in the dirt. Herr Stoltz asked us to meet him here. Said he saw something strange."

The old man was sitting in a buggy beside the graveyard. Wheezing, he stepped out of the cab and down to the ground. I noticed right away that the buggy was pulled by a familiar white horse. I ran to Horace and rubbed his nose. He chuffled at me in delight. Though the Hexenmeister had conscripted him for buggy duty, the old man had clearly been compensating by overfeeding him. Green grass stained his white hide.

I did not speak to the Hexenmeister. I did not want to put him in obvious danger of defying the *Bann* in front of other Plain people. I'd already put my parents under the Elders' critical eye after walking brazenly into my house. There was no point in continuing to endanger those I loved.

A gray shape flowed from the buggy to the ground. I heard clicks and the shuffling of guns behind me.

"No!" I said, casting my arms out. I was well aware of how fearsome he looked. "Don't shoot him."

Fenrir bounded up to Alex, then to me, slobbering all over our faces. I smiled and stroked his sides.

"Where'd you get the . . . ah . . . dog?" a soldier asked.

The Hexenmeister shrugged. "He showed up awhile back. He's a good dog."

Fenrir wagged his tail, wriggling his entire backside in good humor.

The soldier gestured to the graveyard. "Tell us what you see."

Herr Stoltz leaned against his cane. "I see nothing. But the animals do. Let me show you."

He led Horace to the graves. Horace docilely stepped over the old, settled mounds and most of the new hillocks of dirt before stopping before a fresh grave. He refused to step over it, shying away and stepping around. I knew what that meant.

"Mark that grave," Herr Stoltz said.

I glanced at the headstone. It belonged to a widower in his eighties. That he could have died during the simple shock of these events was no surprise.

A soldier came forward with a can of spray paint and painted a large red X on the dirt. We repeated this process with the rest, and Horace was as pliant and docile as a horse could be.

"I don't get it," one of the soldiers said.

Herr Stoltz nodded to himself. "The animals know when something is amiss. A white horse is a particularly pure creature. He will not walk over the graves of the restless dead."

"So . . . it's sort of like dogs sensing earthquakes?"

"*Ja,* it is much like that."

"Doesn't seem very . . . scientific."

"My boy, there is nothing scientific about this pursuit."

Fenrir crept to the graveyard, his nose to the dirt. He wound around the simple grave markers. I followed behind him, watching. He paused at the spray-painted grave and began to dig. I stepped aside as he threw up clods of loose dirt.

The soldiers' hands flexed on their guns. "There's a vampire down there?"

"*Ja,* I believe so. And the dog thinks so too."

Fenrir dug to the depth of his back hips in the dirt and retreated, growling. I brushed the dirt from his fur and peered into the grave.

I had the sense of looking into a dark corner behind a shutter where a spider had made a home. Thin filaments of cobwebs crossed the edges of the grave, spun silk clinging around the egg sac of a corpse.

One of the soldiers swore. He tried to push the gossamer filaments aside with the barrel of his gun, but the threads clung. Another man brought shovels from the truck, and they pulled the sticky mixture of milky material and dirt away to reveal a corpse at the bottom of the hole, surrounded by the fragments of a smashed coffin.

I had seen many dead bodies. Plain people didn't preserve their dead or install them in concrete vaults. We washed and dressed them straightaway, and put them in the ground as soon as possible in simple wooden boxes, buried with their feet facing east. Even in that short time, I had seen cheeks grown sunken and smelled that soft scent of decay that begins to cling to bodies dead from natural causes.

This was not such a corpse. It lay on its side in a fetal position. Its black hat covered its head, and its hands were tucked in the dirt and splinters, away from view.

"Burn it," the Hexenmeister breathed.

One of the soldiers led Herr Stoltz away, mindful that the old man not trip over clods of dirt. I was heartened by that bit of tenderness.

I glanced back at Elijah and the other Amish man. They stood at the edge of the grave, the knuckles on their rifles white. They knew that man, as well as I did. And they knew that what they were doing was not a proper burial according to the *Ordnung*.

I wondered how they had decided which rules to follow and which to ignore. Elijah had been baptized, joined the church, and then chose to rebel. In the eyes of the *Ordnung,* his sin was worse than mine, the rebellion of an unbaptized woman who had not wholly agreed to follow the path of the Lord. And I felt a pang of jealous anger that he was not shunned the way I was.

I turned back to see a soldier uncapping a metal container that smelled like gasoline. He poured it into the grave, and the fumes shimmered in the cold air. Another stood away, struck a match, and threw it into the hole.

The flames rose up in a *fwoosh*. I crept closer, wanting to make well and truly certain that the body was alight. Through the smoke and orange flames, I could see the body curling in on itself. I hoped that he would burn peacefully.

A skeletal hand reached up, snatched the blazing hat from his face. Black eyes burned from a pale face, the wrath as palpable as the heat.

"Watch out!" I cried. "It's—"

"It's coming out!" Alex echoed my thought. He pulled me away from the conflagration. I reached down to pick up one of the abandoned shovels. Pure habit now. Instinct.

Bullets chewed into the dirt, obliterating any speech. I flinched back from the sound of the guns, but not the burning creature clawing its way out of the pit.

Its eyes fixed on me. And it lunged for me.

CHAPTER TWENTY-THREE

I knew, in daylight, I was just as vulnerable as any other human.

But the vampire was vulnerable in daylight, as well. I could see it smoking and withering.

It gained purchase on the edge of the grave and leaped toward me, but I was ready.

We were ready.

Alex had snatched up one of the other shovels. Before the creature's steaming hands could reach me, he'd slammed the shovel into its chest. The vampire snarled, and Alex flung him to the dirt. He pressed all his weight behind the shovel, forcing the point through its ribs, splitting them open under the sharp point of metal so that the wooden shaft impaled him.

I didn't hesitate. I rushed to Alex's side with my own shovel. With all my strength, I slammed the point of the shovel down on the vampire's throat. I saw a glimmer of something human in its expression. Something familiar. But that didn't stop me. I put my foot to the shovel, feeling it split sinew and bone. I tried to imagine digging through a recalcitrant tree root to plant a new garden.

I felt the creature moving under me, but the soldiers' shovels were sharp. The old man's head split off, like the head of a daisy from a stalk. It rolled three feet, coming to rest next to the boots of the soldiers. Its hair was still on fire, smoldering in the sunshine.

The soldier looked from the head to me, Alex, and back again.

"Nice work, you two."

Behind them, Elijah stared at me, blinking.

"God looks kindly upon those who do his dirty work," I murmured immodestly.

Pride was a terrible sin, but I allowed it to flicker through me, just that once.

It felt warm.

The soldiers treated Alex and me differently after that. I expected them to shrink away after that display of brutality, to treat us as if we were animals. Indeed, violence was something to be ashamed of. It was not a quality cultivated in Plain people.

But to the soldiers, it was as if we had completed some rite of passage. They offered me cigarettes, which I declined, and began to laugh and joke with grim humor about the corpses they were finding. They offered Alex a pistol and instructed him on how to use it. They set a can out on the edge of a fence post and cheered when he was able to shoot it off.

These things did not interest me. I felt the Hexenmeister's smile on me, and that meant more to me than the approval of the soldiers.

Fenrir was not fond of guns. He leaned against my side as I walked through the graveyard, running my fingers over the stones of the newly dead. I recognized all of them, of course. I saw all the names of the Hersberger family. Before we had been placed under the *Bann,* I had personally plunged stakes in their hearts and taken their heads.

Beyond them, I saw two other families, parents and children. I paused to pluck some late-growing weeds away from the stones. These were the families who had been burned in my absence. Odd that I felt some kinship to the soldiers in this terrible work.

"Katie."

I looked up. Elijah stood above me.

I turned away. "I am under the *Bann.* If you are a righteous member of the church, you should not speak to me." More than that, I didn't *want* to speak to him. I felt incredible wrath toward him.

It was best that we did not speak

"Katie, I wanted to say that I'm sorry."

My brows drew together, and I plucked more viciously at the weeds. "What for?"

"For . . . for everything. For trying to push you into baptism and marriage. For letting the vampires in. For turning you and the Englisher in to the Elders. I . . . I did wrong."

"According to the *Ordnung,* you did right."

"*Ja,* but . . ." He stared down at the rifle in his hands. "I am not wholly convinced that the *Ordnung* is the only right."

I waited for him to continue.

"I could not have lived with myself, knowing that I caused your death. No matter what kinds of sins you committed, they were not for me to judge. You will stand before God in your time, and so will I. I can never make up it up to you . . . what it must have been like to be Outside." I could tell that his eyes still reflected the violence I'd shown him.

I plucked the leaves from a piece of ironweed. The thorns stung my fingers. "It was hard. And bloody. And we lost Ginger."

"I'm sorry."

I said nothing.

"I just . . . wanted you to know. I was wrong. It may take a whole lifetime to make it up, but . . ."

I shook my head. I didn't like this kind of talk. It was too close to suggesting that he and I would have some kind of relationship. "I don't want you to make it up to me," I said. "I want you to simply . . . look after my family, as best you can."

He nodded. "I will."

I looked up at the sun in the sky and the purple ironweed in my hands. I had known the harsh dirty work of manual labor. But equally hard was the emotional work of faith. Repentance and forgiveness.

I looked at Elijah, feeling my anger dissolve. There was no point to holding on to the hate. "I forgive you."

He lowered his head, and I could see tears in his eyes. "Thank you, Katie. Thank you."

This time, when I walked away from him, it was without love and without hate. It was with a profound sense of peace that I knew didn't come from my own heart. It came from God.

———

"There's a problem."

When we returned to the barn, Simmonds was waiting for us. His arms were crossed over his chest, and I could tell by the dust on his boots that he'd been pacing.

"What's wrong?" Alex asked.

"Your serum." Simmonds jabbed a finger toward one of the stalls.

We rushed to the stall, peered inside. Tobias was lying on a sleeping bag, glossed in sweat. He was very still. The medic was crouched beside him, pressing a stethoscope to his chest.

"Is he sick?" I said.

"No. He's not sick," the medic said. "Not anymore. Now he's dead."

I stared at the body. He had been incredibly alive, just a few hours before.

"What happened?" Alex demanded.

"He started off sick. Ralphed his breakfast up in a bucket. Then started vomiting blood. He spiked a fever of a hundred and five, and then lost consciousness. He didn't wake up."

"That's not supposed to happen," Alex blurted. "That didn't happen to anyone up north."

"How many people took it?"

"Twenty-five, maybe thirty of us."

"Well, it could be lethal in a significant part of the population," Jasper said. "Or you've got a bad sample."

"I can't lose any more men to this," Simmonds said, from the doorway. "I can't deny the results, but there's something wrong. I can't, in good conscience, ask anyone else to take it."

"But couldn't there have been another factor?" Alex insisted. "Some genetic weakness that interacted with the serum, or some constitutional issue? Or he could already have been infected from handling the vamp you brought in to torture Katie."

"My men are all healthy," Simmonds barked.

I went to kneel beside Tobias while the men argued. I took his hand, which was still supple and warm. I thanked him for his sacrifice and said the Lord's Prayer for him.

When I finished, there was silence.

I looked up to see the men staring at me. I lifted my chin. I would not be ashamed of my treatment of the dead man.

Elijah was with them. He looked at me, then at Simmonds. "I'll try it," he said.

Simmonds shook his head. "For all we know, it's toxic."

"It's our best hope of surviving the vampires," he said.

I raised my eyebrows. "What happened to *Gelassenheit*?" If Elijah was going to gamble with his life, it seemed only fair that I challenge him. That I play God's advocate and make sure that he was not acting out of guilt or some perceived balancing of the scales against me.

He rolled up his sleeve. "I want to."

Simmonds stared at him, hard. "You're not one of my soldiers. I can't tell you what to do."

"I know, Captain."

The medic looked at him. "I'll get the jar and a needle."

———

There are no secrets in a Plain community.

Not for long. The material that holds it together is as

transparent as air. Gossip gets from one house to the next, by horseback and on foot, faster than sparrows fly. I had heard it said that the dead travel fast, but news moves faster.

I stood in the shadow of the paddock door, watching Elijah. The medic had scarcely left his side, hovering with needles and thermometers. I simply did as Frau Gerlach asked and brought buckets and sponges to mop his brow.

I was surprised that he had volunteered. He was risking either death or censure by our community. The Elijah whom I had known had been determined to follow the *Ordnung*. In fear, he'd retracted behind the gate of rules, thinking that would make him safe.

Perhaps time had taught him that nothing could keep us safe. Perhaps he had changed. I knew that I had changed; I could feel it deep in my marrow. Perhaps Elijah was not merely looking upon this act as one of repentance out of some debt that he owed me. Maybe he really wanted to survive, to help us all live.

"I don't trust him."

Alex was at my elbow. I looked up at his face, and it was creased with skepticism.

"There's no reason for you to trust him," I said.

"But you do. After everything he did to us."

I was silent for a long moment before I spoke. I suspected that Alex spoke out of uncertainty as much as he did out of skepticism. And jealousy. He knew what Elijah and I had been to each other.

But that was a lifetime ago. I set down the bucket and reached for his hand. "I forgive him. Which is not to say that

I have any feelings for him beyond a brother in the faith. I do not forget what he is capable of doing."

Alex nodded and kissed the top of my head. "You're a far better person than I am, Bonnet."

I shook my head. "Forgiveness is a small thing I can do for him."

I stared into the half dark, watching Elijah sweat and spit into a bucket. It was hard not to feel sorry for him.

Voices rose out front in a cacophony. I followed Alex to the front of the barn. We were shielded from direct view by the side of a tank, but I could see through the door. The Elders were gathered on the brittle grass like a murder of crows holding lanterns aloft, ringed by other men in our community. The Bishop was at the front of the group, arguing with Captain Simmonds.

"You've brought poison into our community." The Bishop's voice rang out as clear as a sermon. "Your soldiers are no longer welcome here. We are asking you all to leave. Take your poison and the people under the *Bann* with you."

"Be reasonable," Simmonds said. "We have a chance to save humanity. And we're your best bet at protection from the vampires."

"You've gone too far. You want to alter us—make us less than human. A procedure that we will not survive."

"Nobody's forcing anyone to do anything."

"I survived," I said, stepping forward. "I survived, and vampires cannot touch me."

My heart hammered, but I knew that I had to speak. I stood in the doorway, half in the artificial light in the barn and half in the warm lantern light. "I mean not to force this elixir on anyone, but to give people the option to choose."

The Bishop's finger pointed to me. "She is unhinged."

That was a charge that was leveled against anyone who disagreed with him. Ginger had been marginalized by the label of insanity when she was here. But I would not let that happen to me.

I squared my shoulders, walked out into the darkness among the Elders and the soldiers. In that weak light, I began to glow.

The men at the margin of the circle began to back away, clutching their lanterns, muttering to themselves. They turned their backs to me, but I knew that they had seen me. And that they heard me:

"I am changed, but not unhinged. I've seen the world beyond here, the devastation." My voice sounded high and clear to my ears. "I came back to bring a defense against the Darkness. Though you have placed me under the *Bann* . . . I still love you."

I would not have been able to say that before this moment. I had felt so much anger, so much betrayal, when they cast me out. I had felt it burning in my chest, scorching my throat and lungs. It had poisoned my words and my thoughts. That rage had chewed me up and spat me out. But now . . . I could feel a sense of calmness pervading me. It felt like love. Pure. Clear. Cleansing. Like fire. I took a deep breath. When I exhaled, the ghost of my breath glowed green in my reflected light. I glanced behind me. Alex was at my back. Where he always was. Part of me and part of that light.

The Elders were afraid. They shrank away from me, like shadows. The light of their lanterns seemed very dim.

I didn't see what happened next. I don't think that anyone really did, not even the soldiers. It could have been that one of the Elders knocked over a lantern, stumbling backwards. It could have been that one of them purposefully hurled a lantern toward the barn.

Whether it was clumsiness or malice, I couldn't say. And it didn't matter. I saw a streak of fire in my peripheral vision, rushing along the ground. I smelled spilled kerosene, felt the heat of fire along my skin. The blaze licked up against the wall of my beloved barn.

My calm broken, my incandescence fading in the greater light of the conflagration, I screamed at the fire.

All around me, I could hear soldiers shouting. The Elders melted away into the darkness. Alex pulled at my arm, dragging me away from the mouth of the barn.

"No!" I gasped. "Elijah is still in there."

Alex's hand was caught around my wrist. I could see a mixture of feeling in his eyes: anger, frustration, fear.

"Let the soldiers find him."

"We need to get him."

"Damn it!" He swiveled back to the barn. The west wall was rapidly being engulfed in flames. A stream of soldiers ran out, hauling supplies. None of them was carrying a Plain man. From within the walls, something exploded, sending a firework-like streak of orange through the roof.

I gave Alex a tug toward the door. Swearing, he followed me. That was why I loved him.

Chapter Twenty-Four

Thick smoke stung my eyes. Keeping Alex's fingers laced in mine, I plunged into the searing heat. I knew every loose board and broken shingle in this barn. This was my realm, and I could navigate it even in heat and dark.

I pulled him left, unerringly, toward the stall that held Elijah. We crawled on hands and knees in the straw. Sparks spilled overhead in the smoke like stars. I could hear the *pop-pop-pop* of soldiers' ammunition sizzling, but it was cool and the air was relatively breathable this close to the ground.

My right hand felt shoe leather, then a leg. I crawled up beside the body, shook it.

"Elijah!" I coughed.

He grumbled and twitched. Alex grabbed his arms and I lifted his feet. We made to go back the way we'd come.

But the fire was too thick. It roared in a way louder than any flame I knew, impossibly loud. It was then I realized that someone had started up the tank that had been parked inside the barn, trying to salvage it. It was moving forward, crushing into the front wall.

The supports of the barn creaked and shrieked. A wall collapsed over the tank. I could hear men screaming. A sheet of fire swept behind the tank's treads.

There was no escape there.

"It's blocked!" Alex shouted.

"This way!" I crawled to the back of the stall. I ran my hands over the wood. Part of it was rotted, weak, the same spot I had halfheartedly worked at earlier. I lay on my back and kicked at it.

Alex wriggled down to the ground beside me, pounding at the wall with his boots. We struck at the wood until I felt it splinter and I could feel cool night air rushing in.

I turned over, grabbed one of Elijah's hands. Alex snatched the other, and we hauled him through into the blessed cool of night.

We dragged him back, back into the darkness. Fire licked through the seams of the barn's slats, and the soles of Elijah's boots smoked. The barn creaked and howled under the roar of the fire.

Transfixed, I watched the remains of my beloved hex sign painted above the front door blister and blacken.

Alex had to tear me away. I grasped Elijah's smoking boots in my apron, and we fled with our burden into the night.

———

"No one must know that you are here."

"We had . . ." I panted. "We had nowhere else to go."

"I understand. Come."

The Hexenmeister ushered us into his home. Elijah's arms

were draped over our shoulders, and his feet dragged soot over the threshold. Fenrir sniffed at him and growled. Herr Stoltz wiped the telltale signs of soot away, lit a lantern, and directed us to a hatch in the floor.

The Hexenmeister's root cellar was dug into the earth below his cottage. He lifted up the hatch and bade us climb into a dark chamber that smelled like earth and musty onions.

I shivered, climbing down a rickety ladder to the rough-hewn crawlspace. It was close and cold here, the ceiling so low that I could not stand upright. I scooted to the back of the cellar, sat down against sacks of potatoes, onions, and sweet potatoes.

Grunting, Alex levered Elijah down into the dark. With a distracted sense of hopefulness, I noticed that his skin had begun to glow faintly.

Alex clambered down behind him. Herr Stoltz handed down a mason jar full of water and a blanket.

"Hide yourselves," he said. "The Elders will be coming soon."

The door in the ceiling closed. I heard scraping of something moving over the hatch.

I turned to Alex, shivering. I could see him glowing in the darkness. He kissed my forehead. He wrapped the blanket around me and I pressed my head against his chest. His shirt smelled like smoke.

I glanced at Elijah's prone form, draped across a sack of potatoes, dimly shining.

"Do you think he'll live?" I asked. My voice felt hoarse from the smoke. I reached for the jar of water.

"He'd better. I still want an opportunity to beat him to a pulp."

I smiled. "I hope you get that chance."

I heard thumping upstairs, and I turned my eyes toward the ceiling.

Alex began to say something, but I brushed my finger to his lips.

I realized that the sound was rapping at the front door. I heard Fenrir growl, then the tripartite thud of the old man's feet and his cane on the floorboards and the scrape of the front door opening.

"Herr Stoltz."

My blood quickened, hearing the Bishop's voice. The clomp of many sets of shoes on the floor told me that he was not alone. The footsteps thudded all around the first floor.

"This is a late hour for visitors." Herr Stotlz's voice was fainter.

"Have you seen Katie or the Outsider man?"

"No. Not since I brought them to the soldiers."

"You should have brought them to us."

"I did what I could. Is this what brings you to my house?"

"There is a problem. More than the *Bann*. They brought with them poison."

"Poison?"

"They say that it is a way to deter the vampires. It tampers with biology. It killed one of the soldiers."

"And what are the soldiers doing about this?"

"Nothing. Which is why we asked them to leave."

"You asked them to leave?"

"*Ja.* They must. We must be united in telling them that they are not wanted here."

"I do not understand. At first, we were to welcome the soldiers. They have destroyed a great deal of Darkness . . ."

"And they have tainted us. We have sent them a message that they are not wanted."

"And that would be the orange flame on the horizon?"

The Bishop said something unintelligible, and then voices clambered over themselves in argument. I drew myself into a ball under Alex's arm.

"It is finished!" I heard the Bishop say. "Their poison has been destroyed. The soldiers will come to your doorstep. They trust you. Tell them that they must leave."

"I cannot. They are keeping us safe, as they promised. They are holding up their end of the bargain."

"Tell them to leave. Offer them no food, no assistance. Or else it is you who we will place under the *Bann.* And it will be up to God whether starvation or the Darkness gets you first."

The shoes clattered to the door. I heard it shut quietly behind them, but it had the same force as a slam.

The four of us sat around the Hexenmeister's ink-stained kitchen table. Herr Stoltz sat at the head and I sat to his right. Alex was at the foot and Elijah across from me. Elijah had regained consciousness in the morning, with no other ill effects than startling himself with his glow-in-the-dark flesh. The jar of algae sat on the table among us, and the blinds were tightly drawn against prying eyes. Even so, bits of late-afternoon sun slipped in through the window, casting bright stripes on the floor. Fenrir stretched out under the table, asleep, his belly full of canned hamburger from the Hexenmeister's pantry.

"I don't see any other way," Alex said. "They don't want us here. We have to go."

I sighed. We'd debated it all day. He was right, but the truth made my chest ache. I had sacrificed everything to come back. But my community was already poisoned. Tainted. And I was unwelcome. That was the hardest part of it to swallow. I had idealized it to such an extent for my whole life . . . and now I felt that I had an Outsider's grim perspective on it.

"They think you're dead anyway," Herr Stoltz said. "They won't be sifting much through the wreckage of the barn. They'll count their own heads and assume that the missing are dead."

There was a peculiar freedom to that. Not having to say goodbye to my parents. Being able to slip away into the dark. Which was what we intended to do.

Elijah's gaze was on the jar. "The . . . culture can be divided?"

"Ja," I said. "It should be broken into pieces, daughter cultures. To bring it to people who want it." I tasted some bitterness in my voice, and fell silent to keep it from overtaking my speech.

Elijah nodded. "I will take some to the soldiers and leave with them."

I blinked at him in startlement. "You won't stay?"

He shook his head. "No. They need to know that the elixir works. And they have the ability to cover a lot of ground, reach a lot of people." He glanced at me. "I hope that you will forgive me for not watching over your parents."

I sighed. "They would not allow you to."

Alex challenged Elijah. "And this would fit within your definition of what God wants for you?"

Elijah shook his head. "I have come to accept that I have many amends to make on my way to heaven. I have broken my vow of obedience to the church. But the Bishop would turn me out anyway, for taking the 'poison.' There's no other choice."

"What about your father?" I asked. Elijah was the last surviving son of his home. He had been determined to do all he could to be there for his father, and now . . . I felt that, in some ways, he was a toy soldier. He always was one to be told what to do. If not the Elders, then the army men.

"My father will not understand. But I am a man now. My choices are my own, for good or ill. If I am a tool of the Devil, then . . ." Elijah trailed off, and shrugged.

I had not ever heard such reasoning from him. Perhaps if I had heard that months ago, things would have been different. He seemed resigned now. Broken, in a way.

Now, all I could offer him was my friendship.

"And the two of you?" Herr Stoltz prompted.

Alex and I exchanged glances. "We will not go with the soldiers," Alex said.

"No?"

"Not after how they treated us," I said. "There is a capacity for cruelty there. While I can understand that the ends justify the means, I won't support it."

Alex nodded. He reached across the table to take my hand. "It'll just be the two of us."

"Come with us, Herr Stoltz," I urged.

The old man shook his head. "I would not get very far. I'm too lame to follow." His gaze fell on the jar. "But I will take a portion of this elixir. For safekeeping, with the rest of the secrets. In the event that things change around here . . . some may wish for the elixir long after you're gone."

"Unlikely, but understood," Alex said. I could see that he'd had enough of this place. I wished that I could have shown him the good in it, what was bright and shining. But it seemed that all he saw was the cloudiness.

"When will you leave?" Herr Stoltz said.

Alex squinted at the orange light. "Tomorrow morning, Herr Stoltz. If that's all right with you."

The old man nodded. "*Ja,* that's good. That will give me time to feed you properly. And to pray for you."

I reached out for the hands beside me, bowed my head, and began the Lord's Prayer. For Alex and me, for the Hexenmeister and Elijah. And most of all, for my old home, which seemed so dark and so lost.

There were few rooms in the Hexenmeister's house, but they were by far the most comfortable accommodations I'd experienced since the lake.

The old man had invited Elijah to sleep in his room. There

were two other rooms, one with a guest bed, which was as-
signed to me, and one in which the Hexenmeister had set
up a cot for Alex. Though we had been traveling together for
months, Herr Stoltz wordlessly insisted that we maintain a
sense of propriety. And I would not break the old man's sensi-
bilities in his house. Alex had been good enough not to grum-
ble when he was half crowded out of the cot by Fenrir. The
wolf was beginning to think he was human.

But again, I could not sleep. I tossed and turned, and my
glowing fingers chewed the edge of the blanket tugged up to
my chin. I despaired of walking the open road again. Winter
was upon us, and I had no idea of where we would go.

Perhaps we could make our way back to the safety of the
lake. Or perhaps we were meant to walk the earth as Elijah
was going to, and spread the vaccine among the survivors who
were left. We had not discussed or decided. It was only understood that we would go wherever we were going together.

But I would miss this place, this last bastion of my hope.
I rolled out of bed and stared out the warbled glass window
tucked under the eaves. Snowflakes spangled the darkness, a
veil against the stars.

I gently worked open the window, lifting it up an inch. I
wanted to smell the air of this place that I'd known as home. I
wanted to feel it, unhurried, unwatched, to sense some of the
joy that must surely still remain in it.

I heard singing.

My pulse quickened. It was a thin, faint sound, vaguely
singsong and unaccompanied by instruments. I knew the song
— my lips worked around the familiar words from the *Ausbund*.

It must be Sunday night. I was ashamed to admit that I'd lost track of the calendar days in our time on the road, as obsessed as I'd been with the hours of sun and night.

I bent closer to listen to that pure, joyful sound. Amish youth gathered on Sunday nights, unaccompanied by parents, to socialize at the schoolhouse or various barns. In summertime, we gathered in open meadows. The Singings, as we called them, were our magical hours of freedom. They were the times to find partners, to gossip and giggle and play among ourselves, under only the watchful eyes of God.

I frowned. I knew that the soldiers had imposed a curfew. It was surely too dangerous to be roaming out at night. And yet . . . some of the young people must have rebelled, must have sneaked out of their parents' houses to revisit this simple joy and normalcy. The Singings were a much-loved tradition, hard to abandon.

I breathed deeply of the cold, clear air. A snowflake slipped past the window and melted on my glowing hand.

I wanted to eavesdrop on this, just one last time. I wanted to know this fragment of joy again that would forever be taken from me. I would not hear those voices again in heaven, and the only time was now.

I dressed quickly in the dark, snatching my shoes and my heavy English coat. I paused for a moment outside Alex's door. I heard Fenrir snoring behind it. I thought to ask Alex to come with me, to experience this sublime thing that was part of me and part of this world.

But I didn't think he'd understand. He'd consider it to be an unnecessary risk, sentimentality. He would not want me to go. He would capitulate, finally, and come with me if I insisted. But this was something purely for me, something I wanted to do alone.

I turned away. I padded down the stairs and jammed my boots on my feet. I tugged open the door and slipped out into the dark.

Snow was falling fast, leaving more than an inch on the ground. I lowered the hood of my coat to cover my face and plunged my gloved hands in my pockets. Snowflakes became trapped in my eyelashes and stuck to the velvet interior of my hood. I had walked alone across this land many times without trepidation.

But never with this sense of yearning.

I made my way across a field, toward the old schoolhouse. It was a one-room structure, built with thick walls and heavy white wood siding to withstand the ages and the winters. Lights were on inside, warm and yellow lamplight. I approached, keeping to the shadows. Holding my breath, I peered inside a window.

This was a much smaller group than usually attended the Singings. But there were still almost two dozen young men and women inside the blackboard-lined walls. The women sat on one side and the men on the other, with their *Ausbund* hymnals open on their laps. I saw girls I'd walked to school with and boys who'd helped my father harvest wheat and haul produce. I saw a girl who had wanted to become a school-teacher making doe eyes at a boy who was apprenticed to the blacksmith. There was innocent flirting and blushing, surreptitious giggles and flashes of smiles.

It seemed so ordinary. So lovely. I stood outside in the snow with my breath fogging the glass, wanting desperately to be that naïve again. I wanted to be on the inside, feeling that warmth and hope for the future. My fingers pressed against the cold glass, smearing light against the pane.

There was no going back. I knew it. But this spark of warmth gave me some hope, hope to spark life into my memories and sustain me going forward.

I turned away.

And was confronted by the glimmer of red eyes in the darkness.

Chapter Twenty-Five

"The night belongs to us, little one."

Wind snagged in my coat, billowing it around me like a black flag. Red eyes converged in the white, embedded in shadows. I counted six, seven pairs of them. They were in Plain dress. I recognized them as members of a family who lived on the edge of the settlement—the father, mother, and four children. There had been a baby, I recalled, but I didn't see it among them.

"No," I said. "It doesn't."

I lowered my hood. Green light reflected from my skin. I could see it shining in the snowflakes.

The creatures paused, squinting. This was something that they had never seen. I could sense their confusion.

It gave me enough time to slip around the edge of the building, to the door. I burst inside like a gust of wind, a force of nature.

The singing broke off abruptly. I slammed the door shut behind me, locked it. Eyes looked upon me in fear and trepidation. These young people knew me. They knew that I had done something terrible to myself. They knew that they should neither speak to me nor look upon me.

But they were frozen in shock, in that moment, at my wild appearance, at my heavy breathing and panicked expression.

"The Darkness," I panted. "The Darkness is outside."

The silence fractured. Wails and chatter broke out. The young men and women rose from their benches, coming together in the middle of the room in a tangle of arms and voices. Some rushed to the windows.

"No!" I shouted. "Don't look at them. They will bespell you."

One of the young girls began to cry.

I knew that it was only a matter of time before the vampires called to them, summoned them outside. They knew these people, could draw them out by that simple tie. I had to keep them from listening.

I jammed an *Ausbund* under the nose of the nearest girl. "Sing," I commanded. "Listen only to the words."

"What should we sing?" she gasped.

"Start at the beginning. And don't stop until dawn."

There was panicked murmuring. Copies of the *Ausbund* were gathered from the floor.

Something scratched and growled at the window.

"You must," I said. "Sing to the Lord and pray that he keeps you safe."

One voice began, then others. The young men and women huddled in the center of the floor, far away from the windows. The song rose up, reaching up to the dark rafters.

My heart hammered in my chest. I sang too, feeling the old songs swelling within me. I had always felt the most at one with God while singing. It was a sense of being a part of myself, part of a larger collective will.

But I was not still. I scurried around the classroom. I snatched up yardsticks, ripped down a loose piece of chalk rail. Any piece of wood that I could find was torn free and gathered in my arms. I broke the edges of the yardsticks under my shoes, to make sharp points. I emptied a duffel bag full of volleyballs and jammed the stakes into the bag. The balls rolled around my feet.

A girl tugged at my skirt. "What are you doing?" she whispered.

I lifted a jagged piece of chalk rail. "Going to fight the Darkness."

Eyes fell upon me.

"Alone?" she gasped.

"Stay here," I said, loud enough that the others could hear. "Keep singing until the sun comes up. Lock the door behind me, and do not open it for anything."

I took my coat off, let it puddle in an inky shadow on the floor. I rolled up my sleeves. The sack of makeshift stakes swung over my shoulder, I opened the heavy door to face the Darkness.

I slammed the door hard, heard the lock snap shut behind me, the sound of voices that shook the glass. I swallowed, feeling the cold cutting through my thin dress and realizing that the Darkness had gathered while I was inside.

There was no longer just one family. I saw a dozen more pairs of eyes milling around the schoolhouse. I recognized a carpenter, a dairy farmer, and the daughter of the blacksmith.

These were my people.

And I meant to kill as many of them as I could before they got to the young people inside.

I clutched a stake in my hand.

The carpenter came to me first. I aimed for the space of white shirt beneath his arm. He reached for me, flinched, and I drove the stake deep into the ribs. Black blood stained snow as he staggered back, landing in the skiff of perfect white.

I reached for the next stake. A stray nail cut my palm as I hurled it at the blacksmith's daughter. She shrieked, clawed at my arm as I drove it into her right eye.

Part of my soul collapsed in on itself and covered its head as I worked. But the rest of my soul needed to protect the people inside the schoolhouse. I was tired of fighting, of running, and wanted to simply make a stand. And there was no better place to do it than with God's music ringing in the back of my skull. My lips worked around the song, and I tasted snowflakes.

I kicked, fought, punched, and stabbed. The other vampires were wary, coming in twos and threes. They realized that they could not touch my skin, though they tried. The sleeve of my dress was torn from my shoulder, and my apron strings were snatched away. One of them grabbed me by the waist. I leaned back and pressed my cold, burning cheek to his. He screamed and let me drop like a hot coal, the side of his face smoking.

But there were too many of them. The carpenter, still bleeding from his wound, ripped a loose brick from the foundation of the building and hurled it at me. I tried to duck, but it slammed into the side of my head. I landed on the ground, dazed, tasting dirt and snow and blood.

A shoe pummeled my ribs. I felt something crack. I reached for a stake and thrust it into the leg of my attacker. He howled and leaped back, but the others swarmed me.

If they couldn't eat me, they were determined to crush me.

I glanced up at the sky, feeling the music in the back of my skull and the blood pounding in it. I felt bright pain . . .

. . . and saw bright light.

A burning blue-white light washed over the land. I blinked against it, unable to see anything. There were men shouting, gunshots.

I felt cold, glowing hands around my face. I looked up into Alex's phosphorescent eyes.

"Damn it, Bonnet. You are the most frustrating woman on earth!"

I closed my eyes and fell into darkness.

I awoke in sunshine.

And I hurt. My head pounded, my ribs throbbed, and I felt as if I were covered by a single large bruise. I focused on the sharp pain that came with each inhalation, staring up at the ceiling.

It was a familiar ceiling. I recognized the slant and light of my girlhood bedroom. I turned my head, taking in the plain closet doors, the chest of drawers with no mirror, and my sister's bed across from mine. My hands smoothed the worn surface of the quilt pressed over my chest.

I was home. The place I most wanted to be. My vision blurred with tears of joy.

"Hi, Bonnet."

Alex sat in a rocking chair beside me, Fenrir and a heap of golden retriever at his feet. His fingers were interlaced in mine. I scarcely noticed him over the racket of the pain in my chest.

"Hi." My voice sounded weak and tinny. I began to form questions with my mouth, but my lungs wouldn't cooperate.

"Don't try to talk," he said soothingly. He poured water from a pitcher into a glass and pressed it to my lips. I drank a few sips, the liquid cold in my throat and tasting like familiar iron.

"You got hurt pretty bad," he said. "Broken rib, they think. Bruised lung. The medic sewed up your head."

I reached up to my scalp. I felt stubble and the prickle of stitches. I felt a pang of vague panic. I had been growing my hair since I was a child. Plain women didn't cut their hair.

My hand fell. It didn't matter. A dog tongue licked my palm.

"Frau Gerlach's been feeding you some nasty-smelling tea. She says it'll help you heal."

I swallowed, whispered: "The people from the Singing . . ."

"They're all right." He stared hard at me. "I couldn't sleep without you. So I got up in the middle of the night, then saw that you were gone. But you'd left tracks in the snow."

My face flamed. I felt ashamed that I hadn't been honest

with Alex, hadn't tried to share what I felt, what I sought. Though we were different, there was no reason that he couldn't have respected or understood my feelings.

"I got the Hexenmeister and Elijah up. I thought that the vampires had glamoured you . . . taken you away." He shook his head. "Elijah went to get the soldiers. Fenrir could find your tracks in the snow . . . and we saw you at the school-house, whaling away on those vamps."

"Did they get away?" I hissed.

"Nope. Soldiers chased them down. Elijah actually did pretty good with the fighting thing, too. But the kids in the schoolhouse wouldn't let anyone in. Not until dawn."

I cracked a smile. That hurt, so I stopped. I stared at the ceiling. "But we're still under the *Bann* . . ." I didn't understand how we were here. Home.

"You've been out for a few days, Bonnet. There was some thing of a town meeting. The Hexenmeister got pissed as hell. As near as I can tell, the Elders got voted down."

I drew my eyebrows together. I didn't understand how that could happen.

"The Bishop got . . . I dunno what you guys would call it, but he got defrocked. The community voted to keep lodging the soldiers and to lift the *Bann*."

I blinked back tears. In the sunshine, they shimmered.

A small knock rattled at the door. I turned my head to see Sarah rushing in, holding her doll. She pounced on my bed, causing my head to thud.

"Katie." She snuggled close, beneath my arm, slapping her

rag doll down on my belly. "They said you fought the Darkness off. All by yourself."

"Not by myself," I croaked. "With a lot of other people. And God."

I looked past her, at my parents in the doorway. My mother came to kneel beside my bed, kissed my forehead.

"Welcome back, *liewe,*" she said.

Tears gathered in my father's eyes. "I'm glad that you're home, Katie."

And I was, in a way that I had never been before. In body and in spirit.

———————

The winter passed slowly. Storms moved in, blanketing the land in snow.

The army set about offering vaccinations against the Darkness. Most of the Plain people and all the soldiers took advantage of it, except for the very old or sick. My parents took the serum. Even Sarah stood in line to get her shot. She was very brave, announcing that she didn't cry and showing me the red spot on her arm where the needle had gone in.

And after many Amish had been inoculated, something strange happened. We used fewer lights at night. We could see well enough to get around through our own light. Through my window, it was not uncommon to see soldiers on patrol, glowing like green plastic figures in the darkness. An old man who took the serum died. But no others. Those were acceptable risks.

Alex slept in our living room until I was well enough to

ambulate. When I was, he bundled me up in a wagon and took me to the Hexenmeister. I loved being home, eating my mother's mashed potatoes and listening to my father read the Bible, but there was also something for me at the old man's house.

It was work. Strange work. I hunched over Herr Stoltz's drawing table, with my bonnet covering my stubble and stitches. I traced the figures as he explained them to me, followed examples of his calligraphy in old letters. Sitting in his chair, he schooled me on how to mix the paints and inks, and I wrote down the instructions in painstaking detail. Alex worked around the old man's house, feeding Horace and learning to hunt with Fenrir. He would disappear with the wolf for hours at a time, coming back with a string of rabbits for stew.

The Bishop became a recluse. It was as if he'd imposed the *Bann* on himself, withdrawing into his house and speaking to no one. He refused the vaccine. One cold winter morning, someone went to check on him and found him frozen in his bed. He had not fed his fire for days.

We kept a few cultures of the vaccine in various homes, including the Hexenmeister's. The army clucked and muttered over the rest, and they took it with them when they fixed their tank and rolled out in late February. Simmonds said that they had a duty to bring the vaccine to the rest of the world.

Elijah went with them. I understood that he was searching for something, something that had been unfulfilled at home. I had been there, and I wished him well as he marched away with the soldiers, the only Plain-dressed man in their green ranks. I had given him Ginger's wedding rings and her glasses, asked him to find her husband and give them to him.

And there had been no more attacks of the Darkness since the schoolhouse. Alex speculated that somehow, the holiness of our land had been restored.

I wasn't sure, but I wanted it to be that way. And I tried my best.

As the ice thawed, I slowly climbed up on ladders and began to paint hex signs. I painted one over the door of my parents' house, another over the Hexenmeister's. I painted them on every barn and house I could find. The work helped me grow stronger, as the ground softened and the grass began to push up from the mud. My parents had even gathered a group of people to do a barn raising, to rebuild the place that had been my sanctuary before the soldiers had taken it over. I had considered moving Horace back into it, but he had grown attached to the Hexemeister's horses. The three of them were inseparable, and it seemed cruel to take him away.

Alex had begun to work his way into the fabric of the community, the way that he had worked his way into my life. He started teaching at the schoolhouse. No Outsider had ever been allowed to teach in that room before, but he had a gift for helping the boys and girls understand their numbers and letters. And the older ones felt safe in asking questions about science and philosophy, things living vibrantly in the vast library of his mind. The students would often stay after class, sitting on the steps of the schoolhouse with him and Fenrir and a couple of puppies that looked like wolves with floppy golden retriever ears, listening to him talk about lightning and geography and the history of the printing press. I would come to the school at the end of each day, and we would walk away, hand in hand, with the dogs bounding around us. I knew that the children had never seen this kind of relationship before—a partnership of equals, a Plain woman and an English man.

Things were changing. I think that we were keeping to the root of who we were, not giving that up. But we were adapting.

I was working paint into the side of a barn one morning in March when I heard a sound that I hadn't heard in a very long time: the caw of a raven.

I turned around to gaze at the field behind me. A solitary raven was walking along the base of a fence, his head bobbing. He was looking at the sky, calling.

I watched him.

More of his fellows came. They came from the trees and the blue sky, hundreds of them chattering, swirling in black. It was as if they'd been separated on grand adventures and they were eager to tell each other of their exploits.

I smiled, knowing that we would have a future. It wouldn't be a future any of us expected or imagined.

But there would be a future.